PIXIE'S B & B

Anna Contrell

Author/Publishing Anna Contrell
www.annacontrell.com

Publisher's Note: This is a work of fiction. Names, characters, places, and incidents are a product of the author's imagination. Locales and public names are sometimes used for atmospheric purposes. Any resemblance to actual people, living or dead, or to businesses, companies, events, institutions, or locales is completely coincidental.

Book Layout © 2017 BookDesignTemplates.com

Pixie's B&B/ Anna Contrell. -- 1st ed.
ISBN 978-0-9997981-0-2

In three words I can sum up everything I've learned about life.
It goes on.

— ROBERT FROST

Contents

Charlie is late. The salad will wilt soon; I should have just poured the dressing in a container on the side. It looked crisp and vibrant when I plated it, now it just looks like, well...like an old salad.

"So much for making a surprise dinner." I tell Buca; slumping into my chair and letting out a sigh. Buca jumps into my lap and head-butts me. My nose is tickled by a fluff of orange fur before he settles down on my thighs and purrs. I need a bigger cat. Or smaller thighs. A cat in the lap should cover the whole lap. I stab a piece of the wilted lettuce and eat my share of the salad.

I prepared Charlie's favorite meal tonight. Almost. His favorite is pork chops, handmade applesauce with a side of yams and green beans. But what I made is better. Mainly because I can't cook pork chops. Scratch that. I can only *overcook* pork chops, which I guess is cooking them, but Charlie has told me, more than once, he'd rather I didn't attempt that particular dish since it's inedible by the time it hits the plate.

Instead, I made roasted chicken breast with baked potatoes and a side salad. Or at least there was a side salad before I ate it. Buca protests when I abruptly stand up and send him flying. Opening the oven where the chicken has been left to warm, the air fills with the lovely aroma of sage....no, that's not quite right. Rosemary? Damn it. Where is the box?

Digging around in the trash, I shudder when my fingers push past the wet fur ball I tossed in earlier. With my eyes squeezed tight, I push further till I find the box, hidden inside the bag the salad came in.

Charlie will ask what I seasoned the chicken with, and he'll know the right herb. *"Thyme."* I say it to the cat a few times before shoving the box back into the trash. For good measure, I move the fur ball on top of it again.

Maybe I need another dirty pot too. Earlier I smeared butter on three of them, now tossed catty wonk into the sink to give the appearance that I cooked tonight. I love my husband enough to know I'm a better heater then I am a cooker. Therefore, I heat. But the potatoes I made from scratch. They were raw before I put them into the microwave and that totally counts as cooking!

It's after six. I click on the TV and roam the news stations but they are all covering the same story, a traffic jam shown from various helicopter angles. That's not going to help things.

"Maybe my phone is off and he tried to call." Buca seems to agree, and follows me to the door where I retrieve my purse off the hook.

The phone is not in the side pocket. As usual, I've lost it at the bottom of the purse. Plunging my hand into the cavernous depths I remind myself to buy a smaller bag. One by one I drop items on the floor: hand sanitizer, hair brush, the silk scarf my mother-in-law gave me. I should wear that sometime. It would be lovely with the green suit…no, there is no way the suit still fits.

I wrap the scarf around my throat but gag on the musty smell assaulting my nose. This thing needs to get washed! Do you machine wash and dry silk or is it one of those things that melts? Silk comes from worms so it shouldn't melt, but being from worms, is silk actually worm poop?

Buca decides the scarf makes a good cat toy. "I wonder what kind of fabric we could make out of cat poop?" I quip. The cat ignores my joke.

One pen.

Two pens.

Red pen, blue pen. "Why do I have six pens in my purse?" Buca doesn't answer. I could test them and see if they all still work. Do I have paper in here? Oh, there is the phone!

No missed calls.

I press a few buttons just to make sure it's charged. It is.

Damn it. It's 6:20. He never comes home late without calling. But if I call, he'll know I planned something.

"It's still a surprise even if he finds out ahead of time, right?" Buca stares up at me and purrs louder. The surprise is me cooking dinner instead of ordering out. Because I always order out on Tuesdays. And Wednesdays. And any day we don't have enough leftovers and which Charlie isn't home to cook. Which lately is…always.

Charlie gave me an apron and cooking lessons for my birthday. I meant to go to the class. I really did. But the timing was all wrong. I agreed to help with the summer play and the kids wanted to rehearse on the weekends and I couldn't say no. How do you say no to a group of seven-year-olds with their beaming cherub faces?

Maybe I didn't have to convince them to do it exactly on Saturdays at 11am. Charlie knew I was going to school…I just didn't clarify I was going to the elementary school and not the culinary school. Small fibs - every marriage has a few.

Charlie knew I couldn't cook when he married me, but we both thought I could learn. I do want to learn.

I will learn.

But between grading tests and designing new lesson plans who has the time to watch water boil?

Doing chores could help pass the time. I rock on my heels and survey our studio apartment…I already put away my laundry, and Charlie's is still sitting in the basket for him to tackle; we have different techniques. I don't see the point in making everything all neat and uniformly square in a drawer – it gets all messed up when you dig for that perfect pink cotton tank, what is the point of spending all the effort to tidy it? Stacks of files and papers cover his desk, but I wouldn't know where to start with that. In contrast, my own pile takes over a third of the floor around the couch. Well, pile isn't quite the right descriptor. More accurate is aftermath of a tornado of arts and crafts supplies. No, no way I'm starting on *that*.

Footsteps. I catch the sound of our neighbor, Freddie, walking down the hall. I know it's him and not Charlie because the Spaniard is humming and jingling his keys to some tune he plays over and over. I stand perfectly still until his door clicks into place, not realizing I'm holding my breath till I exhale.

Freddie is okay, but he talks a lot and he's nosy. If he knew Charlie was running late he'd offer to keep me company and then talk my ear off about the weather or speculate why the news is still focused on the traffic. Small talk. Just the thought of it makes me shudder.

That's one of the reasons why I like working with kids. It's not all jibber jabber with them. They ask important questions like how can water be both a lake and rain? Or who created the alphabet?

The sound of a police siren pulls my attention to the window. Charlie's parking spot is still empty. I watch the road for a few minutes but there is no one coming.

Buca joins me at the window sill and looks outside, too. He spies a bird in the tree and his tail twitches enthusiastically.

"You can't reach it, that's all in your head, buddy." Even seven-year-old cats have a good imagination, I suppose. I scratch his head and clutch my silent phone.

Charlie always calls. Unless something is wrong.

No. I won't let myself think like that.

Clearly, I have thought about it, or I wouldn't have to tell myself not to think about it. I only think about it enough to know it could be a reason but it's not a reason therefore there is no reason to…wait, I'm lost in my own reasoning.

Sighing, I punch in Charlie's number and it goes directly to his voicemail. Well that explains it, his phone is off. He probably has no idea what time it is.

"This is Charlie! If you're calling about insurance, you've come to the right man. If you're not calling about insurance, you should be! Leave me a message and I'll get back to you lickety split!"

"Hi, love. Hurry home okay? I've got a yummy surprise for you and it's getting cold!"

6:45. Something is wrong.

"Mrs. Gibbs? Mrs. Gibbs, are you listening to me?"

I can't look at Principal Jackson; my eyes are locked on his window. It's recess and the children are running across the playground. Taking turns down the slide. Standing in line for the swing. Everyone is so happy.

I remember happy. Happy was being with Charlie.

We talked about having kids one day, two girls. We would buy a house first, something with a yard; we could have our own swing set in the back with a swing for each of them. Charlie wanted girls, daddy's girls, and I love him for that.

Loved him.

Everything in past tense now. There will be no little Charlie-look-a-like girls swinging on our backyard playset because there will never be a backyard with Charlie in it.

Principal Jackson pulls up the seat next to me and sits down. He takes my hand in his. But I can't drag my eyes away from the playground.

"Mrs. Gibbs. Melanie, please look at me." I give him my eyes. Few people use my name these days, it's all "you poor dear" or "sweetie" or just that look with the bite of the lower lip and the raised eyebrows that says the same damn thing without saying it.

"Melanie, have you thought about talking with Miss Finch?"

Is he serious?

"The school guidance counselor? She's trained to work with kids who have lisps and bad hygiene. Why would I talk to her?" Secretly, I have talked to her already. She held my hand and patted my shoulder. She's a twenty-two-year-old bottle blond who wears clothes too revealing for elementary school. Her advice was to smile more because 'if you smile on the outside, you will remember to smile on the inside.' I wanted to punch her.

That might work for the kid who got left off the birthday invitation list to help her feel better about herself. But it doesn't work for me.

"We're all worried about you. You really need to talk to someone about…about Mr. Gib-" he clears his throat, "Charlie. You need to talk to someone about Charlie." I can see his face morphing from the stern Mr. Jackson I-Am-Principal face he uses when kids are running in the hall, to that crestfallen I-Think-I'm-Your-Friend-So-I-Pity-You mask. Oh yup, there it is. The eyes are wide. Mouth drawn down into a forced frown. A little shoulder shrug with the head leaning to the side. And now it's a pity party.

"I'm fine. Totally fine!" My words snap out a little rougher then I intend. Mr. Jackson removes his hand from mine and rubs it on his thigh. As if he must wipe me off him.

"Right. You're totally fine." He stands up and paces. At least he's back to his Principal self. But now I'm nervous. Even teachers don't like to be in the Principal's office. He sighs and pity is threatening to slip back onto his face. I look down and notice I've twisted my skirt up into my hands and I smooth it over my lap, trying simultaneously to brush orange cat fur off onto the floor.

"Melanie, we all know this has been a very hard year for you with your husband's…" he trails off. How kind of him to not say the word *death*. Like it's a curse word. "I think you should take some time off." He stops pacing and stares at me.

"Oh. Time off." *Gather yourself Melanie, stay calm.*

"Like taking time off is going to bring my husband back?" *That is not staying calm.*

"Or do you think I should take some relaxing vacation so I can remember I am completely alone? So I can watch all the other couples in love strolling the beach with their hands entwined!"

Really, Melanie, stop it.

Mr. Jackson adjusts his tie and licks his lips before raising his eyes to mine. "Melanie, you have a problem and we want to help you find —"

I stand up and cut him off. "Frankly Mr. Jackson, I'm upset that you think I need coddling or need more time off. I do not have a problem!"

I just yelled at my boss.

Ok. I have a problem.

Mr. Jackson flops back into the chair and puts his hand over his eyes. Did he have that grey hair above his right ear before? Or did I just cause a spontaneous color change?

"Melanie. Please." He still won't look at me, smoothing his forehead with his fingers. Did I cause that wrinkle there? "The kids adore you...but I've received some complaints about your behavior from the other teachers. Melanie," he clasps his hands and touches them to his lips before going on, "I've even heard from the kids about how worried they are about you. They say you're crying in class."

"No I haven't!" Well, maybe just a few times, but I didn't think the kids saw me.

"And you took Valentine's Day off the calendar in your classroom?"

"What? No, it must have fallen off." Fallen off? What the hell am I saying?

The Principal leans towards me and makes sure he has my attention before going on. "You took the holiday off the calendar and you told the class it didn't exist anymore. Then you told them no one should exchange cards this year because they shouldn't fall in love."

I cover my mouth with my hand. Tears press behind my eyes. Oh god. I remember. I did say that. I said it to a classroom of seven-year-olds who still think holding hands is icky and like to celebrate this holiday because they get cupcakes. Or they should have gotten cupcakes, but I erased the holiday.

A shriek pops in from outside. I look out the window again. Those innocent children, laughing and playing with no idea you can be stripped of your happiness in the time it takes to heat up a potato in a microwave.

"You've been a walking zombie this entire year. You should have taken more time off after the funeral. Melanie, we have to do something about this. You used to be bubbly and charming, the center of the room." He stands up then and goes back to his desk. "Frankly, if you don't get yourself together, I'm not sure we can invite you back next year."

Would that really matter? *Does any of it matter?*

"I've discussed it with the school board and we'd like you to take a few extra weeks off. Spring break is coming up and I think it best if you prepare some lesson plans and take off the first of March and we'll see you at the end of the spring break."

A kid in a yellow shirt has started a game of tag. His mouth is open in a laughing grin and his arms are flying through the air in glee as he chases after another boy. 'Round the swing set and through the tunnel by the slide. So carefree. So innocent…I will never get to see Charlie's girls run around like that.

"Okay." It comes out in just a whisper. I nod my head for good measure in case my voice didn't carry across his desk.

"Okay?" Mr. Jackson seems pleased. No. Relieved. What would have happened if I had said no? Fired on the spot instead of finishing out the year? "Three weeks off, Melanie. It will do you good. Refreshing. You'll see."

I straighten out my skirt and take one last look at the kids on the playground. They are lining up to go back to class. Which is where I must go too, with a plastered-on smile as if I had not just been reprimanded for wallowing in my sorrow.

Three weeks off, what the hell am I going to do?

TWO

"What the hell am I going to do?" The phone is pressed between my ear and shoulder while I punch in the buttons on the microwave to heat up dinner. "Three weeks of staring at Charlie's stuff and being in this apartment all alone with the cat?" Buca stares at the spinning tray of food, oblivious of my insult of him.

"No, you are going to take a vacation and relax, just like they asked you to do. I think it is a good idea." Karen, despite her eccentric way of viewing life, is always down to earth when it counts. She flew to San Diego the minute she heard the news and stayed with me through the funeral. But she had to go back to Florida to her own life afterwards.

Even my parents couldn't stay more than two weeks. That's the problem with living so far away from family. San Diego was a business move for Charlie. It made sense to live here when he was here.

Charlie had worked for the insurance agency for a year after a career change from massage therapy. That's how we met, I was his client. Which isn't appropriate, I know. But he had hands of gold.

Karen and I got each other the same congratulatory gift to celebrate the end of our college life, a day at the spa. I remember his voice in the candle-lit room telling me to relax, how I was instantly turned on and not relaxing as instructed. The almond oil hitting my skin and then his warm hands, as if he had been holding them over a heater before he touched me.

Despite the warmth, my skin responded with goose bumps. And despite his skills, I couldn't relax. I was holding in my stomach, as if he would notice an extra five pounds under the towel as I laid there in nothing but my panties while he touched every inch of my body. Well, not every inch. There were some parts he didn't get to touch till much later.

After that massage, I couldn't stop thinking about him. We barely exchanged two sentences and I kept telling myself it was just some benign crush. I'm sure a lot of girls crave guys who give good massages.

Who are also sexy, and tan, and have silky blond hair.

With hands of gold. Did I mention those yet?

I held off for two weeks before I couldn't take it anymore and booked another massage. And then just a week before the following one. After my fourth visit, we'd spoken enough for me to know he was at least flattered by my repeat business and probably single.

After the fifth visit, I gave him my phone number along with his tip. I stared at the phone all weekend.

He called on Monday. "You know I can't date my clients." Not even a hello. Just straight to the point.

My heart dropped. "Oh, right. I knew that."

"From now on, your massages will have to happen outside of normal business hours. Pick you up at 8?"

And that was the end of my single life. We dated for three years and got married at his family's place in St. Augustine with just our closest friends in attendance. A polite and short wedding compared to some of the theatrical ceremonies my friends have dreamed up.

I moved into Charlie's cottage and we didn't need much. I liked being a substitute teacher and worked at a summer camp with a swimming pool we could use. We were carefree for a while. Then the owner of the spa sold it and the new guy laid everyone off. We moved to a larger apartment and the second bedroom became Charlie's space to see clients.

Strangers coming and going all day long made me nervous. I didn't have anything worth stealing, but I didn't like the idea of all those people in my space. Touching *my things*.

The perpetual smell of the massage oil was no longer a fond aromatic telling me Charlie was home…it was the bane of my existence, following me in an almond cloud everywhere I went.

We tried to make it work. Some weeks Charlie saw five or six clients a day, and I tiptoed around the apartment avoiding the client quietly sitting on our couch, holing up in my bedroom to avoid small talk. Both of us tried to get full-time work: me at a school, him at a new spa.

The months passed and there were fewer options and more debt.

He went back to school part-time to learn the business of insurance and got an internship leading to a decent starting offer, but it was in San Diego and we made the move across the country. We got the studio apartment. Adopted a cat.

Charlie liked his new career and his boss. I secured a full-time job teaching. We bought a new car. Charlie started to talk about babies and getting a house and giving up apartment living. He had a plan.

And then he died.

That's a sucky ending.

"Melanie…hello?" Karen's singsong voice breaks through my daydream.

"I'm here, I'm here." I sigh, "Just heating up some dinner."

"What is it tonight? Pizza or Chinese?" Anyone else would have said that with a condescending tone, but Karen says it like she's asking me if I want merlot or chardonnay.

"Neither. Meatloaf with potatoes and corn. And some apple tart thing…kind of looks like a brown glob."

"One day, Mel, you'll have to grow up and learn how to cook something that isn't out of a box, okay?"

"Yeah, yeah." The microwave is spinning my dinner tray so I turn my attention to feeding the cat. His food comes out of a can and he never complains about my lack of cooking skills. Loud purrs confirm he prefers the canned slop I dumped into his bowl on the counter.

"So, vacation. Any ideas?" Karen is persistent without being annoying. A quality I adore. I imagine her sitting on the other end of the line, phone in one hand, and scrolling through the internet looking for great vacation spots.

"I don't know, Kay. I do know I can't stay in this place for three weeks. I see him everywhere. I can still smell him here and I can't—"

"I know, love." Her voice is quiet now, strong. No trace of pity. Exactly what I need.

"What if I come and visit you?" I ask before I even finish thinking it through. And immediately remember why I shouldn't have.

"Oh Mel, are you sure that is wise?" No. It's not. She just got engaged and her fiancé, Edward, moved in. Here I've been talking for over an hour about how I can't stand watching people in love.

"Well, maybe I can just come to Florida and see you and my parents. I'll just stay at a hotel or something." I can hear her thinking it over, she'll talk me out of it if I let her.

But I don't want her to.

This is the first idea that brings me any hope.

"It will be fine, Kay. I promise. You can even pick the hotel, okay?"

THREE

Why did I say she could pick the hotel?

I know better. This is NOT a hotel. It's a cottage. Worse, it's a frilly little candy-colored Victorian cottage. Who puts a pink door on their house? And pale green garden planters with white daisies in every window. Swirly wood scrolls frame every door...in more pink? I feel like I'm trapped inside the story of Hansel and Gretel.

There is no way this is the right place. I'm supposed to be going to...where is that paper I wrote the address on?

Several pens scatter on the pavement as I dig through my purse to retrieve the Target receipt I wrote the information on the back of. *Ah ha!*

375 Cricket Lane

I lean forward to look at the street sign hidden from my view by a tree branch. Yup, Cricket Lane. But this cannot be the right place. This is where witches turn children intro pastries. Maybe my hotel is at the other end of the block. But the Uber driver did pull up here...and he had a GPS. Plus, he said "Here you are, three seventy-five, Cricket Lane".

This looks like a giant version of a play house. Something I remember from my days subbing at a preschool. Where the inside walls were made of chalkboard and the kids could draw on them and invent their own stories about the people who lived inside.

Why would Karen put me at someone's house? A house with white spindly banisters and...are those rocking chairs on the porch? All you need is a little old lady in a bonnet with an iced tea pitcher to make this the worst possible scenario.

Oh, my god! I'm dreaming, I know I am. No sooner do I finish the thought and the front door opens to reveal a granny carrying a silver tray with a few glasses of lemonade on it. In my head, she should be wearing a grey dress with an apron, but the woman in front of me is wearing jeans and a snazzy blue polo shirt with embroidered doves on the collar. She sets the tray down on the table between the two rocking chairs and turns to me with a grin on her face.

I stare back, mortified.

Granny-lady cocks her head to the side and raises her hand in a little wave. A bracelet of yellow stones sparkles on her wrist. Her curled grey hair frames ice-blue eyes.

I raise my hand barely higher than my hip and twiddle my fingers back at her. To break the stare, I dig my phone out of my purse. I glance up at the lady who is still looking at me. Embarrassed, I turn my back on her while quickly sending a text to Karen.

Kay, what on earth is this place?

My cell phone sits quietly in my hands. Come on Karen. *Write back.* I can feel the lady still staring at me, I can't look. The phone is getting sweaty in my grip and I'm squeezing it a little tighter than necessary. But as soon as I let the tension go, it slips to the ground with a not-so-great cracking sound.

Oh no. Please be okay! With my eyes closed in fear I pick up the phone and turn it over in my hand to face me. Barely opening one eye, I can see the screen is still on and breathe a sigh of relief.

"Is everythin' okay, dear?" The lady must have come down from the porch, she is standing right behind me. Her question takes me off guard and as I turn around, the phone drops again.

"Ahh!" This is not happening.

"Oh my, let me get that for ya." She bends down to pick up the phone which has landed near her foot. "You seem to be having a hard time holding on to that slippery little bugger." A chuckle escapes her lips as she hands it back to me. "You must be Melanie Gibbs. My name is Betsy-Lou Ringley. I've made you some lemonade. Long flights always dry a girl out and I heard ya came all the way from the West coast!"

I nod but I can't seem to speak. Betsy-Lou continues, "My now, I do hope you like sweet lemonade, most of my guests like it with extra sugar. You just let me know if ya like it to be on the sour side and I'll fix up the next batch to suit you. Come now, let's get ya settled in." While she spoke, she picked up my luggage and climbed the porch steps. Spry for someone her age. Maybe eighty-five?

I glance around the street. but seeing no other option I follow the old lady into her house. As soon as I put a foot on the steps my phone vibrates in my hand. Finally, a text back from Karen.

Pixie's B&B. You'll love it!

B&B? That's when I see the sign by the door. I missed it earlier. The baby blue sign is engraved with gold letters.

375 Cricket Lane
Pixie's Bed & Breakfast

Well, at least a few things are cleared up. This is not someone's home.

I am *so* going to kill Karen.

Betsy-Lou has put my bag at the bottom of the staircase and is watching me take in the lobby.

"You are standin' in the very center of history, young lady. This house was first built in eighteen eighty-three and housed several prominent people over the years. There was a fire in the nineteen-fifties and it was rebuilt as a guest house while the family who owned it lived next door. I stay there now." She points out the window to a more modern looking white clapboard structure. "And this place was turned into a Bed & Breakfast twelve years ago. Your room is on the second floor, you have the Mint Suite. You're stayin' with us for three weeks, is that correct?"

My head nods as I take it all in. The lobby's staircase softly curls up the wall with a wood rail polished to a sheen I can see my reflection, I can see all the way to the third floor's vaulted ceiling. Each doorway of the lobby is trimmed in a dark stain with a scroll of carved wood at the top. An oval sign plate held with delicate chains telling the name of the room is on every door. Kitchen. Rosemary Lounge. Cherry Suite. Cinnamon Room. Closet.

Really? They put a sign on the closet?

Betsy-Lou is smiling at me when I look back in her direction. I might have guessed wrong on her age. Her hair is curly and grey like a granny, but her face looks younger up close, her eyes more powerful. Maybe seventy-five?

Who knows, she could have had a facelift.

"There are three other guests here right now; I believe they are all out and about today. But you'll be seein' them over breakfast tomorrow." She turns to pick up my bag when I interrupt her.

"Over breakfast?" My stomach knots up, not at the thought of food but at the instant understanding that it's a social event, with strangers.

"Of course! Breakfast is served between 7 and 9am, I like to keep it short so ya can all enjoy the day." Her open smile and shrug of her shoulders remind me I am out of my element. "Any special requests while we're on that subject, dear?"

Breakfast requests? When was the last time I ate breakfast? "Um, just coffee is fine."

"*Just* coffee? Surely there is somethin' ya like to munch on in the mornin'?" She looks at me with wide blinking eyes, clearly planted in place till I give her a response. Maybe she makes breakfast as part of her contract. *Think*. Name something people eat in the morning.

"Toast…with jam?" Yes, that should suffice. Jam sounds better then saying plain toast.

"Toast. Tsk tsk."

Did she just *tsk* me?

"Deary, what about some eggs and a muffin? Perhaps a frittata or waffles?" Betsy-Lou hasn't moved yet, and is still holding my bag. She's too strong for seventy-five…seventy-two?

"I don't want to be any trouble, just toast. And coffee." I rub my face. This isn't going well, I'm more stressed now then I was from leaving my cat with my neighbor for three weeks. Freddie better remember to feed Buca. I reach for the phone to punch in his number.

Betsy-Lou shakes her head, and sighs. She turns with the bag in her hands and nimbly ascends the staircase. Did I just insult her?

After sending a quick text to Freddie to check on the cat, I climb the steps after her. From the landing of the second floor we face four more doors and a mahogany hall table with a milk-glass water basin on it. As I pass the mirror hung above it, I pause and get a good look at my reflection.

What a sight! My eyes are puffy from the crying every night, waking to a damp pillow, and my arm reaching for Charlie, where he should be sleeping next to me. But he's not.

My hair is a mess from the plane. Or it's always a mess. Either way, it's unsightly with stray hairs falling from my pony tail, the frizz making a brown halo around my face from the Florida humidity.

I used to think I was okay looking. Blue eyes, brown hair. My skin freckled from the sun by monitoring recess; and I know how to dress smartly on a tight budget.

In the past six months, I feel like I've aged ten years.

My eyes don't shine. My skin has dried out, and there are lines in places I don't remember them being. I've become pale from hiding indoors, holding Charlie's shirts to my face for hours on end. I'm not me anymore.

I'm a widow. And I certainly look the part.

"Melanie?" Betsy-Lou leans out of the doorway and waves me over.

Right, my room. The little oval plaque clearly says Mint Suite and there is a reason for the name. The walls are a pale green and the décor is, well, minty. A king size bed fills the center with a Victorian headrest, stained and carved to match the door frames. A large wardrobe stands at one side of the room, a writing desk at the other.

The bed is covered in a quilt, probably handmade. And old. The material is faded in some spots but the patterns on the fabrics are florals in various shades of green. On the desk sits a milk-glass lamp with a pull cord, and a writing pad with a pen.

Small oriental rugs dot the wooden floor and to my left is the bathroom. At least I have a private bathroom.

Betsy-Lou has apparently been telling me about the room. "…and you'll notice this window overlooks the upper veranda. You can access it down the hall there between the Nutmeg and Basil rooms."

I look back towards the hallway and see the door which opens to the balcony. There are wicker chairs and a table out there. A gentle breeze shudders through the trees surrounding the house, bringing the salty scent of the sea with it. Moving from one coast to the other, you would think the smell of the sea would be the same. The Pacific Ocean doesn't have the homey, memory filling aroma the Atlantic brings when it caresses your face. I close my eyes and inhale deeply.

"Your bathroom has a nice tub, perhaps you'd like to unwind from your journey with a hot bath?" I think I nod. When I open my eyes again, my attention is caught by the framed black and white photo on the wall above the desk. A portrait of a married couple. She's wearing a high-necked lace gown and he is in some sort of military uniform.

Betsy-Lou follows my gaze and walks over to the picture to remark on it. She points to the woman. "Pixie. She was the original owner's daughter. There is a different photo of her in every room of this house. I think this was her first wedding."

She has the stony gaze people in these old photos always have. Where they are told to stand stock still and not to blink because the cameras took several minutes to process.

"Her first wedding?"

"My, yes. I do believe she married four times." I can't understand that. I know it's common to re-marry; but after divorce. Their exes are still alive, and it just wasn't meant to be.

Charlie and I were meant to be. Till death do us part.

And then she asks it. Gesturing to my wedding band she says, "Will your husband be joining you on this vacation or is this a retreat for yourself?"

I can hold back the tears. I know I can. Except for that tiny little one sneaking out.

I don't want her pity too. I want to be *away* from the pity.

Far away.

"No. Just me. Here to visit some family, and my friend, Karen."

"Oh yes, the lovely girl who booked this reservation for you! You should invite her to breakfast tomorrow."

What is with this lady and breakfast?

"Being that it's a Saturday, and I know all you young folks will want to spend the day out on town, I start fixin' the meal at 7, but you are welcome to eat any time ya like up till 9 when I close down the kitchen."

Betsy-Lou's eyebrows are knitted together atop her creased forehead, her hands folded gently on her stomach. She's looking at me like she needs me to say something. It becomes an awkward staring contest until her eyebrows can't possibly be raised any higher.

I clear my throat. "Um, well I'm still on West coast time, so I don't think I'll be down quite that early." For good measure, I add, "For my coffee and toast."

Betsy-Lou's entire face slips into a frown for just a split second before she recovers her smile. "Well, maybe on Sunday mornin' you'll have more of an appetite. Now. I'll just leave ya to unpack, and then you're welcome to join me for some of that lemonade downstairs."

FOUR

I don't go downstairs. I don't unpack. And I don't take a bath.

I do take the photo off the wall and hide it in the desk. The walls used to be a darker shade of green, now clearly exhibited by the jade green square on the wall where the photo used to hang.

Karen has texted me a few times to see how I like the place. I only wrote back to let her know I was not happy with her. Then I felt guilty.

Here I am, on a forced vacation to relax. Everyone hoping I'll find my way back to being a happy school teacher, and my friend, my best friend, finds the most cheerful looking cottage in the whole town.

And all I can do is sit on the floor and cry over some stupid wedding photo of people who died a century ago.

I have to get a grip. When my grandfather died, sure, I cried. I was sad. We all gathered at the funeral and said our good-byes. But he was old; everyone knew he wasn't going to be around forever.

But Charlie...

You were just getting started. *We* were just getting started.

I did see a real counselor last week. Miss Finch had tried to see me again, she'd been sent by Principal Jackson, so I knew to make some sort of effort to show him I was taking this seriously.

So, I saw this counselor and what he said made sense. But I haven't come to grips with it just yet.

"People around you are telling you what to do, right?" I nodded.

"They have your best interest at heart but you don't take their advice because they are not grieving like you." I nodded again, with more interest.

"They say you should cry more. Or cry less. Go out more. Or stay home more. Get rid of his belongings, or maybe turn them all into keepsakes." Maybe he knows what he's talking about. People do keep telling me these things; each person contradicting the last.

"Wear black, wear red. When someone asks you how you are, with that forced sympathy, you don't know if you should smile and say 'fine', or crumple and let them see you surrendering to the grief." Wow. *He's good.*

"So, here is what I want you to do, Melanie Gibbs," I held my breath and leaned forward in anticipation of what this wise man could offer me. "Ignore them all and do what your heart tells you is right."

I paid $300 for that? Ignore everyone. Crying more is going to get me fired. Crying less makes me feel like I didn't deserve Charlie in the first place. I don't own anything red and all my black is washed out to grey. When I stay in, he haunts me. When I go out, I feel too vulnerable. What if some guy tries to flirt with me? Just the thought freaks me out. Not that anyone would flirt with this mess.

The tears are coming harder now and I bite the olive-green pillow to soften the sound of my sobs. This results in me sputtering out dust-flavored fibers, stuck to my chapped lips.

What does my heart want? There must be something I can get out of these three weeks to cheer me up.

The Atlantic breeze sweeps into the room again, the curtains billow gently into the room. I see them as ghosts.

It's hopeless. An hour later. I am still on the floor, eyes damp, and I'm pretty sure the pillow cover was not ripped when I arrived.

I've written an apology to Karen, and she's invited me over to her place for dinner. I haven't seen her new condo yet; she just bought it a few months back. She also wants me to meet Eddie, of course, but said he didn't have to be there. I told her it was okay.

Now I just have to get myself ready to go out. I can do this. A little makeup to hide the dark circles under my eyes.

Okay, a lot of makeup.

A few brush strokes through my hair, and I've got it back in a ponytail. With a lot of frizz. I need to pick up some gel or I'm going to have an afro by the end of the week.

Perhaps some earrings to add a little sparkle to distract from my red eyes? Damn. If only I had packed some. There might be a pair at the bottom of my purse, since everything seems to eventually find its way there. A meager search with my fingers comes up with a single gold hoop. Not helpful.

The purple swoop-neck top always makes me feel brighter. But after a look in the mirror, the wrinkles and the bleached spot on the hem are all I can see. That won't do. I opt for the white cotton top instead: my good ol' stand-by jeans and flip flops finish it off. I'm in Florida, after all.

One last glance in the mirror and I feel…defeated. But oh well. The puffy red eyes are not going to magically disappear before I get there. Karen will understand.

But Betsy-Lou does not.

"Oh my!" She exclaims as I come around the corner to the steps. She was apparently bringing me the lemonade since I never came down. "Are you okay, dear?"

I wave my hand flippantly, avoiding eye contact by trying to look engrossed with my fingernails. "Oh, I'm fine. Just heading out to dinner with a friend." But Betsy-Lou doesn't move aside. In fact, she's squinting at my face. Hard. It's rather uncomfortable.

"Hope you don't mind me saying so dear, but you look quite upset. I do not think everything is okay." Well, that's kind of intrusive.

I flick my eyes to her for just a moment and back down to her dainty house shoes. "Betsy-Lou…".

She interjects "Bee. Just call me Bee."

"Right, sure. Bee. I'm fine. Really." I make my cheeks rise up in a pretend smile and dare to hold eye contact. Her smile falters.

She doesn't believe me.

I don't believe me.

She's put the lemonade down next to the white ceramic water basin on the hall table and is looking me up and down. She twists her mouth to one side in thought and shakes her head disapprovingly.

"No. This won't do."

"Excuse me?" Won't do for what? It's my dinner out, not hers.

"Your eyes are too puffy and that outfit isn't cheery." She continues, "We need to get you fixed up."

"I don't have time for this, Betsy…Bee." I protest.

Her eyes flick up at mine, and for a moment I think maybe she's going to let me get past her, but I'm wrong. "Twenty minutes. Then you can be on your way. I'll even ring up the taxi for ya so it's waitin' and ready. In twenty." Her tone implies there will be no negotiating.

I want to keep protesting.

But I haven't plugged in my request for an Uber driver, and I do feel gloomy. Might as well see what she thinks she can do with this mess. I give her a nod.

"Excellent!" She claps once in glee, then continues, "First things first, let's go to the kitchen." Bee turns on her heel and heads down the stairs.

This should be interesting. How is little old granny going to fix me up? Pink rouge on my cheeks and a cardigan with embroidered flowers? I can see myself in clip-on earrings and a big beaded necklace. It almost brings a smile to my lips. Almost.

I follow her, and after only a slight pause, turn to pick up the lemonade glass and sip it on my way down.

Bee is rummaging in the massive refrigerator when I walk in. The kitchen is quaint in a shabby chic way. A shiny stainless steel oven and dishwasher stand out next to the Victorian tile embellished with purple lilies covering the wall and countertop. The fridge is also steel and exploding with food.

My fridge at home is never full. Unless it's stuffed with leftover take-out cartons and pizza boxes. Lately there are more leftovers than usual. I forgot how much Charlie ate compared to me, and I still cannot correctly guess the amount of food I'm supposed to order for just myself. I should probably text Freddie and tell him to eat my food while I'm gone. Bonus payment for taking care of Buca.

In Bee's left hand is a potato, she pulls a knife out of the drawer and places both on the built-in cutting board while she pushes her sleeves up.

"Um, I'm going out to dinner, I don't need you to cook anything." Maybe she didn't quite understand where I was headed. Or perhaps she is just forgetful, we came in here to fix me up and she's making fries.

She slices the potato into thick discs. "It's not for eatin', it's for your eyes. We have to get the swellin' down, and the starch from this here potato will do the trick in fifteen minutes."

"Right." Put potatoes on my eyes? Is she serious? I've seen the cucumber thing of course, but that's just a gimmick.

Apparently, she is serious. Bee ushers me into the lounge and instructs me to lie across the sofa. She props my feet up with a pillow. "Now close your eyes." I refuse. She repeats the command in exactly the same tone. I sigh and give in. I feel something cool and moist gently placed over each lid.

Ten minutes later, I'm still resting with two potato discs on my face and a refilled glass of delicious lemonade in my hand.

"I've rung for the taxi, Melanie, another five minutes with those taters and then we'll finish ya up." Bee set me up in here and then went off to do the rest of her 'preparations.' Whatever that may be. I've tracked her footsteps going upstairs to my room and back down.

At first the idea of her going through my bag made me cringe and I almost got up to stop her. But I talked myself into calmness. What's the difference? She'll be in there to clean anyway, and oddly, these potatoes do feel good against my eyes.

Besides, is it wrong to lay here and relax, and sip the lemonade? Bee refilled the glass a third time, repositioned the straw she's added to the glass, and told me to think like I was in a day spa by the ocean. The mention of being at a spa reminded me of how I met Charlie and I almost melted down again. But then she turned on a CD of the ocean crashing with flute notes above it. And I did relax.

I needed this more than I knew. Chasing after the kids all day at school was a great distraction, but not relaxing. I'll have to thank the Principal properly when I get back to work.

I can hear Bee humming in the lobby. She's trying to follow along with the flute, but it isn't lining up well and…I want to giggle.

I want to giggle! Amazing.

Fifteen minutes with potatoes on my face, some extra sugary lemonade, and I can feel a real bubble of laughter rising in my core. It's almost surreal, and as I think about it…I shouldn't have thought about it.

Charlie is dead. Just six months ago. I shouldn't be this happy. Not as sad either. I feel at odds with my heart.

"Okay. Let's get those taters off of ya and see our results." The woman has incredible timing. She picks the discs off, and I flutter my eyes open. My face feels tight and I stretch out my jaw to get all the muscles loose.

"Yup, you just get used to the light again and then sit up. The potatoes will have dried ya out quite a bit, rub this in." Bee hands me a little pot of cream which I dab on with my pinky finger the way I recall from the TV show *Top Model*.

I was never one for make-up and beauty tips. But when you spend all evening locked in your house with nothing to do but cry in front of the television, I learned you can pick up all sorts of tips binge watching Tyra Banks. Not that I've used a single one of those tips until today.

"Next, we're changin' ya out of that outfit. You're in the sunshine state and you should embrace it." She holds up the yellow dress I packed on a whim. She ironed it. The dress has spaghetti straps, so I couldn't wear it to work and when I tried it on for Charlie he'd said it was too bright for his taste.

"Oh, that dress. It's a little too big for me. I don't even know why I packed it."

Bee holds up the silk scarf in her other hand. Damn, I'd meant to take that musty thing to Goodwill months ago. She went through my purse too? Does this woman have no boundaries? She smiled. "This scarf as a belt, and we'll pair it with these shoes." She brandishes my white sling-back sandals. "Come on now, your taxi will be here in a few, get changin'."

All in, I shrug and take the clothes from her and head upstairs to change. She calls after me, "I didn't see any jewelry in your stuff, so I laid out some of my own on the desk for ya!"

I roll my eyes to the ceiling.

Great, here come the beads and clip-ons.

Back in my room I strip out of the jeans and the shirt and pull the dress over my head. Already I feel lighter. The skirt moves freely when I twist, I can't help but twirl all the way around. Kids do know what's best.

Right, the scarf-belt. I twist it around itself, and then around my waist and into a bow on the side; check the mirror. The bow looks ridiculous. Trying again, I let it sit widely across my hips…no. Twisted up was better. Maybe just a knot with the ends hanging in front. Wow, the dress looks like it was made for my body.

"Tyra was right, a good belt makes all the difference." I muse aloud. The image staring back at me is of a slimmer girl. Someone in bright yellow with a smile on her face.

That's me, smiling.

I'm smiling.

Don't think about it. Charlie would want you to keep the smile. Keep smiling, keep smiling… no use. I can't keep it up, but I'm not going to cry right now. Those potatoes got the puffiness down and I refuse to waste another fifteen minutes going through the routine again.

"Melanie! Taxi is here." Bee calls up the steps.

Bee's jewelry is still on the desk. Ladybug earrings and a butterfly charm on a small chain for the necklace. Whimsical, just like the rest of this place.

I quickly throw on the ornaments and slip the sandals onto my feet before heading downstairs.

Bee is waiting at the bottom with her arms crossed, giving me a head to toe look-over as I walk towards her. "Much better," she appraises. "You'll be needin' some gel for your hair if ya want to get rid of the frizzies."

My hand automatically goes up to smooth them down.

She humphs through closed lips, "You got gel magically built into your hands? Here." She holds out a little tube of clear gel and squirts a bit of it into my palm. "Try that again."

I rub the gel between my palms and then over my head. When I reach the mirror by the front door I have to admit, I do look a lot better. "Bee, where did you learn all these tricks to cheering up a stranger?"

"Ya spend enough time runnin' an inn and ya learn all sorts of things." She snaps the lid back on the gel and says, "Now go, have fun with your friends tonight. The door stays unlocked all night, but the lights will be low. I'll see ya in the mornin' over breakfast. Coffee and toast." The last bit she says with a little extra *humph* on the end of it.

Okay, now I know for sure I insulted her earlier with my breakfast remarks. "Well, maybe you could make something else?"

"Such as?" Her grey eyebrows arch over her eyes.

"Um, well… I don't really…"

Bee holds up a finger and suggests, "How about a frittata? That will give ya the right pep to get your mornin' goin'."

"Sounds great. Sure. Awesome." What the hell is a frittata?

The cab honks out front. "I should get going." I shoulder my purse and adjust the butterfly charm so it is centered on my neck. I am going to have an okay night. It's going to be…fun.

***

Karen's apartment is only a few miles away, I could probably walk there. I could use the exercise. Maybe I'll walk back!

When she opens the door to her flat she grabs me into a tight hug. I see the open bottle of wine in her hand and know I'm not walking back.

She's dyed her hair a bright red, tipped in yellow, and shaved off the underside so the top part flops over like a wave. Karen gets away with creative looks better than anyone I know.

Memories flick through my head: a spiky black Mohawk, frosted ringlets, braided extensions down to her knees. Once she even dyed her hair in blue and purple stripes. And it looked amazing.

That is the advantage of being an artist. I guess you are expected to look as interesting as your pieces. She's a sculptor and the apartment shows off her talents well. The entire place is stark white, just like an art studio. The kitchen counters, the furniture, even her dog, Daisy, is pure white.

In sharp contrast, there are several beautiful glass mobiles hanging from the loft's ceilings, vases made from old shoes displaying origami flowers. Lamps of welded silverware sitting atop the cubed end tables, and in the corner a large…um…

"Karen, what is that supposed to be?" I point at the six-foot tall creation. It kind of looks like a tree trunk with snakes all over it. The snake-ribbons are made up of little blobs from every color under the rainbow.

"It's a gum tree." She says this nonchalantly over her shoulder as she pours the wine, as if it should be obvious.

"A gum tree?" On closer inspection, the little blobs are chewed pieces of gum. I crinkle my nose at the thought of all those germs. Not a very sanitary art piece.

"It's my new concept for the show coming up this summer. '*Leftovers*.' I'm making all sorts of pieces out of used coffee cups and French fry cartons, the bones from buffalo wings, peanut shells, that sort of stuff. This is going to be the centerpiece!" Karen is looking at her tree with all the admiration of a mother watching her child learn how to walk.

Now I see the cases of gum stacked up by the base of it on the floor. Every possible gum you could think of. There is also a bin of gum wrappers. No doubt she plans on using those for some other sculpture.

"Here," she bends down and picks up a few packets of gum, "pick one and chew it for a little while and then stick it on. I could use some help with this piece." Obligingly, I select a white square of Dentyne and pop it in my mouth. Although I now have a dilemma with the wine glass Karen has handed me. Merlot and mint. Not happening.

A dark-haired man dressed in a crisp blue shirt with turned up collars steps into the room. "I see she already has you working on her art? Karen darling, mint isn't exactly a complement to the wine." It's like her new boyfriend - wait, fiancé - read my mind. He's different than I expected. More normal. Karen usually goes after creatives like herself. Guys with piercings in odd locations and tattoos everywhere. Once she dated this guy with the word 'Earth' tattooed across his forehead with the 'A' replaced by a green and blue orb that did not look anything like Earth, or the letter A for that matter.

Karen was a vegan during that relationship. Thank god she is over the diet restrictions! I can smell the steaks cooking on the grill through the open door to their balcony.

"You must be Edward." I say, reaching for his hand and right away noticing his manicure.

"It's Eddie. And as my soon to be best-friend-in-law, you get a hug."

"Oh!" The exclamation escapes me as he wraps me in his arms. He lifts me from my feet in a hug-twirl.

"Eddie!" Karen hisses. "I told you to stay cool."

"It's okay Karen, I'm feeling…better?" Yes, better I guess is a good word.

Surprisingly, I mean it.

"Eddie, go check the steaks, please." Eddie taps her butt as he walks past her. Karen shoots me a glance to see if it's bothering me to watch them flirt. It does. It's painful. But I'm smiling on the outside, just like I am supposed to.

He's taller than Charlie was. Broader. Darker. And clean-cut. "He's not your usual type, Karen. Where'd you meet him again?"

"He's an international art dealer. I met him at one of my shows." She adds in a mock whisper. "He hates my work."

Really? Her work is awesome, sells for bundles. Well, looking at the gum tree, maybe her newer stuff is not as universal.

Karen must be able to read my face because she laughs and says, "It's okay. It doesn't matter if people like my artwork, it only matters that they find it interesting. The more people talk about it, the better the piece is. And Eddie likes to talk about my work. He tells everyone who will listen how horrible it is and then they cannot wait to see it for themselves." She takes a sip of wine.

I take a sip too, and immediately sputter. Pulling the gum from my mouth, I choke out "where should I stick this?" The white gum has turned lightly pink from the wine sipping debacle. I've helped Kay with art projects in the past, even let her make twelve molds of my right leg for some freaky super human sculpture piece she worked on in college. But tonight, I'm going to contribute only one piece of gum.

Karen looks from the gum in my hands to her tree, and studies the sculpture for a second. She points to a spot between a red blob and a yellow blob, and I dutifully press it into place trying not to think about whose salvia I might be touching. Karen sways a little to the left and right, studying the new addition and then nods her head, satisfied. She walks to the open door.

Following her outside, I watch as she goes behind Eddie and lazily drapes her arm around his waist. They discuss the grilling times of the steaks and the asparagus while I sip my wine. It is hard to watch them together. But it's a good challenge. I can't hide from all the people in love. I can't just delete Valentine's Day from the calendar.

Oh, wait, I did that. *Grr.*

Karen has turned back to me. Her eyes narrow, and a smile spreads across her face. "I love those earrings, Mel. I've never seen you wear stuff like that before, they're fun."

Automatically my hand goes to touch the little red bugs in my earlobes and I think of Bee today, insisting I cheer up before I came over here. I owe her a bigger thank you. A total stranger, observing and interjecting where most people would turn a blind eye. At a regular hotel, no one would have noticed if I was upset or crying. Or they would have noticed, but then looked the other way. Not get involved. No one wants to get involved with strangers.

But Bee did.

Chills radiate across my shoulders causing goosebumps on my arms. I rub them away with my free hand. "I meant to thank you, Kay. For putting me up in the candy house. I've never stayed at a place like that before."

Her face splits into a wide grin. "I knew it would grow on you. I also knew you would protest if I told you about it before you got there."

A memory comes to mind of the time she tricked me into attending a Sting concert by randomly saying she was in the mood for ice cream, and then kidnapping me for the two-hour drive to the venue. With a bag packed of concert appropriate attire for me to change into when we got there, of course. Had she told me beforehand about going to a music concert I'd have found twelve and half reasons to back out. It was one of our best nights together back in college. I would have regretted not going. Yeah, she knows me so well. Too well.

I sip at my glass. God, this wine is good. And that was my last sip. I've drunk the entire glass already. Seeing the problem, Karen goes back to the kitchen for a new pour.

Eddie turns to me. "I have to say, Karen warned me you were down and out lately. But you seem to be doing okay, Melanie."

He's a straight shooter, no small talk, I love him already. I nod. "Yeah, I'm starting to get somewhere."

"Where do you want to get?" He turns away and moves the asparagus off the grill as he says this.

Back to happiness. Back to knowing my life is going to work out okay, even without Charlie. Do you have any idea how many plans we had for our future? The kids. A house. A trip to the Bahamas. A dog. He was going to coach little league and I was going to run scout meetings. You don't even realize how many unmet plans you've made with someone till they are gone. We had a whole lifetime of events laid out. Milestones to surpass and goals to reach.

With a deep sigh I say, "Right now, I just want to get to that steak." The downside of ordering out all the time is the aroma isn't ever quite right.

Eddie turns back to me with the steak and asparagus on a platter. A wide grin across his face, "Well, you are in luck my dear. Because dinner is ready."

After the meal, the three of us sit outside sipping the last dregs of the second bottle of wine, and they reenact the proposal for me. I had to insist I really, truly was going to be okay hearing the story.

Eddie had been out of town collecting art for an auction and was flying home. He asked Karen to pick him up from the airport and they met at the baggage claim. While they were waiting for his luggage to come around, he went to the bathroom and told her what his bag looked like in case it came around while he was gone.

Karen takes over telling me the next part. "I waited for the bag to come around, and waited and waited. Eddie was gone for quite some time and most of the bags were gone. I'm starting to think his luggage didn't make it on the plane."

Then she spotted a red ring box coming down the belt with a little handwritten sign sitting on it with cursive font that spelled out "Marry me."

Since she wasn't looking for a ring box, she was looking for luggage, Karen watched it go past and looked around the crowd for the lucky lady who was getting proposed to. Which is when Eddie yelled out to her from the other end of the belt "Karen! That was for you!"

At this point in the story they both laugh. Their hands are entwined and their eyes sparkle as they look at one another. Karen always exclaimed to whoever cared to listen that marriage wasn't for her. She didn't believe in the conformity of it all. But Eddie swept her off her feet in under a year and apparently changed her mind about the whole governance of marriage. They are clearly each other's yin and yang.

Of course, she said yes, and they moved in together.

My engagement to Charlie was quite the opposite. We dated for three solid years and then, though we planned a small wedding, waited seven months after the proposal before we said 'I do.' A small ring in a small box, presented to me on bent knee at a candlelit dinner in the only four-star restaurant we could afford. I set up a drawer with my nightgowns at his cottage; he had a spare toothbrush he left at my place. But we didn't move in together until after the wedding, So freakin' cliché. I never doubted for a moment he'd propose, never doubted we'd have a simple and loving life together.

Forever. Till death do us part.

I'm smiling on the outside with what I hope looks like a loving, toothy grin pressed out of my wine-numbed cheeks, but I want to cry so hard on the inside.

7:30am...*that don't mean I've forgotten where I came from...*
7:41am...*spent his whole life spinnin' his wheels...*
7:52am *...but that could never be, you got a hold on me...*
8:03am *...wish I could start this whole thing over again...*

Okay, okay. I'll stop hitting the snooze button. I let the radio keep playing this time, some Toby Keith song, and stretch my arms out from the warm covers. I'm feeling well rested, more so then I have in a long while. I don't recall waking up at all last night.

This bed is really comfy. Or maybe it was the wine last night. Or that yummy steak. Or...oh the wonderful aroma of coffee!

A robe hangs on the back of the suite's door, I slip it on. Green, of course. Just about everything in here is green, as if I'm inside a honeydew. After washing the sleep from my eyes and checking my jaw line for those annoying little white zits I squeeze out every morning, I see the corner of a paper wedged under my door.

I pull the paper into my room. It's a handwritten note from Bee.

There will be more coffee when you come down for breakfast.

More?

Upon opening the door, I find the most petite little pot of coffee sitting atop a lit steno on a silver tray. A flowery coffee mug, with a little silver milk pitcher, and a matching dish holding a pyramid of sugar cubes sits upon it. I didn't think sugar actually came in cubes outside of the movies.

After mixing my coffee to taste light and sweet, and crunching a sugar cube just because I can, I sit back on the bed and let the wonderful liquid cascade down my throat. I can feel the warmth spreading through my veins.

A quick shower and I toss on the jeans and shirt I had planned on wearing last night, before Bee talked me into the dress, and head down the stairs.

All the doors are closed but I can hear the voices from behind the one marked Rosemary Lounge.

"Larry! Use your fork!" screeches a woman, her sooty voice reeking of decades of cigarette smoke.

"Bacon tastes better when you can suck the fat off your fingers," Larry replies in a deep baritone.

"Ohhh Larry! That's disgusting!"

"Mmm mmm." *Slurp.*

I push open the door to see the couple sitting at the table with the same china as my morning coffee in front of them, the plates covered with the remains of their meal. The guy, who must be Larry, is popping one chubby finger into his mouth at a time and sucking the bacon grease off through his pink lips.

The lady sitting next to him is watching with a face of horror, her fork frozen in mid-air with a dollop of her breakfast about to roll off it.

Larry reaches for another strip of bacon and tilts his head all the way back, raising the meat to dangle above his open maw and slowly lowers it in.

I cough a little to announce myself.

Larry pulls the bacon from his mouth and turns to look at me, he puts the bacon back on the plate and tries unsuccessfully to pick it up with his fork. The woman shakes her head and moves the fork at her mouth, but the eggs wobble and fall in her lap. In a fury of fluttering hands the fork clatters onto her plate and she turns towards the open door and calls, "Bee, I think I will take you up on that offer for a Bloody Mary after all!"

Larry wipes his mouth with the cloth napkin tucked into the collar of his shirt and gestures for me to join them at the table. I've been standing frozen in the open door, and jolt myself into taking a step forward opting for a seat at the other end.

"Good morning young lady. Bee told us you might be joining us. Uh...Renee right?" Larry is a portly man; I couldn't appreciate his roundness from the side when I first entered the room. From this angle he looks, well, kind of like a pumpkin.

I open my mouth to correct him when Ash lady interrupts. If at all possible, she looks even more upset, "Renee? Where did you get Renee from? Bee never said her name was Renee. Isn't that the name of your new secretary? Were you thinking about her just now!" Larry puts his hands up in defense but can't swallow his food fast enough to speak. "Larry! Were you thinking about your secretary while we are on our anniversary trip?"

Larry swallows loudly. "No, no, Love. I wasn't thinking about anyone but you. Just you, dear." Beads of sweat are breaking out on his forehead. "Just you my sugar muffin." One fat finger reaches up to touch her cheek but she turns away. Margie looks like she is trying just a wee bit too hard to look young. Thick eyeliner and mascara make her eyes pop, but almost too much emphasis on the *pop*. And while the skin on her cheeks is tight, the wrinkles on her neck indicate something has been worked on.

She rolls her eyes. "I'm Margie and this is my soon to be ex-husband, Larry." She unfolds her arms to flip a hand in his direction.

"Oh, don't say that dear, you always say that. I would never leave my muffin-wuffin." Larry succeeds in stroking her cheek this time and Margie turns further away from him and crosses her arms again.

"Melanie, good mornin'!" Bee's sing-song voice fills the room as she comes in and places a Bloody Mary in Margie's hand with a wink in my direction. In a fluid motion, she plops a few more strips of bacon on Larry's plate, then is by my side depositing another cute little cup of coffee in front me. She moves like a young waitress around the table, not really pausing, her lavender dress breezing away from her body. Embroidery decorates her collar and a little bit of lace peeks out below her hem.

I bring the coffee to my face and let the warm steam fill my lungs.

"I take it you have already met the Hellins?" Lowering her voice for my ears only she adds, "Don't mind them dear, they come here every year for their anniversary and they fight like this each mornin'. By tonight they'll be swoonin' again. I always make sure they are on a floor all to themselves so no one else has to…hear." She winks at me again and heads into the kitchen in a swirl of chiffon.

Hear them fight or hear their making-up from a fight? Or both? Margie would have to be on top or bent over the bed because Larry's bulk would surely crush her in the missionary position.

Oh, now I have an image in my head I *really* wish wasn't there. Margie takes a drink of her Bloody Mary and lets out a scratchy moan of pleasure.

Coffee. Focus on the coffee. The cream and sugar are near Larry and as I am about to ask him to pass the tray he pops another strip of bacon into his mouth sucking on his fingers again.

I guess the moment of decorum when I first entered has already passed.

Charlie and I never fought like that. We loved each other too damn much to fight. We always smiled and gave each other little kisses for no reason, and held hands whenever we walked around town. God, how I miss snuggling on the sofa to watch a movie, and making love every night before we slept.

Well maybe not *every* night.

Wait.

I haven't thought about this is in a long time. I know we hadn't made love during the first weeks of September, but Charlie was working on a big project. He was so exhausted by the time he came home; that's to be expected. And those last few weeks of the summer where I stayed up late to get ready for the school year, and new students, he'd often be asleep by the time I turned out the lights.

Did we really spend our evenings like that? Our noses stuck in work and in totally separate rooms. Our own anniversary. Yes, I remember we had a romantic evening that night. But that was all the way back in July.

"Your frittata!" Bee places a plate down in front of me and I blink a few times to get the image of Charlie stooped over the table in our kitchen chair out of the way so I can see what is in front of me.

On the plate is a square hunk of yellow with hints of green and red dotting it. Some sort of white sauce adorns the top of it and a bright assortment of fruit slices are on the side.

"You don't strike me as a bacon person, but I could make some if ya like."

"I'll take some more, Bee!" Larry mumbles around a mouth full of his last stick of meat.

Margie swats his arm, "No you won't. You've already had seven pieces and your doctor said you aren't supposed to have any! None, zero, zilch."

"But dear, we're on vacation!"

I shake my head more to myself then to anyone. "No, this…this looks amazing Bee."

Bee has a smirk on her face. "And what about some toast? I could crisp up some bread and bring out the jam if ya still have a cravin'?"

"Thank you, no." I still feel guilty about that, but she doesn't have to rub it in. "So…what exactly is this?" I poke at the square with my fork, it's firm but wobbles a little.

"A frittata!" Bee shrugs her shoulders like that is supposed to explain it to me.

Right. So, I guess I'll just eat it. Bee waits, with her hands on her hips, and watches me take my first bite.

In fact, the Hellins are watching me eat.

Why do I suddenly feel like I am on a game show? *Welcome to 'Guess the Ingredients'. And now, Melanie Gibbs will attempt to figure out what the hell is in a frittata. Come on folks; let's all watch her decipher the mystery ingredients!*

The texture is creamy, and it is easy to tell the main component is eggs. I take a second mouthful as they all continue to watch me. Well Larry isn't watching me. He's trying to fish the bacon scrap off his wife's dish while she is distracted.

Chilies. Tomato maybe. There is something white in here too. "Potato?" I examine the next bite before popping it in.

Bee claps her hands in glee and nods her head, setting the little pearl bracelet adorned with insect charms jingling on her wrist. "That's the trick to gettin' a nice firm frittata that sits upright like this. Grated potato. Lots of cheese. A hint of spice balanced with a soothin' crème fraiche on top. With one of my favorite flavors, sundried tomatoes."

"Yumm!" I manage, and pop in another forkful with gusto.

Pleased with my response, she heads back into the kitchen and the door swings behind her.

"Bee likes to experiment with new dishes. Every time we come here, we try something we've never had before." Margie has drained her Bloody Mary and is nibbling on the remains of the red stained celery.

"She said you were here for your anniversary, congrats." I lift my coffee mug to them in a toast and take another sip.

"Humph! Like it's a joy to still be married to this lump." Margie gestures with her celery to Larry who has finally stopped scrounging for more to eat and is finishing his coffee.

"Love you too, dear." He utters from behind the cup.

"We come here every year mainly because of Bee's cooking. It's always a surprise to see what she's serving."

I continue to eat the frittata and a few pieces of fruit as Margie continues. "We came here the first time for our thirtieth anniversary. I can still remember the lime muffins Bee served with cilantro jam. Tomorrow it will be forty-two years since I married Lawrence." She has a serene look on her face as she says this. But that quickly falls as she adds with a jab of her thumb, "And now I'm stuck with Larry here." She makes air quotes when she uses his shorter name.

"Hey!" Larry has finished his coffee and is getting fidgety. His eyes keep dropping to my plate and the remains of the frittata.

"Larry is twice the man Lawrence was. If you get my drift." Margie stands up and places her napkin on the table. "Excuse me dear, I need a ciggy. Come on Larry."

Larry pushes his chair back and it takes him a few tries to get to his feet. Margie ticks her fingers on her leg, the cigarette already in her hand.

I wonder which will go first. Him from all the food, or her from all the smoke? And immediately, I regret the thought. I wouldn't wish the vacancy in my heart on anyone. Not even these two.

They exit the building and I can hear the rocking chair creak in protest as Larry takes a seat on the porch. Faint traces of Margie's smoke wisp by the window. At least it's quiet now.

I munch on a grape and cut up the remainder of the frittata with my fork. I can hear Bee in the kitchen washing dishes. That ocean music with the flute notes is on.

Yesterday, in this room with the lights down, and potatoes on my eyes, I didn't get a chance to look around. I first seek out Pixie's portrait, which is easy enough to spot. A large painting of a young girl holding a puppy hangs above the fireplace. I've a hunch it's Pixie.

A filled bookcase fits between the windows that look out to the porch where the Hellins are sitting, and I make a mental note to peruse the titles later. The sofa is creased tan leather with matching wing chairs on either side, all surrounding a glass coffee table that has a collage of photographs stuck under the surface.

The wind blows through an open window and another scent catches my attention. The smell of rosemary must be coming from the large potted plant on the mantel, giving the room its namesake. The walls are a soft yellow and the room feels grand. You could host a decent sized party here.

In fact, this table could seat eight and with another five over by the fireplace, I bet you could pull in a few more chairs and—

"Can I get ya any more coffee, Melanie?" Bee comes in and starts to clear away the dishes from the departed guests. She has an apron on over her dress now, a white cotton thing with blue birds and red roses that reminds me of the cross-stitches they made us do in home-ec class. Maybe she likes to embroider in her down time? Does she have down time?

"Oh no, two is my limit." I used to drink more. Charlie would make a full pot every morning, and I am pretty sure I drank more of it than him since he left before I did, and I could not stand to toss out the leftover. But I couldn't figure out how to work the pot after he was gone. Now I just pick up a coffee from the corner deli on my way to work and grab another cup from the teacher's lounge.

"Bee?" She looks up at me but her hands keep working the table. "Didn't you say there were three other guests?"

"Oh yes! Roger. He had breakfast right when I opened the kitchen and headed out to the beach. Unless ya get up early, you probably won't see too much of him. Beach bum that one!"

"How many people does this place hold?"

"Well." She puts the stack of dishes back down on the table, and gestures as she speaks. "There are seven rooms so that would be your main fourteen. Plus, there are two rooms with sofa beds so you could get another four there. And if you count babies, the Vanilla Suite up on the third floor has a crib in it, there could be nineteen total. Plus, me of course. But with all the ins and outs there are usually only ten or twelve at one time." Bee picks up the dishes in her wrinkled hands and retreats to the kitchen.

Twenty to be full, and there are only five of us here now. Including Bee, of course.

"And you cook for everyone all by yourself?" I call after her. I can't even cook for one. This wiry lady is cooking for a whole army, every morning.

She pushes the door open with an elbow just enough so I can see her face. "That's what we innkeepers do ya know. Cook and clean. Clean some more, and then cook again."

Putting the cup on the plate, I carry my own mess into the kitchen for her.

"Oh, thank you, Melanie. You needn't do that. I trust you'll be headin' out to have some fun today?" The sink is full of soapy water and Bee is up to her elbows in it, the tops of pink rubber gloves barely visible above the deep basin.

"I'm not sure about that." Fun. Ha.

"Did you enjoy your evenin' out?" I notice the little bumble bee earrings peeking out between Bee's curls. I need to give her the jewelry back.

"I did, yes. Thanks to you. You were right; wearing yellow helped. And my friend loved the insect charms; I have them upstairs for you." I turn towards the door when she interrupts.

"That's okay dear; you just leave them up there. I'll pick them up when I make up your room later today. Okay?" Bee has finished scrubbing whatever was down under all the suds, rubber gloves removed, and is drying her hands off on a towel attached to the oven door. She tugs open the oven door to peek inside.

The most wonderful fragrance wafts to my nose and despite my full stomach, I start to salivate.

"Bee! What is that…it smells incredible!" I inhale so deeply I actually close my eyes and sigh.

"You tell me. What do you smell?" I breathe in a deeper whiff, and I have it. The smell of yeast. I know that smell. We have a lesson on yeast in my classroom and all the kids experiment with making yeast bloom in little hot water dishes. "Bread."

"What kind of bread?" Comically, she waves her hand to send the aroma in my direction before closing the oven door. I try again. It's something sweet, like a summer garden.

I'm shaking my head without a thought in mind when the memory suddenly hits me. My brother's fruit-stained t-shirt. The same sweet scent all around us. My mom used to take us to the U-pick fields every summer. We would spend the afternoon running through, and jumping over, the rows of strawberries. Our fingers stained red as we popped them into our mouth instead of into our allotted buckets.

"Bringin' back some memories there? Good food will do that." Bee is grinning ear-to-ear when I open my eyes. I can feel the smile on my face, too.

"Strawberries. We used to pick them as a kid. Strawberry bread. I never heard of such a thing."

"You just wait till tomorrow's breakfast. This here," she pats the oven, "is just the start of what is on the menu for tomorrow. Sundays, I go all out. Tradition, ya know? There will be a few more people comin' in today to stay for the weekend so I have some preppin' to do."

"Right. I should get going anyway, and let you get on with it." But I don't move. Despite the closed oven door, the sweet smell of warm strawberries is still present and I want to breathe in every last drop. The scents are bringing back such wonderful emotions. The sea breeze last night was the start of it. The strawberries today are helping. My chest shakes with my next inhale, just a little. I squeeze my eyes a tad tighter to ensure no tears are going to well up, not this early in the day.

"You never answered my question earlier, what will ya be doing today?" Bee says this with her back to me now, her hands busily clearing away a space on the counter and setting up different size bowls for her next concoction.

When I still hesitate, she adds with a wave of her hand, "Don't you worry, never mind. Just have fun with whatever it is you are doing, and I'll see ya in the mornin' unless ya need something from me later today!" And with that she dismisses me from her kitchen. I reluctantly move one step at a time until I've left the warmth of the kitchen. When the door swings closed behind me, my instinct is to run back in and tell Bee what I need to do today, because I don't want to be doing it, and maybe she can talk me out of it. But I have to.

SIX

What I am doing will not be fun. It will be a chore. While coming to Florida to see Karen is always a positive, it also means seeing my parents. Which is not a *bad* thing. It's just, well, a chore.

We didn't grow up down here. My parents migrated to the good ol' state of Florida when my brother and I were in high school. They picked our town for the name alone, Pelican Bay, although I'm not entirely sure why. As far as I knew, we didn't have any affinity with pelicans.

My family came from further up the coast in New Jersey. My Aunt Julia still lives up there, but she is always traveling so I hardly ever saw her even when we were nearby. We had the beach at our doorstep every summer, and snow would fall every winter and in between the two spring flowers and autumn leaves.

In Florida, there is the beach of course, but it's crowded with tourists all the time, not just in the summer, like at home. And there is no snow. In between summer and not-summer is hurricane season. I could live without winter, but I missed spring and fall. San Diego gave me no respite from that, out there it is just summer, more summer, almost not quite summer, and summer again.

If you go for a hike in the woods at home, you might run across a deer. Here, if you go for a hike, you might step on an alligator. We stopped hiking when we moved to Florida, took up urban walking instead. Not always safer though, still had crazy drivers and the occasional stupid teen skateboarding over your toes. But at least no gators to drag you down into the mud never to be seen again.

When you are sixteen years old, you don't care what your parent's reasons are, you just hate them for doing things you don't want to do, and making you come along. I had to leave behind my friends and I swore it would be impossible to ever meet anyone down here that I would like. In the times we had visited, I most often encountered old people and college kids. But we visited only on school breaks to visit my grandfather. He had his house in Florida for the winters, and the family house in New Jersey for the summers. But as he got older, his time in Florida grew longer.

We spent every holiday down in the warmer state, and each time we visited, my folks talked about how great it would be to move here. When dad got hurt on the job and his company offered early retirement, they hesitated long enough to find a golf course they wanted to live by. Enter Pelican Bay into my home address after that.

I hate golfing.

So, I wasn't exactly excited about the move and starting a new school right in the middle of my sophomore year. For a while, I was pretty much the outsider, till I met Karen in junior year in an art class. While I kept busy trying to paint the perfect rose petal, she poked holes through canvas and sprayed the ripped edges with hairspray to make them stand erect.

My brother, Todd, took to Florida much better than I did. For starters, he loves golf. So clearly, he is the family favorite. He hadn't started high school yet, and had worried about fitting in. It was a good move for his sake.

He lives in Miami now, with his partner Bill. They both work at a hospital, which is how they met. Todd is an RN and Bill works the front desk in the emergency room. I don't get to talk to them very much these days although they did fly out for the funeral.

Todd was mad at me for leaving the state and moving so far away. I knew he'd have an issue with it. He spent months debating the decision to move to Miami for work and that was only the other side of the peninsula. Charlie and I moved to the other side of the country.

The last few years have been a little tense between us. Bill did his best to keep me in the loop with news on with my brother or my parents, more so then they themselves ever did. But I learn more about their lives through their Facebook posts than firsthand. Apparently, they've refinished their bathroom recently, joined the *People who like macaroni and cheese* club, are fans of their local indie movie theater, and have over eight-hundred friends. They share a profile, I have no idea if they both like everything on there, or if one likes it, and the other just deals with it.

Charlie used Facebook to stay up to date with his clients, watching for posts about upcoming skiing trips or overseas travels so he could remind them to update their insurance plans. I didn't get too into Facebook. After seeing all the sympathy posts people starting authoring on my behalf, and tagging me, I closed my Facebook profile entirely.

In the few conversations we have had since the accident, Todd has already started suggesting that I should move back to Florida.

"Come on Sis, move closer to your family, where we can support you." Is what he said the last time we talked.

The idea of getting support from my family isn't the problem. True, I went straight from my parent's home to living with Charlie. I never really did the independent thing.

But that doesn't mean I can't!

So what if I tried to live at the dorms during college and moved back home after a month? That had nothing to do with me being able to live alone. It had everything to do with sharing a bathroom with five other girls. When I noticed someone had been using my razor…well, it just wasn't okay!

I can live alone. I just need to learn a few things. Like how to program the DVR. And I need to make the door hinge stop squeaking. I'm sure I can figure out how to get the bills on auto payment in a new account. Right now they are still coming from our joint account, with Charlie's name on everything.

Ok. So, Charlie took care of me. But I can do it myself. I'm sure of it.

I guess I should learn how to use the coffee pot first.

But I can't leave during the middle of the school year anyway. So I haven't given Todd's suggestion much thought.

Of course, Mom has.

It takes her all of fifteen minutes after I arrive at their home for her to bring it up. I use the term 'home' loosely. I'm sitting on a patio chair on the deck of their boat which is docked amongst forty-nine other boats at the Pelican Bay Marina. Last year they sold the house and most of their stuff. They keep some travel items and holiday decorations in a storage locker but downsized enough that they could live on their boat full-time.

Apparently, a lot of people do that. Several other boats at the dock also have clusters of people sitting on them, sipping an early gin and tonic or playing bridge.

"Does anyone actually take their boat out, or do you all just stay docked here?" I turn three-hundred sixty degrees. Parked boats full of folks in every direction.

"Don't you go be changing the subject now Mel-Mel. I wanna know whatcha gonna be doing this summer? Are me and your pops getting our little girl back home or not?" Mom is wearing red from head to toe. Long pants and long sleeves, even a straw hat with a red bow atop her head. Hair dyed brown as if she had never aged. Gold bangles adorn both wrists, and matching earrings swing from her ears. A toe ring catches my eye, peeking out from her red sandals.

Retired life has suited her pretty well. Course, she didn't actually retire. She was a full-time writer for the newspaper back home and now writes columns for the local paper down here. These days she writes about boating and golfing, and other leisure events. Once a month I get an envelope in the mail with newspaper clippings of her columns. Along with any other columns she thinks I might like to read.

I tried to tell her that I don't need her to send them. Her paper is online and I could just look it up if I wanted to read it. Which I don't. All those clippings are stuffed in a drawer at home, unread. Any time we talk about her not sending more, I think she's finally going to stop; and then the end of the month comes around, and there is the envelope with her handwritten address label on it.

"Isn't that right, Richard?" Mom doesn't turn her head; she just says this louder so her voice will carry to him.

All I can see of my father is what's left of his grey hair on the top of his head. Right now, he is standing on the side dock, polishing the metal inlays on the side of the boat.

"Of course!" His voices booms with authority, that deep tenor that he's always had when he speaks.

"Dad, do you even know what she's asking you?" I sit up in my chair to make eye contact with him over the railing.

He shrugs. "Does it matter? I'll end up agreeing at some point, might as well be now and save us both some time."

I twirl the ice around in my glass. Mom keeps a perpetual supply of Diet Pepsi on board. You don't get asked what you want to drink when you visit her; it's always Diet Pepsi, and nothing but Diet Pepsi. When she came out to San Diego in

October, she went to Costco's and stocked up. I still have a case left over at my apartment.

While the thought is on my mind, I get my phone out and text Freddie to drink the soda, too. He already happily replied last night about eating the left-overs. Then followed with an afterthought text that my cat was just fine.

"I don't know, Mom. A lot has changed over the last couple months and I don't really want to make too many more changes." God, I hate these pointless conversations with my parents.

"Why the heck not! This is the best time to change. Change everything all at once, that's what I say. Get it all over-de-dover with." She pours out the rest of the can over the ice in her glass, and pops another can open to top off mine. "Todd could fly out and drive back with you."

"Todd is allergic to cats, and I'd have to bring Buca with me." She isn't listening.

"There is a preschool just across the street for all the kids from the boat owners." She taps her chin thoughtfully, "Well, grandkids I think for most of them. 'Cept for the Hell Fire owners, I think that is their actual child. You know those biker types, having babies when they're in their fifties!" And raising kids on parked boats. Or docked. Parked?

"Where would I stay?" Oh, that was a mistake. I know better than to ask questions that continue the theme of the conversation I desperately do not want to be having.

"Here, of course!" She puts her hands up in the air and twists around like Vanna White displaying the grand prize.

Delightful.

A room aboard a small boat with my parents. Every widow's dream.

"I'm twenty-eight, mom. I can't live with my parents."

"And just why not, you tell me one good reason why a child cannot move home with their mommy and daddy?" She leans in to squeeze my chin and puckers her lips to give me an air kiss.

"That's just it! I'm not a child." I slam the glass down on the table and stand up in frustration. The problem with a boat deck is that you can't pace. So, I step off, onto the dock. I pick up a rag abandoned by my father, and start polishing the portholes.

For a few minutes, we do this in silence. My dad tenderly shining the railings, and me getting all my pain out onto the window casings. I don't think I'm being very effective though, they are just as smeared as before. I'm just swirling the streaks around and around.

"Ya' know Mel, you don't need to do what they want you to do. You have to do what you want to do." Dad says this quietly, straight forward. He always says things matter of fact.

I nod. He isn't looking at me, but I know he saw it.

"You just have to figure out what it is you want to do, now."

As if it was that simple.

I don't have any reason to stay in San Diego other than my job. It's only my second year though, and they aren't happy with me right now. I have a few friends there, but no one like Karen.

But just the thought of moving back to Florida feels…it feels like I'm giving up.

Yeah, for a while I did want to give up. I was a useless wreck after the police told me about the car crash. Charlie had died on impact and they wouldn't let me see him. Even after they had cleaned him up, the mortician refused to let me see him, and insisted that we hold a closed-casket ceremony.

My therapist said I wasn't granted the closure I thought I was due. I didn't get to say my good-byes to a tangible object. But that's all he was at that point anyway. An object. Not Charlie anymore. I had to say my farewell to his pictures. And his watch. And the clothes in his closet. And all those boxes of paperwork his office delivered, still stacked up around the house.

I hated him. I hated him for dying like that. If he had to die, couldn't it have been after they had him at the hospital, and I raced to his side, and he got to tell me how much he loved me and that I should go on without him? If I have to be a widow before I'm thirty, why couldn't I have the fairytale accident and death that the movies always show us?

He didn't tell me what I should do if he died. We never talked about it.

The first time someone said, "Charlie would have wanted you to go on with your life." I thought, really? Are you sure?

Because he never said that.

What if he didn't want me to go on with my life?

What if he was like the Egyptians I teach my kids about. The ones that died with a list of the other people that had to die too, so they could all be together in the afterlife. Favorite servants, siblings, even their pets. They were all sacrificed to be buried with their King.

Charlie was my King, and maybe he would have wanted me to follow him. Sacrifice myself upon hearing of his own demise, or throw myself on top of his coffin after it was lowered into the grave. What if his spirit now hated me for not being with him? Was I so selfish to be alive when he was gone?

I suddenly realize my dad is holding me, and I'm crying on his shoulder. We've dropped the rags into the water and I've collapsed into a heap on the dock.

"Shhh, shhh," Dad soothes. He isn't sure what to do with his hands, they float between rubbing my shoulder and patting my head. "Charlie wouldn't have asked you to follow him."

Oh god, did I say that out loud?

I'm lying on the round bed in the 'guest' bedroom of the boat with a cool towel across my eyes and a refilled glass of Diet Pepsi on the table.

Mom had rushed onto the dock when she heard me sobbing and went on and on about how this was exactly the reason I should move home. Dad kept telling her this wasn't the time to discuss it and had shepherded me into the cabin and told me to rest up. Somehow, he talked Mom into leaving me alone, and they closed the door so I could have some peace.

I'm all cried out again. My eyes sting. With a little smile, I wish I was at the B&B so I could get some potatoes from Bee.

My shoulders ache from the sobbing. My neck is stiff and I can't turn it to the side without wincing. Reaching for the soda, my arm feels like a lead weight. Everything hurts when I cry like this. But I've gotten used to it.

At least once a day I collapse back into this grief. But it's progress! That first month, I barely remember anything. Crying was all I did, all day long.

I had flipped through the television channels trying to tell myself everything was okay, he's just gotten delayed. I had called his office, but of course no one was there. I realized for the first time that I didn't have any personal numbers for his co-workers.

The chicken had gone cold. The salad had wilted beyond edibility. I had eaten part of a potato while I alternated my stare between the door and my phone.

The knock at my door came at 11pm.

I felt it in the pit of my stomach. I just knew it was bad news. Charlie hadn't called. He hadn't come home. His phone was off. I must have called it a dozen times.

I let myself think that he was cheating on me. That he would come home smelling of perfume and we'd have a big soap opera style fight about it, and he'd bring me roses for days after to apologize. And then I thought, maybe he had been invited out with the guys and would come home smelling of cigars. Or maybe he had a gambling problem I didn't know about, and he had lost it all, and was stalling to come home and tell me.

In every bad scenario I could dream up, he came home.

He apologized, I forgave him, we had wonderful make-up sex. There might be counseling to follow, some more missteps, but we'd be okay.

But my Charlie didn't come home. If it was him, I would have heard the key in the lock. I would have seen the handle turn and I would be prepared to be standing there with my hand on my hip and a glare pasted on my face demanding to know what had kept him. Why he would let me sit there worried for all these hours?

So, when I heard the knock. The sharp rasp that you just know is someone of authority. Not the kind of knock that is your neighbor asking if you have extra laundry soap. I closed my eyes, and allowed the one scenario I had avoided flash across my mind. The one where he had been hurt and the police were coming to my door.

By the time I saw that it really was the police on the other side of the door and they asked me if I was Melanie Gibbs, I was numb all over. In my mind, they were telling me he was badly hurt and they were here to escort me to the hospital. But they didn't usher me out of the apartment. Instead, they asked if they could come in.

I know they told me about the accident. I know they told me that Charlie had died instantly, hadn't felt a thing. But I can't recall their words. Someone made coffee for me and somehow I had a phone to my ear and I was calling Karen.

Karen called everyone else for me so I didn't have to repeat the news over and over. The commotion in my apartment had caused Freddie to come see what was going on. When the police finally left, after asking a bunch of questions I can't recall, Freddie stayed till Karen arrived the next day.

Freddie played host for me. He'd always been a nice neighbor but we weren't really friends. Without him, I don't know how I would have gotten through that week. Charlie's parents arrived the next day, followed closely by my folks, and then Todd and Bill. The guys stayed across the way at Freddie's and Karen stayed at my place.

Charlie's parents went about the process on autopilot. They had done this before. Charlie's older brother had died the year before I met him. If I hadn't been such a wreck myself, I would have been more considerate of their needs.

They booked the closest motel for ten rooms. My parents stayed there with them, and as more family arrived, they filled up the rooms.

Within a week, the Gibbs had planned out the entire funeral. The casket, the flowers, the sermon. They wanted to fly his body back to Florida to be buried next to his brother, and I didn't protest. They asked me what type of music Charlie might like playing.

Like that is a conversation we had? "Deary, by the by, if you happen to die soon, what kind of music do you want playing at your funeral?"

Charlie had been into Fleetwood Mac at the time. We played Landslide. I realized much later that he only listened to that kind of music when he was working out; it was probably the wrong decision.

There weren't too many people there, maybe fifty or so. A lot of his friends and family chose not to fly out to California, preferring to attend the burial in Florida.

Just eight days after he died, I watched his casket get loaded onto a van headed for the airport. His parents flew out, and I waved good-bye.

All the family left.

Only Karen stayed behind.

She had gone with me to the police station to collect his personal effects that survived the wreck. She had helped me call his office, and they sent someone over with a box of his stuff from his desk. It's still sitting untouched in our apartment. Buca started to sleep on top of the box as soon as it arrived, and I just couldn't deal. Now, I just think of that box as the cat's bed.

There were papers to sign, and people to call, and I wouldn't have been able to do it without her. Freddie brought home food every night for us, I didn't have to think about it. I still didn't think about it. If Karen wasn't there, I'm not sure I would have remembered to eat.

I chose not to go to Florida for the burial. I had already said all there was to say at the church. I just wanted to get on with it.

I needed to get on with it. But then Karen got a call from her dealer about an art show where she was supposed to appear, and she couldn't stall any longer. Even an artist has deadlines and people to report to. I put on a brave face and remembered to eat dinner that last night, to show her I would be okay.

And then she left too.

I didn't go out.

I didn't answer the door when Freddie came by with some burgers. He left them in the hall, and I brought them in hours later to throw them out.

Principal Jackson called to find out when I might be ready to come back to work. I said I was fine. That work would be a good distraction. That the kids wouldn't be able to tell the difference in me.

And the very first day when I heard over and over "Mrs. Gibbs". I ran from the room to the bathroom to cry. Biting on my fist to keep from sobbing out loud.

After that, I got most of my crying out of the way in the evenings. Lying in bed staring at the side where Charlie slept. Trying to imagine his shape there. The way he looked when he slept. The sound of him snoring. Floating my hand in the air, and trying to remember what it felt like to have his warm body next to me. I bought a bottle of almond oil and scented his pillow with it, with my eyes closed I could pretend he was there.

I sat in the teacher's lounge during lunch and tried to chat with everyone a little bit. I had to keep up the image that I was okay. At home, Freddie was still leaving take-out containers at my door. Which I was still throwing away uneaten. Finally, I picked up my own food and brought it home, making sure to time it so I got to the building same as him, and I waved the Wendy's bag, and he smiled.

He stopped bringing food for me after that.

I still didn't eat much. By December I started to get my appetite back. My clothes were hanging on me then and people had started to make comments. I avoided going home over the holidays. It was the first in many years that I didn't fly home. I couldn't let them see me like that. It was much easier to pretend I was doing better if all I had to do was say it over the phone. At least I was hungry when I was supposed to eat. I felt like that was progress too.

Sitting up in the bed, I sip the Diet Pepsi and press my fingers over my eyes to relieve the stinging.

Outside, I can hear my parents discussing me. Or more correctly, my mother discussing me.

"Richard, you saw her! She's not okay." My mother says defensively.

"I know, Gloria. But you can't force her to come home."

"I'm her mother, and she needs me right now. Either she comes home or…or…I'm going to have to go to her!" Oh boy, that would not be fun. Me, my mom, and my cat all in my closed up dark apartment. Yay.

"You will not meddle unless she asks for it." *Go, Dad!*

"Meddle?" Indignantly, Mom continues, "I am not meddling, Richard! I am looking out for my baby. I know what she needs right now and—"

I can't hear Dad's reply.

"Richard! How dare you! You know I would have stayed out in California longer if I could have, but we had the golf tournament!"

Again, I can't hear what my father says.

"Really now. Don't be like that, darling. You know how important that tournament was. It was for charity, I had to be here." Mom sounds like she's been scolded.

"You chose the tournament over your son-in-law's burial, Gloria. You can't just pick and choose your moments to be her mother." Wait, hold up. She didn't go to the burial? I thought they had gone. They told me they had gone, and how many people showed up, and about the clouds parting to let the sun shine down on the casket just as they started to lower it.

That does sound made up. Damn it.

I get up and head back out to the deck. They are both sitting in the lounge chairs with Diet Pepsi in their hands.

"You didn't go to the burial, Mom?" The sun is blinding, I hold my hand over my eyes to try and see her.

I can't read her face. She says "Well, it just wasn't good timing. I had this...there was an obligation and I couldn't reschedule it. St. Augustine is not exactly a quick drive you know. I guess we could have flown—"

"Dad, did you go?" I interrupt her and turn to him.

He looks uneasy. He tries to look me in the eyes but quickly take a drink of his soda instead. "Well, honey. We tried to go, really, we did. But you weren't going to be there and your mother had…we just didn't make it."

"And Todd and Bill couldn't get any more time off work, right?" This is just great. No wonder I haven't heard from the Gibbs. They bury their son, and no one from my family attends.

"Sweetie. We were all there for the funeral. We all said our good-byes. "

"Dad, that's not the point! I needed you to be there. For me."

Mom clinks her ice in her glass, "You weren't there yourself."

"Gloria!" Dad scolds her.

"All the more reason you should have been there!" I talked to Charlie's mom the morning of the burial. She told me about the flowers and how the stone wouldn't be ready for another month, but she described to me the style they had picked out to match his brother's.

I went to the cemetery once with Charlie. We were engaged at the time, and it was just a quick visit. Charlie put a little wrapped gift on top of the headstone, knelt down and said a few things. To be honest, graveyards freak me out. In our family, we cremate our departed and spread their ashes.

I asked Charlie what was in the box as we left the cemetery. He kicked a rock off the path and replied, "Just something he had said he always wanted. I never had a chance to give it to him." It wasn't until our wedding day that Charlie told me what he had left for his brother that day. An invitation to our wedding. They had an agreement that they would stand as best man for each other at their weddings. Which is why Charlie chose not to have anyone with him when we said our I dos.

How could no one go to the burial?

The Gibbs only called me once since then, letting me know they were heading out of the country for a while, to travel the world. They didn't fill in the details. Now, with both of their sons gone, there was no one left for them.

We had never really grown close, and there was no reason now to try and fix that. But thinking about what they lost only reminded me of my own emptiness.

We spend the rest of the day on the deck of the boat not talking too much. Dad and I play a few hands of Canasta. Mom pulls out her writing tablet and starts in on an article. I can only assume it's about tennis, as every few minutes she swings her arm around in an imaginary stroke.

At 4:30, we head over to the marina's restaurant that caters to all the avid boaters. My parents were more than delighted to learn about the early bird dinner service. They get up to play golf or tennis by 6 on most mornings; everything is moved up earlier in their day.

They avoid bringing up Charlie or where I should live for the rest of the evening. Instead we talk about Mom's newest columns and how the marina produces a monthly bulletin that she might take over writing. She finds the current one to be 'old fashioned' and 'quite boring.'

Dad talks about the boat. And fishing. But Mom doesn't want to take that boat fishing. After all, they live on it now and they must keep it very clean. The idea of bait and fish guts on her deck causes her to wrinkle her nose in disgust. Admittedly, it brings a smile to my face, and I encourage Dad to take it out fishing while Mom is at her yoga class someday.

By 5:30 we are done with dinner. I tap my phone to call an Uber to head back to the B&B. Mom tried to talk me into moving onto the boat for the rest of my vacation, but thankfully Dad pointed out that Karen had already paid in full for my room, and that would be very wasteful.

We make plans to get together in a few days and I kiss them both on the cheek before climbing into the sedan.

Relief.

Back at the candy colored house I find two new couples sitting on the front porch, holding glasses of Bee's lemonade. Inside, the Hellins are in the lounge laughing it up with a young family; a little girl of maybe eight or nine is sitting on her father's lap playing with a doll that looks exactly like her, wearing the same outfit even.

I give a polite wave to these people as I pass, and try to head up to my room. But Bee is on her way down, blocking my way, and greets me with a huge smile.

"Well, Melanie!" Her arms are full with a laundry basket of sheets, and I have to press against the rail so she can get past. She doesn't go by, but instead stops to chat.

"Hi, Bee." I glance hopefully up to my room to indicate I would like to escape.

"Did ya have a good day?" She sounds suspicious, and is peering closer at my face, no doubt noticing the traces of the earlier crying session around my eyes.

"There are certainly a lot of people here today." I change the subject and slide up one more step.

"Yes, yes. Let's see, the Tanners and Petersons are in the rooms up here with you, and the Goldens, they have the little girl, they are up on the third floor with Roger."

"Only one room left then?" I take another step up, but Bee moves the basket ever so slightly, just enough to block me from sliding any further without pushing into it.

Bee nods her head. "And that will be filled tomorrow by two sisters; Yvonne and Vanessa, I believe are their names. Spring break, ya know? The next few weeks will be filled up by younger and younger crowds with all the tourists we get during the college breaks." She says this with a hint of a sigh, but the smile never waivers.

Right. I forgot about that. Going to college in Florida, Karen and I always left the state for spring break, going somewhere with snow. But for most of the country, they come here for the beaches.

"So. Breakfast at 8am again?"

I smile. "Sure thing! I can't wait to see what you are going to do with that heavenly strawberry bread."

Bee gives me a wink, swings the basket to her other hip, and then continues down the steps with the laundry.

Back in my room I see she's made up the bed, and hung up my clothes in the wardrobe. Did she iron my shirts?

She ironed my shirts.

Amazing.

The amazing part isn't that she ironed my clothes, but that I don't feel violated by it. She picked up the clothes I had left in a heap on the floor last night, she touched all my stuff. And I'm okay with it.

There is this vibe from her that I can trust her. I don't feel like I have anything to worry about.

It's strange, really. I always had my own room growing up, and when we moved to Florida, I even had my own bathroom. I like my stuff a certain way. Living in that dorm with those other girls for just a few short weeks made me realize just how much I like my own space. The television remote was always in a different spot. Chips would disappear. A full bottle of juice would magically become empty, and I had no control over it.

Moving in with Charlie was stressful. Thankfully, he knew by then just how picky I was about my living space. He let me set everything up the way I liked it, and then whenever he used something, he put it back where I had it before. The remote was always left on the coffee table. When the juice was half empty, he bought a back-up. If I was reading the paper and then he read it, he'd leave it open to the exact page I had left off on.

We both put away our own clothes. We each had our own toothpaste because I liked to roll the end of mine up and he didn't.

He made it work. When I got upset over the way he left his shoes in a pile by the front door, he changed his habit. I got used to him spreading his work out, but he'd always clean it up and stack it on the side of the room, out of the way. I could deal with that. Even though I left my own stuff spread out. But that was my stuff, my mess. Only I should touch my stuff, it's why I hated when Charlie brought his massage clients home.

That's why I like hotels. Everything in its place. The maid comes in and resets the room exactly the same way it was when you first arrived, around all of your personal stuff.

But here is Bee, just organizing everything to suit her own style. She's even lined up my bottles along the tub in order of height. Cute.

In some ways, this feels so inviting. So different from home.

I can hear the chatter of the two couples coming up from the open window. The laughter of the little girl downstairs in the lounge mixed with Larry's baritone of a rumble.

The aroma of fresh lemons and warm baked goodness envelops me.

Being surrounded by this many people in this type of setting should be making me antsy. I like to retreat to quietness. To aloneness. Close the door, pull the drapes, wrap myself in a flannel blanket and top it off with my cat, until it's time to be an extrovert the next day. Use up that small dose of social energy and retreat once again.

But what I really feel like doing right now is going downstairs and joining in.

I've almost talked myself into doing it. Going downstairs and pouring myself a glass of that lemonade, and chatting with the rest of the folks. But I hear the honk of a taxi.

I look outside to see the four people from the porch climb into the cab. Right. It's only a little after 6. Most of them are going to be heading out to dinner.

Leaning over the railing outside my door, I watch the family step out of the house. The little girl grins up at her dad, "Can I have a giant stack of fries for dinner?"

"No." Her mother immediately squashes the request.

"Lighten up, we are on vacation! How about one giant plate of fries for us to share?" The dad picks her up and plops her on his shoulders as they walk away from the inn.

That leaves just Larry and Margie. Well, they can still be good company I suppose.

But just as I start to walk downstairs I can hear Margie giggling from the Rosemary Lounge.

"Oh Larry! Stop it." She laughs from deep in her ashy throat.

"My love, you are just as beautiful as the night of our wedding." Larry croons.

"Larry!" I hear a playful slap.

"And it's all I can do to keep my hands from pulling that dress right off you!" Another giggle from Margie.

I shudder. Bee did say they got frisky as the day progresses.

"You've been a very bad boy this year, Larry. I think someone is due for a spanking!" Another playful slap, but louder this time.

I tip toe back up the stairs as they make their way to their room on the first floor and I lock myself in.

I can still hear Larry through the closed door saying "Yes mistress, I've been *very* bad!" Again, that image I conjured up this morning of Margie riding atop Larry as his thunderous stomach rolls in waves from her rocking above him appears in my head, and I'm mortified that I can't seem to keep it at bay.

Turning the radio on, I start running a bath, and trying to sing along to the country song that comes on. Looks like I'll be spending my night with a book.

"Oh, Larry! Yes, right there."

And ear plugs.

SEVEN

I'm awakened by the smell of coffee. With the robe on, I look out my door and find the coffee pot set up, just like yesterday. There is a matching tray across the hall at the Nutmeg room, set for two.

Downstairs I can hear the clink of dishes and some of the chatter from the guests. I sniff the air for strawberry fields, but all I get is the coffee aroma.

I don't hurry. I crunch on another sugar cube and let the coffee cool off in my mug before taking a sip.

My skin is radiant from the bath last night. Bee had placed some sort of honey and herb mixture next to the tub with a handwritten label that declared it was Bath Sugar. Somewhat skeptical, I poured a little into the hot water and it flooded my head with all the fragrance of lavender. The honey did wonders, leaving my skin feeling soft all over.

It also helped me sleep. After Margie and Larry finally quieted down, I didn't hear anyone come back last night. Assuming they came back.

After putting my hair up into a braid and slipping into a blue sun dress for the day, I head downstairs. The Goldens are already heading back up the stairs.

"Good morning." I say as we come towards each other.

"Cheerio!" says the dad.

The woman taps his shoulder with a laugh. "Are you trying to be British, Doug?"

"We didn't have Cheerios." The little girl is looking between her two parents, confused.

They usher her forward so we can pass on the steps with another smile exchanged. As they continue up to the third floor I can hear mom telling her daughter to hurry up and change into a bathing suit. No doubt they'll be spending the day on the beach. It's what most people do on a day like today.

In the lounge, I find the Hellins at the table with one of the other couples and Bee clearing away the plates from the family.

"Melanie! Good mornin'." Bee looks up with a smile. "Come on in and take a seat. I'll have this reset for ya in a moment."

I smile to everyone else at the table and take the offered seat. They are all happily munching on what looks like French toast. Except for Larry, who is eating more bacon. I can't look at him, I just can't.

When Bee brings out my coffee and breakfast I inquire about the strawberry bread.

"Well, this is here is the same bread." She spins the plate a little so it's centered in front of me. "After it cooled off yesterday, I sliced it up and let it dry out overnight. See, that makes it primed for the custard this morning."

"Custard?"

"Oh yes, dear! Custard. You'll never get the right mix of crispy and creamy if ya use just eggs for French toast. You must use custard." Bee looks around to see if anything else is needed and retreats to the kitchen.

On the plate before me are three thick slices of golden brown French toast, what I can only assume is fresh whipped cream, and slices of strawberries.

Cutting into one triangle I can see that this is truly the pink strawberry bread she was baking yesterday. How clever!

After I take a few bites the blond gentleman across from me catches my eye. Swallowing some coffee to clear my throat, I say, "Oh sorry. We haven't been introduced yet."

He reaches across the table for my hand, "Mike Tanner, and my wife, Sally." He gestures to the forty-something matching blond woman seated next to him.

Sally and I exchange a wave. "Melanie. I'm staying up in the Mint Suite."

"Ah!" Mike toasts his coffee mug towards me. "Our neighbor. Bee tells us you are from California?"

"Oh well, no actually I'm from here, well not here, but Florida. Or, I guess I'm really from New Jersey. But I live in California right now."

Mike is shaking his head in response to my confusing answer.

"Let me try that again. I flew in from California, yes." When did I become so horrible at small talk? Oh right, always.

"For business or pleasure?"

Now there is a hard question to answer. What is my trip about? "Well," I take another bite of toast to stall, "to relax. So, I guess pleasure."

Thankfully, Sally decides to supply all the answers to the same questions since no one is in fact asking them of her, "We're here for business. Mike has been offered a job here and we're checking out the area. We live in Chicago, this would be a big change for us, but we are starting a family and I just don't think we should do that in the city. Right, honey?" Sally puts one hand on Mike's arm, and the other she rests on her extremely flat stomach and turns doleful eyes on him. She's either wishing she were pregnant real soon or she's got the tiniest baby ever in there.

Larry clears his throat. "Ah, Pelican Bay. If I could talk the missus. into moving here, I would."

"Larry, you would not!" Margie admonishes him. "You'll have to ignore my husband, he's always talking about moving, but we're not leaving our home."

"But dear—"

"No, no. We've talked about this before." Margie sips at her Bloody Mary. Does she drink these every morning?

Larry picks up another slice of bacon and sucks it out of his fingers. Chewing in silence, he just shakes his head at his wife. "We have come here every year for the last twelve years and you always say it's your favorite place to come to. Why not just move here?"

"We are not leaving our home. I want to be close to the grandkids."

At this, Larry rolls his eyes. He leans over to Mike and says in a mock whisper, "She means the grand*puppies*."

Sally drops both hands to her stomach in a protective move as if her fetus, if there is one in there, is somehow being insulted, and asks what I am sure we are all thinking. "I'm sorry, puppies?"

Margie waves her hand at Larry in annoyance and hisses, "How dare you!"

Larry puts his fork down and sighs. "Honey. This is absurd."

I'm on my last piece of toast. Bee pops out to refill our coffees and has a platter of more toast. "Anyone want seconds?"

I take another slice, as do Sally and Mike. Larry reaches for more but gets slapped by Margie and declines them instead.

"So I hear Larry is tellin' ya about the grandkids?" Bee says after we've all started in on the toast.

Margie crunches loudly on her celery.

"Margie had a prize-winning collie some years ago. She used to bring the dog here with her. Brighty was her name. Right, Margie?"

Larry reaches out and gives Margie's hand a little squeeze. But Margie just takes another bite.

Bee goes on to tell us what Margie clearly can't talk about herself, "Brighty passed on a few years ago, but Margie still throws birthday parties for all of Brighty's puppies. They gather at her house every year, and are each presented with a little dog shaped cake."

We're all a little stunned. Margie is clearly embarrassed by this, but you can also see it's something very close to her heart.

Sally breaks the silence first and goes for it, the thing that will help make this normal. "How many puppies are there?"

Margie hesitates but she wants to talk about it. "My Brighty had nine litters, sixty-three puppies total. Although, some of them are no longer with us."

"And...and you throw them a party every year?" Mike chimes in awkwardly.

Larry shakes his head, "Nine parties a year, every year."

"For the grandkids." I add. Yup, this is totally normal. Puppy parties.

Margie nods, and then chews on her celery stick looking around to each of us, waiting to see who is going to start laughing at her first.

"Isn't that just splendid!" cries Bee with a little clap of her hands to break the silence that has swept the table. "Every year she gets to see all those beautiful dogs as they grow up. How many of them have won prizes like their mother?"

Margie sits up straighter with pride. "Seventeen now."

"Marvelous." Bee smiles and heads back to the kitchen.

"It's just...well, we couldn't have any children—"

"Margie. You don't need to explain." Sally gives her a sympathetic smile. "We have a dog too. He's like our son, we'd never think of leaving him for much longer than a quick trip like this."

Sally looks at me and raises her eyebrows, "Right, I have a cat. Um...and he's like a son to me too."

Margie puts down her celery and begins to tell us all about the last puppy party. The banner announcing their eighth birthday. How one of the dogs decided it would be fun to jump in the pool, and then three others followed him, so the rest of the party decorations got ruined when the wet dogs started running around the yard. "And this year I gave all the puppies gift certificates to my favorite groomer." Larry rubs her shoulder and the rest of us collectively exhale now that she seems done with the story.

After everyone finished their breakfast, the Tanners excuse themselves by announcing they are spending the day with a realtor looking at open houses near Mike's potential new office. As they exit, Sally pockets a handful of sugar cubes stating, "Eating for two you know!"

The Hellins are heading to a local dog breeder. Margie is apparently considered an expert on breeding collies and always stops in to see to give advice on pairings to get the best quality puppies.

I lied and said I have a full day planned in town. As the others departed, I accepted one last pour from Bee when she was clearing away the coffee, and settled into one of the chairs by the fireplace. I leaned in and studied the black and white photos under the glass tabletop.

I find Pixie in most of them. I can see her growing up through many of the pictures. She smiles from two different wedding pictures in the mix. In another she is pregnant, and then in sequence, several of her holding a baby.

"Mind if I join ya?" Bee is holding her own mug of coffee. After I nod she sits in the other chair.

"She was a lovely lady, wasn't she?" Admiring the photos, Bee smiles. She points to one where Pixie is sitting with two children. "That girl with the glasses, that was my mom."

"Pixie was your grandmother?"

"No. My great aunt. But my mom spent a lot of time over here, playin' with her cousin. Pixie's own children didn't want to live here, so my parents moved in, and this is where I grew up. It was my mom's idea to turn it into a Bed & Breakfast, but it didn't happen while she was alive. We had started the process together, gettin' everything ready, but I had to finish it on my own."

I take a sip of my coffee. "I don't think I could do that."

"Oh, it's just a few nails and some paint. Anyone can spruce up a place, just takes time."

"No, not that part. The sharing of my space with strangers." Bee gives me a quizzical look. "You grew up here! Isn't it...I don't know...strange to have people going in and out of your home all the time? You never know if they are going to steal something or break a trinket. I just don't think I could do that."

Bee stirs her coffee around before replying. "You're right, it was hard at first. I lived here on the first floor for the first couple years before I moved next door. The first time a picture was broken I cried. But then I cleaned it up and put up a different picture. When the hand-knitted doilies were taken out of the Cinnamon room, I thought, 'How lovely, they took home a souvenir because they wanted to remember this place'." She shrugged, and continued, "You adapt. And now I can't imagine it any other way."

"Well, you are a stronger woman than I, Bee." I shudder just a little thinking about all those people in my apartment, and around my things.

"Nonsense!"

"No seriously!" I laugh, "I couldn't do all this by myself. I can't even figure out how to open my husband's toolbox." My smile drops when I say that. I close my eyes and wait for the wave to pass.

Bee patiently waits till I open my eyes and look at her again.

"How gone is he?" Her eyebrows are knitted atop her forehead again.

"Sorry?"

"How gone is Mr. Gibbs? Just out of the house, or has he left this earth?"

"The second one." I bring the mug to my lips but realize I'm out of coffee, and lower the empty cup to my lap. I brace myself for the phrase that is about to come my way. The one steeped in empathy. *Oh, I'm so sorry to hear that.*

"Well you better buck up, then." Bee slaps my arm as she says this.

My head darts in her direction and I cock an eyebrow. *Buck up?*

Bee chuckles. "Don't you be playin' the war-torn widow on me Melanie. I know a thing or two about widows. I'm one myself. You'll be gettin' no pity party from Betsy-Lou Ringley."

I blink in astonishment and find myself nodding. We both sit there for a few more minutes looking at the photos of Pixie and her family eternally frozen under the glass.

"Well, I had better get to cleanin' the place." Bee stands up and reaches out for my mug, which I hand to her.

I clear my throat and stand up. "Right, I have a busy day too. Going to be spending it with my best friend. So, I had better get going."

"Okay, dear. Have a fun time!"

After Bee heads back into the kitchen, I text Karen.

> What are you doing today? Should we go shopping or to the beach?

Almost immediately she writes back.

> Oh Mel, I can't! E's parents r coming in today to discuss wdg plans. Din ltr?
> Okay. Buzz me when u r free.

Crap. Now what am I supposed to fill my day with?

Before I can answer my own question, I hear the doorbell ringing. And ringing. I wait for Bee to pop out of the kitchen but I don't hear her. The doorbell rings again and a voice is calling hello.

Oh, what the hell, I can answer the door. The bell rings two more times before I make it to the front door.

"About time, what took you so long? Like, we've been waiting." Before me are two very tan, very blond, very out of place, girls with large bags all around them on the porch.

"Can—can I help you?" They must be lost. Not that I could actually help them find where they need to be.

"Like, yeah." Snaps the other girl. "You can take these bags to our room."

I shake my head, "Oh no, sorry, I don't work here."

"Then why are you answering the door?" Asks the first girl.

"Vanessa, are you sure this is the right place?" The second is tapping on her phone without raising her eyes.

I offer "Pixie's B&B. This is the place. You must be Vanessa and Yvonne?"

The one named Vanessa rolls her eyes "You don't work here but you open the door and you know our names. Just show us to our room, 'k?"

Bee still hasn't come out to greet them but there is only one room left, the Cherry Room, right next to the Hellins. I step back and point.

Yvonne snorts. "This is fucking hilarious. Not only does Pops set us up in the *most* lame town in Florida, he puts us in a room named after cherries!"

Vanessa smiles. "What'ev'. There are cute boys in every town. Besides, there will be less competition out here."

"Yeah, but we can't exactly bring them back to this junk box."

The girls are checking out their room, and I take the opportunity to sneak out. I am *not* going to get caught up in their mess. And I'm certainly not going to help them bring their bags inside.

I spend the day walking the beach and watching the boats out on the water. I left the house without my bathing suit or towel...or anything really. Thankfully I had so much to eat at breakfast that I didn't need to buy any lunch.

I tried my best to stay in the shade but I can still feel the prickling of a sunburn coming up across my nose and on my shoulders. But the sand felt so wonderful under my feet. I haven't been to the beach in ages.

Even living in San Diego, there just isn't much call to go to the beach where the water is frigid all year long despite the warm sun. But here. Here you can stroll the water's edge and let it splash against your legs as you walk and it is the most delightful feeling - the salty spray licking your skin and the moist sand sliding away from under your toes as the water draws back into itself.

"Harry, stop, wait up!" A little girl is chasing a toddler across the sand, both with buckets swinging in their hands. Their parents are dutifully alert but keeping watch from the shade of their umbrella parked over their towels.

After watching the duo running around looking for seashells, I decide to do the same. I don't run, and I don't use a pail, but I do look for seashells. I watch the sand as the waves bring up new batches of shells to the shore, and dive my hand into the surf to grab the ones that look promising.

The few early ones I picked up, I tossed back into the ocean after finding better ones. I decided on purple as a goal. The larger white shells with the purple insides, and only if they are whole, without any nicks. Those are the ones I'm collecting. For what purpose, I don't know.

I've found nine so far. I'm determined to find number ten before I leave the beach. But my feet are starting to ache, and despite a few stops at the public fountains, I'm parched. And I really do need to get out of the sun before I regret the sunburn.

I can always find the tenth shell tomorrow.

When I make it up to the street, I realize I must have been wandering for quite some time. I'm at least twenty blocks from Pixie's. After brushing the sand off my feet, I put my sandals back on and start the walk back.

My calves are protesting now. At least I got a workout in!

But after just three blocks, I have to stop and rest. It was much easier to do this walk when I was distracted by the waves and beach goers.

Why didn't I grab my wallet at least? Or my cell? Then I could at least get an Uber back.

I'm not even sure what time it is, my watch is sitting up on the dresser next to the jewelry Bee has yet to reclaim from my room. I look down at the nine shells in my hand. They are pretty. And useless.

Well, this is getting me nowhere.

I start out again, and now my legs are really stiff from giving them that break. But I can muster through. I know I can!

Hard to believe now, but I ran track once. In my freshman year of high school, I made it on the track team. But I never competed. In truth, I joined because I had a crush on one of the soccer captain, Ricky, and running track allowed me to watch him practice. I trained all that year and then of course, we moved the following year and it was too late in the season to join the team at Pelican High. By Junior year, I had given up any interest in being an athlete.

Charlie always stayed in shape. He went running every morning. I tried to go with him a few times, but running and I don't mix too well. I would get the most awful shin splints and I couldn't keep up the pace, or run as far as he could. So, we agreed it was better he went running on his own. I said I would take the steps at our apartment instead of the elevator.

Our place was on the third floor, so that wasn't too hard to do. Three flights, twice a day. Unless I wore heels to work. That was the exception. I wasn't going to go up and down all those steps in heels.

I wore heels a lot.

And then I kept forgetting to take the stairs, remembering after I was already on the elevator, and swearing I would take them the next time.

Has it only been five blocks? This is going to take all night.

The problem with quaint little villages like this is no mass transportation. You can't just flag down a taxi; you have to call for one. There is a regular bus, but it only goes through the center of town. And I am not near the center of town.

Maybe I can hitchhike! I'm sure it's safe to do that here. Haven't heard of Pelican Bay being aired on 20/20 or America's Most Wanted, so it's probably not full of rapists and murderers. Or they are might just be super savvy here, blaming disappearances on the alligators.

I take a break at a stop sign, and for a moment, watch the road for cars. Well. In order to hitchhike, there must be passing cars. Of which there are none at this present moment.

The first car to pull up at the stop is full of college boys and what I am pretty sure is cans of beer in their hands. That won't do. I divert my gaze the moment one of them looks over at me.

Figuring I might as well keep walking while I debate this option, I carry on down the street.

Another car whizzes by, it comes and goes so quickly I don't even have the chance to look at the driver.

I try to think of what Charlie would do. Without cash and without a cell, he'd probably come to the same conclusion as me. Hitchhike. Or maybe he'd pick me up onto his back, and carry me the rest of the way.

But that would be absurd, and I can't very well use that option while I'm by myself. So, when I hear the next car coming up behind me, I stick my thumb out and turn around to face my hopeful ride.

To my amazement, the car slows down and pulls over. A familiar raspy voice calls out of the open window.

"Melanie?"

I bend down to peer inside and see its Margie and Larry. With a sigh of relief, I give them a big smile. "Oh, am I glad to see you guys!"

"You shouldn't be thumbing a ride out here by yourself." Margie reproaches.

I shrug. "I didn't have much choice. Forgot my wallet."

Margie has climbed out of the car and pulled the front seat forward. "Well get in. We're heading back to the B&B ourselves."

Stuffed in the back of their Ferrari, I spend the rest of the ride home getting lectured by Margie about the safety of a young woman out on the streets by herself. How it was going to be getting dark soon, and I would have been out there alone. What if I had met a thief or even a rapist?

Larry tries to interject about how quiet this town is, and in all the years they've been coming here, they never heard of those types of things happening. But Margie just shushes him up and continues on about all the possible horrors that could have befallen me if they hadn't come to my rescue.

When we pull up to Pixie's the first thing I notice is that the lights are not on. Larry and Margie continue their discussion as we all climb out of the car. Maybe it's not that unusual then. But the last two nights, all the lights were on in the common rooms, and the porch and walkway were lit up too.

Margie pulls out her cigarette pack and offers me one.

"No, thanks." I wave her off.

"I've been trying to quit myself." She rasps.

"Since when?" Larry asks quizzically.

Margie shrugs, "Well, I've been meaning to quit."

I thank them for the ride and head up the steps. The girls that arrived this morning are playing music in their room. One of the new pop hits with a lot of bass.

Upstairs, I find my room exactly as I left it. As in, Bee didn't make up the bed or straighten anything up in the bathroom like she had done the previous night. I try to shrug it off. Maybe she takes Sundays off. Innkeepers have to have a day off too, right?

I take a quick shower and the hot steam brings my sunburn fully to the surface. I'll have to get some aloe for that.

Picking up my wallet and my cell, I see I've missed a text from Karen.

> Still on for dinner?

She sent it an hour ago, and I'm exhausted from my day in the sun.

> Just got back to the room, getting take-out. Tmrw?

After just a moment she writes back.

> Sure! Evry thing ok?
> Beached it, sunburnt, tired

Karen replies with a series of emojis that make me laugh.

I take a deep breath before forcing my screaming legs to climb back down the steps.

At home, I have most of the take-out places memorized. If I'm in the mood for something new, I just scroll through my phone till something looks good and order it online. Switching over to the map app, I watch the lovely little buffer button spin and spin, hopelessly trying to pull in enough signal.

Screw it. I know I saw a phone book somewhere.

Downstairs, flipping the lights on in the lounge, I look around for the yellow book. It's not on the bookshelf, but I'm pretty sure that's not where I saw it. It was by the phone. But another quick look around, and I don't see a phone in here either.

It must have been in the kitchen.

I find the light switch in the kitchen and when the lights blink on, I know something is wrong. The coffee tray is still on the counter with our mugs from this morning. There are a few bowls of flour and some other ingredients set out. I watched Bee work; she wouldn't leave the place like this.

"Bee?" I call out.

I poke my head into the pantry and look around again. I'm not sure what to do here.

"Bee?" I call out a little louder.

Panic starts to creep into my body, and my arms get goose bumps despite the sunburn. I quickly walk to the front porch. But Margie and Larry are no longer there. Their car is gone, too. No doubt they went out to dinner.

I stand before the Cherry Room where music continues to seep from behind the door. But then I remember I'm the one who let the girls in this morning. I doubt they even know who Bee is.

I didn't hear anyone else upstairs, though. So, after changing my mind a few times I knock on the girls' room. After a moment, I realize they probably didn't hear me so I knock louder to compete with the music. But they still don't answer.

"Vanessa? Yvonne?" For all I know, they aren't even in there.

I walk out to the porch and back through the kitchen again, calling out Bee's name. But this is getting me nowhere. She clearly isn't in the house.

There is a back door that leads out of the kitchen. I step outside and see there is a path that leads to the house next door. Of course! Bee said she lives there.

I rap on the door and call her name. But I don't hear anything. Trying the knob, I find the door unlocked. I open it carefully.

"Bee? It's me, Melanie." The door opens into the kitchen. The only light is coming from the open fridge door. I stand outside, and take a few deep breaths to steady myself. My heart is racing now.

I take a step inside, and then retreat. Pacing a few times outside the door, I will myself to go in and look around. But I can't do it. Margie's lecture is still too fresh on my brain. What if a robber was in there, or worse? What if Bee...what if she was...I can't even bring myself to finish the thought.

What if I go in there, and whoever it is attacks me, too?

I'm sweating now. With a shaky hand, I reach up to wipe my face and realize I'm holding my cell phone.

Duh! Call the cops.

But you can get in trouble for a false alarm, right? And all I have is a missing innkeeper, and my gut feeling that something isn't right. I don't know this person or her habits, and it could just be her day off. You know, where she leaves food out, and lights off, and rooms unmade despite having a full inn. Sure, totally normal, nothing to get concerned about.

What the hell. If this is a false alarm, I'll pay the freaking fine.

Punching in 911, my phone automatically goes to a safety setting and the face turns red.

After just one ring the operator picks up, "911, what's your emergency?"

"Um, something is not right at my hotel—I mean bed and breakfast."

"Ok Ma'am, how is this an emergency?" I can hear the operator already taking an attitude with me.

"Well, I can't find the innkeeper and all the lights are off…and well, it's just not right."

"Ma'am, I'm sorry if you are not happy with your accommodations but this really isn't appropriate—"

I realize I'm not making this seem important. "No, no! it's not the accommoda—look, Bee, the innkeeper. Something must have happened to her. I can't find her anywhere."

"Are you wanting to report a missing person, Ma'am?" The operator is starting to sound annoyed.

"Maybe. But I think there might be an intruder in her house and I'm worried about her."

"What is your reason for believing there is an intruder?" I can hear the operator typing now, her tone has shifted back to brisk and professional

"Look, could you just stay on the phone while I go into her house and look for her?" I swallow my pride. "I'm scared to go in alone, and there is no one else here."

The operator hesitates and responds in a gentler tone. "Of course. Give me your address and then talk me through what you are doing, when you do it."

At least we are the same side now. I give her the location and then I push the door open further and step inside. "I'm in the kitchen. The refrigerator door is open and I'm going to turn on a light." I flip on the switch and look around.

Walking around the center island I come across a whole carton of eggs splattered on the floor. "There are eggs all over the floor!" I cry into the phone.

"Stay calm, do you see the person you are looking for?" The operator brings in her professional monotone now; we are in this together.

I shake my head, then realize that won't translate. "No. I don't see her". I'm whispering for some reason. There is a smear of eggs on the floor leading out through the doorway. I describe this to the operator.

"Call out to her."

I can do this. I know I can do this. My feet are frozen in place though. "Bee! Are you in there?" No response.

I squeeze my eyes closed for some courage and walk through the doorway and find a light switch on the wall.

"Bee!" I scream when the lights come on.

She's lying on the floor with her leg stuck at the wrong angle. There is a phone broken apart on the floor and in her hand, a broomstick.

"Hello? Are you still there? Can you tell me what's going on?" I've let my hand fall to my side but I hear the operator calling for me.

"She's, she's on the floor. She's hurt." I say into the phone.

"Is she breathing?"

I can't look. But I have to. With shaky hands, I reach down and touch her face. Her eyes flutter open. "Harold?" She slurs.

"She's alive!" I scream into the phone.

"Okay, we'll send an ambulance over." The operator tells me to keep the phone on until the paramedics arrive.

I sit on the floor and take Bee's hand in mine and tell her it will be okay. She keeps asking for Harold.

While we wait, she seems to come more alert and focuses on me enough to realize who I am. "Melanie? What are ya doin' here?"

"I was looking for you, Bee."

"Did you need some coffee, dear? I could rustle us up a pot." She tries to sit up and winces in pain. I put a hand behind her head and guide her back to the floor.

"No thank you, Bee. No coffee."

Bee blinks away the tears that sprung up from the pain. "It would seem that I can't make us any right now, anyway."

I smile down at her. "No, you can't make any right now."

"I slipped." Bee blinks away more tears.

I nod.

"I needed to get some more eggs for the quiche I was working on...I slipped."

"It's okay. We don't need quiche." I give her hand a squeeze. "I was worried about you. So, I came looking to see if you were okay."

"That's sweet of you dear. I figured no one would notice till tomorrow mornin' when there wasn't coffee waitin' at the doorsteps."

"If you slipped in the kitchen, what are you doing out here?"

Bee smiles and looks up at the wall. "I crawled out here and tried to use the broom to get to the phone. But it broke when it hit the floor." The tears are now rolling down her face. "It hurts so much."

"I know. I know." I can hear the sirens heading our way. I pick up the phone and tell the operator I can hear the ambulance. Bee is crying harder now. "Shh, shh, they'll be here any minute and give you something for the pain."

Bee shakes her head. "It's not that. I just realized I'll have to close Pixie's. It will be the first time in 12 years I haven't been able to take care of the place. There has always been at least one guest since the day we opened." Bee starts crying in earnest, tears spilling from the corner of her eyes.

The paramedics step inside, I let the operator know and we sign off.

I stand out of the way while they assess Bee's condition and then lift her onto a gurney. She screams in pain when they move her leg and I bite my knuckles and turn away.

"Where are you taking her?" I ask the paramedic as they strap her down.

"Regent's Hospital. Are you family?" When I shake my head, he replies. "Sorry then, you'll have to meet us over there. It's just a few miles away."

I watch them load her up into the ambulance. Yvonne and Vanessa are standing on the front porch of Pixie's watching too. Those brats were in their room after all!

When the ambulance has pulled away, I walk back into Bee's kitchen and take in the mess. The least I can do is clean up for her.

Some of the egg has dried onto the floor. I work at it with a wet rag to scrub it off. The phone isn't salvageable, so I just throw the whole thing away. Back in the B&B, I toss out the half-made quiche and finish washing up the dishes.

I can hear the Hellins coming home out front, and I go into the lobby to tell them the news.

Larry has hands firmly planted on Margie's ass, and is nibbling her earlobe when I walk through the doorway.

"Oh! Sorry to interrupt." I say louder then I mean to.

Larry stops nibbling but keeps his hands where they are.

"Melanie?" Margie looks annoyed to be interrupted in the middle of her tryst.

I shuffle my feet, "I was wondering if I could borrow your car?"

Margie pulls away from her husband and puts her hands on her hips. "What for?"

"They took Bee to the hospital and I want to make sure she's okay."

Immediately, Margie changes her stance and raises a hand to her mouth as I fill her in on what happened while they were out. "Oh, that poor thing! Come on, we'll all go."

"But, sugar muffin!" cries Larry.

"Oh Larry, not now!" Margie slaps the hand he reached out to her. "In fact, why don't you stay here, and Melanie and I will go to the hospital."

With eyes downcast, Larry nods his head and starts heading into the kitchen.

"No snacks! We just ate dinner for Pete's sake." Margie calls after him.

Grabbing my hand, she pulls me out the front door.

"You poor dear!" She exclaimed when I admitted how scared I was to go into Bee's house alone. I didn't mention that it was her earlier comments about rapists that made me so nervous in the first place.

At the hospital we have to wait for them to find the right doctor to give us an update. Bee was still in a treatment room where they were popping her hip back into place.

Margie gets sucked into a soap opera playing on the waiting room TV, and I absently flip through a magazine.

When her soap is over, I just have to ask. It's been bugging me all night. "Um, Margie?"

She looks at me expectantly.

"I was kind of curious…you don't need to tell me, but you and Larry…" I bring my hands together in awkwardness.

Margie smiles and leans back into her chair. "You want to know our secret? How we go from fighting every morning to lovers every night?"

"Yeah, I was a little curious about that." I don't really know why, but I am seriously intrigued.

"When you get to our age, you and your husband will need to learn these tricks, so I don't mind sharing." I instinctively cover my left hand to hide my wedding ring. I've debated taking it off before. But it feels wrong to be without it. Yet it hurts more to have people assume I'm happily married. "See, the passion is there naturally. When we were younger, we couldn't keep our hands off of each other!"

Margie's eyes are sparkling. I can see the beauty she must have been in her younger years, even beneath the surgically altered skin and the tobacco stained teeth. She's still quite trim.

"But over the years, you feel the passion, you just don't feel like acting on it. So, you find other ways of expressing yourself. And you argue a lot more. But it's not fighting. It's just healthy arguing. Larry complains about my smoking and I complain about him eating. It's a balanced and fair debate. One we've been having for decades."

"Right. But you've been together for forty years—

"Forty-two!" she corrects.

"Forty-two years, and you are all over each other at night." I shrug. "What, what turns you guys on so hard?"

"Besides the simple fact that we are in love?" Margie smirks and then leans forward. In a lower voice she says, "It's the little blue pill."

Really? "Viagra?"

Margie flaps her hand at me to lower my voice. There is no one around to overhear us anyway but she continues in a whisper. "You'd be amazed at how powerful that stuff is. I crush one up into his wine every night at dinner. By the time we get home, he can barely keep his hands off of me!"

"So...Larry doesn't know?"

She seems giddy revealing this to me and laughs while shaking her head. "Not a clue!"

"Well, what does he think is going on?"

"I've been doing it for years. It's just the norm now. Whenever I'm in the mood, I pop a pill into his dinner, and when I'm not in the mood, I leave it out. And sweetie, let me tell you something, these days, I am always in the mood!"

For Larry? Big bacon slurping Larry? Well, they do say you love someone for their inner-self.

"If you want to try it, I could spare a few." Margie offers.

I shake my head vigorously, "No, no! I'm good. Thanks!"

"Nothing to be embarrassed about. We girls have to stick together you know! But you're so young still; you probably have no trouble turning your hubby on, do you?"

I can feel the heat rising to my face, adding to the sunburn.

"Never mind, Melanie. Just remember my advice. One day you'll wonder why your husband doesn't reach out and touch you anymore. Or why you can't seem to turn him on no matter what you do. And then you reach for the pill. Just make sure you're the only woman around when it kicks in!" She winks at me.

I pick up another magazine, and start to flip through it so we can end the conversation. Why did I ask?

The doctor comes out after another twenty minutes and tells us that Bee is recovering from the ordeal and that everything should be okay. In about three months.

"Three months!" I exclaim.

"It takes longer to recover from something like this for someone her age. She'll need to go through rehab to build back the use of that leg after she recovers from the initial pain, make sure the hip doesn't slip out again. But that's after the ankle sprain heals, too." He looks between Margie and I. "Are either of you family?"

We both shake our heads. "Sorry then, you'll have to come back tomorrow during visiting hours to see her. I'll let her know you stayed." With that, he steps out of the waiting room.

Margie and I have nothing else to do but head back to Pixie's. Bee is okay. That's all that matters for the moment.

EIGHT

But the next morning, all that matters is that there is no coffee. I couldn't sleep last night, and after fighting to keep my eyes closed, I give up and head downstairs. It's just after 6am, but when I shuffle into the kitchen I find I'm not the only one up this early. A half-dressed man is looking through the cabinets. A fine specimen of a man. I pull the robe a little tighter and try to smooth down the frizz atop my head.

"Excuse me?" I call behind him.

He turns around and smiles a toothy grin. His teeth shine white against his deeply tanned skin. "Good morning. I'm Roger." Right, the beach-bum Bee mentioned I would never see. "I am looking for the coffee. Bee usually has some made by now—"

"She's in the hospital." I supply.

Roger frowns. "Well, that explains the missing coffee. Guess I'll just grab some on my way to the beach. You have a nice day."

As he walks out, I can't believe he didn't ask after Bee's health. Doesn't he care?

I really need some coffee too. If I were Bee, where would I store the beans?

Roger had already checked the cabinets and came up empty handed, so it would be pointless to dig through those again. I go back to the pantry I looked in last night.

There is everything under the sun stuffed in here.

A whole shelf of canned produce. Pastas, rices…are there really that many kinds of rice? There are bags of flour and sugar on the lower levels, pots of spices tucked into every open space. But I don't see anything labeled coffee. I test a few of the unlabeled jars, but only find more dried herbs and more pasta.

My stomach starts to rumble. All the aromas in here remind me I haven't really eaten since yesterday morning. The M&Ms I got from the hospital vending machine hardly count as dinner.

Charlie used to keep the extra coffee in the freezer.

Bingo!

Feeling quite proud of myself, I look around for the coffee pot. Oh, thank god! It's one of the regular 12-cup models. Not like the digital monster I have back at my place. Charlie got it for me the Christmas before last, but he read the manual and figured out how to use it. I'm sure if I could *find* the manual I could figure it out too.

I can use this kind though. I just need one of those white papery things.

My morning is looking brighter already! The filters are in the cabinet right below the coffee pot. Now, I should probably make a full pot. Others are going to want coffee too.

I pour the water into the basin and place a filter in the swinging arm part. Now I just need to pour in some coffee—*oh shit*. The beans are whole.

Biting my lip I look around for a grinder. There has to be a grinder near the filters. But squatting down to look into the entire cabinet I see a lot of gadgets. Not a one that looks like a grinder.

Maybe you can make coffee from whole beans? No. I shake my head at myself.

Digging through the gadget cabinet I pull out the cheese grater and try to grate one single coffee bean between my fingers. Until I grate my finger.

Maybe just cracked beans will work in lieu of grated beans. I measure out what I think are the right amount of beans and wrap them in a dishtowel from near the stove. Using a saucepan, I bash the bean bag a few times and unwrap the towel to see my progress. No beans are cracked.

"This is going to take forever." Shaking out all but 5 beans, I wrap them up again and bash them, successfully cracking them this time. I repeat this until all the beans are cracked.

I add the cracked beans to the filer and turn the machine on. It starts to heat up right away and within seconds, brownish liquid is dripping down into the pot and it smells like coffee.

Woohoo!

Pleased with the coffee, I dig out some cream from the fridge, and scoop out some sugar from the pantry into a bowl I find in the cabinet. I don't see any sugar cubes, maybe Bee makes them herself? Or do you get crushed sugar from sugar cubes? Which comes first, the sugar or the sugar cube?

The pleasant aroma of coffee is filling the kitchen, but when I look back at the pot, it's not looking like coffee. It's tan, not brown. Perhaps it needs to brew the entire batch and it will get darker.

I tap my fingers on the counter and watch the rest of the pot fill up with the same tan liquid. When the pot stops sputtering the last few drops I pour myself a little test batch.

This is not coffee. Not yet anyway, more like coffee scented hot water. Maybe if I just run it all through a second time it will come out stronger. I pour the not-coffee into the water basin again and start the machine over.

Now, breakfast. Maybe there is some bread left over to make some simple toast? But a quick search reveals there is none in the fridge, and none in the pantry. Would it be too much to ask for a magical loaf of Wonder Bread to be tucked away in here?

A covered bowl on the counter, however, shows a very promising globe of dough that was left to rise yesterday. Bee must have started a new batch of bread before she got hurt.

I know that baking bread normally takes a long time in the oven. But it's already twenty to seven, and the others will be getting up soon.

I got it! The microwave. If the oven takes an hour, then the microwave should have this done in fifteen minutes. I place the entire bowl with the dough ball inside and hit start. With that going 'round and 'round, I pull out some butter to soften. Soft butter with freshly made toast. I'm quite pleased with myself!

The coffee pot is sputtering to a stop again and I have my fingers crossed as I walk over to look. But the liquid isn't any darker. Hoping it tastes stronger than it looks, I pour another sample.

Yuck. Now it tastes like *burnt*-coffee scented water.

While I'm still trying to figure out how to fix the coffee, I hear something hissing. Looking around for the source of the sound, my attention lands on the microwave. Inside the dough is spinning round and round and bubbles are forming all over the surface. One of them bursts with a loud pop. The hissing rapidly turns into more popping and I scramble to press the stop button.

The bowl is unbearably hot as I pull it from the microwave and I drop it on the counter. The dough continues to bubble and hiss for a few seconds and as I watch, starts to deflate into a gooey blob at the bottom. Not bread, not toast, just goo.

This is utterly useless.

I'm about to give up when inspiration hits. I run upstairs and throw on jeans and a t-shirt, grab my wallet and then head out of Pixie's towards the beach.

By 7:15, I am back at the B&B and setting out the last of the breakfast service when the Tanners make their way into the Lounge.

"Good morning, Melanie." Mike greets.

"Good morning to you, too." I'm sweaty, and quite certain my hair is fully an afro by now. Added to the sunburn from yesterday, I must look like a clown sans makeup. But neither Mike or Sally seem to notice.

Sally takes a seat and pours herself a coffee, and then considers the array of pastries in front of her. "This is a lovely assortment. Bee must have been working at this all day!"

"Ah, no." I reply. "Bee wasn't able to be here this morning, so I bought these from the shop down the street." At the store, just two blocks away, I was able to get a whole carafe of coffee, a dozen pastries and a bowl of fruit salad for just forty-five dollars.

"Well, that was nice of you. Where is Bee?"

"She might not be here for a while. She had an accident yesterday and went to the hospital last night." I pour myself another cup of coffee.

"Oh my!" Exclaims Sally. When I look up she is positively horrified, a pastry frozen in mid-air to her lips.

"Is she going to be okay?" adds Mike, equally frozen with his hand hanging over the pastry tray.

I offer a shrug. "I think so. She sprained her ankle, and her hip popped out when she fell, but they put it back. She can't be on her feet for a bit."

Mike leans over to Sally. "Maybe we should check into a hotel today after the interview?" Sally nods in agreement.

"No, don't do that!" They both turn at my outcry with confused expressions. "It's just—Bee wouldn't want you to leave just because she's ill."

"She's not just ill Melanie, you said she sprained her ankle, and popped her leg? How is she supposed to run this place?" Mike shakes his head and takes a bite of the lemon pastry he's selected.

By 8am everyone has gotten up and come through the lounge for breakfast. After everyone learns about Bee's condition, there is a general agreement that everyone will be checking out to go to a hotel.

Everyone but me and the Hellins.

"We were only staying for a few more nights anyway. No worries on our part." Margie dismissed the rest of the comments. "I can drive you back to the hospital to visit her later?" she offered, and went outside for her morning smoke after I nodded. Larry eyes the remaining pastries and I push the plate towards him.

The girls are delighted at the turn of events. As soon as they heard the news, Vanessa...or maybe it was Yvonne, got on her phone and called their father. As they head back to their room to pack, they laugh about how this will show him to not put them in a waterfront hotel in the first place.

With everyone gone, except for Larry who is polishing off the fruit salad, I clear the table.

At least I know how to operate the dishwasher. While I'm cleaning up the kitchen, I watch as first the Goldens pull out of the drive, and then the Petersons. The Tanners decided to check out later, after Mike's interview. He is now smartly dressed in a suit, and they head out as well.

From the kitchen, I can hear the sisters arguing.

"Put more in your bag, mine is full!" One of them snaps.

"Mine is full, too! This pile is your stuff, you find space for it." Apparently, everything they unpacked yesterday is not fitting back into their bags today.

I have four hours to waste before we can visit Bee. My skin is starting to itch from the sunburn; going to the beach again is out of the question. I head upstairs to find my book; I can sit in the shade on the balcony and read for a while.

But when I get to the second floor, the door to the vacated room is open. "What a mess." I groan.

I consider this for a moment. "Well, I can at least wash the sheets." I strip the bed quickly, and figure I might as well do the room the Goldens were staying in, too. There are only two doors at the top of the steps.

"Einy, meany, miney, mo…are you a Chocolate or a Vanilla flavored guest?" I correctly guess they were staying in the Vanilla Suite.

I get the bed cleared off, and find the crumpled sheets from their daughter lying on the floor next to the day bed. When I try to pick up the entire pile off the floor, I can't seem to keep it bundled. As soon as I pick up the last item, I drop another.

Finally, I drop all of it. I'll just have to make a couple trips. At just the thought, my calves start to throb again. Looking down at the bare floor of the lobby, I have an idea. I start tossing the sheets over the railing and they all drift gently down into a pile at the bottom.

Nice.

When I get down there, the girls have finally packed up all their belongings and are pulling them out one by one to the porch.

"I thought you said you *didn't* work here?" chides one of them in my direction.

I shrug. "Bee helped me out the other night. Thought I could return the favor."

The other just looks at me as I kick the sheets into a smaller pile. "What-ev'." With their bags on the porch they both start texting while they wait for a car.

I wait till they've left before I strip their bed too.

Stuffing the towels and sheets into the pillow cases, I toss them out the door onto my other pile. Now, where are the laundry machines?

Three hours later, I've run all the sheets through the wash, and I'm waiting for the last load to finish in the dryer. Of course, the machines are down in the basement. My legs still ache from yesterday's beach walk, and going up and down the stairs is killing me.

I found the cleaning supplies too, and scrubbed the bathrooms in all the vacated rooms while the laundry tumbled. None of the occupants had stayed for long, the rooms were easy enough to spruce up.

Well, except for the Cherry Room. I hadn't noticed it when I stripped the beds but now standing in the center I take in the full disaster. Globs of gel on the floor and makeup smeared across the sink; half-eaten cartons of Chinese food on the dresser are already starting to decompose. I hold my breath while I toss them. I forgot how messy college girls could be. It seems so long ago that I was one myself.

All of the sheets are color-coordinated with the rooms they came from. Easy enough to dress the beds back up. I'm tempted to clean the rooms that are still occupied but I can't make myself invade their space. I'm not sure where the spare keys are anyway.

At quarter to one, Margie comes back to the B&B. "Melanie, are you ready to go to the hospital?" After eyeing me for a moment she adds, "Maybe after you clean up?" I balk at first, thinking that I've just spent all morning 'cleaning up' when I realize she's talking about the way I look. I nod and rush up to my own room to change.

In the car, Margie tells me about the delightful stud collie that she saw today and how she plans on suggesting he breed with one of her grand-puppies.

"They will have offspring with the perfect coat for showing. Silky and long…" She goes on about the future of the show line between cigarette puffs which she is courteous enough to hold out the window.

The chatter washes over me, but I'm not really paying attention.

I just want to get to Bee.

Bee has her leg propped up in a ridiculous apparatus hanging from the ceiling and she is surrounded by floral arrangements. Margie brandishes the sunflowers we bought on the way, and squeezes them in-between two other vases on the windowsill.

"Wow! Someone has an admirer." She teases the older lady.

With a chuckle, Bee replies, "Oh, just a few of my neighbors and some of the local shop owners."

We ask about her leg and if the doctors were treating her well. "They're doin' their jobs, and they are good at it. Makin' too much of a fuss if ya ask me." She turns onto a more serious note. "Now, what did you all do this mornin' for breakfast? I can't tell ya how upset I am that I wasn't there to set ya up properly."

"Oh, it was fine!" Margie waves off her concern and turns to me. "Melanie took care of it."

"You did?" Bee's wide grin lights up her face. "Did ya finish the lemon bread? I had it rising on the counter yesterday so we could have it this mornin' toasted up with a citrus spread and fried eggs."

"Um, no. I didn't see the bread." I fib, hoping the sunburn covers up the blush I feel rising to my cheeks.

Margie claps her hands together. "She was a clever girl, Bee! She went down to that little delicatessen by the beach and picked up pastries."

Bee folds her arms across her chest, "You gave that cranky old Gus my business?"

"Well—" I defend.

"Gus has been tryin' to sell me his crummy old pastries for years! I'm gone for one breakfast and you break my decade long hold-out." She takes a deep breath. "He is never gonna let me live this one down."

"Oh, Bee," admonishes Margie. "Just admit you have a crush on that old wanker and get on with it."

"Margie!" Bee retorts.

"Well you do."

"I do not! That is…that's *ridiculous*. Gus's pot belly makes him look like a whale, and that haircut! He thinks he's still some surfer despite that he's in his 70s."

I've been scanning the flower arrangements, I find what I'm looking for. Pointing to the red roses I ask, "Bee, who gave you those?"

Bee looks where I'm pointing, then rolls her eyes. "Just because *he* likes me does not mean that *I* like him." Margie and I share a knowing smile and try not to laugh. "Anyway, ya fed my guests this mornin'. Thank you."

"She cleaned up too." Margie is adjusting all the flowers so the roses are in the center of the arrangements.

Bee eyes me for a minute. "You cleaned what?" She asks with some hesitation.

"You know, the sheets." And after a pause, "and I cleaned up the bathrooms too."

"In all the rooms?" She peers at me more intently.

Margie answers for me, "No, just the ones that are empty now."

Bee whips her head between us before asking the shocked, one-word question. "Empty?"

I shrug. "Some of them didn't want to stay and be a burden on your recovery."

"Is everyone leavin'?"

Margie takes her hand. "Larry and I are staying till Friday, as planned. Don't you worry. The place won't be empty."

I offer, "And I...I've got nowhere else to be till the following weekend. Oh, and I don't think Roger is going anywhere. But I don't know how long he was planning on staying?"

"Roger comes and goes with the tides. As long as the sun is shinin', he'll be stayin' around." Bee seems to have relaxed a little. "But the others are all leavin'?"

I nod. "The Tanners are clearing out later, but they've already packed up and are ready to go. The rest left this morning."

"Such a shame. Pixie is much happier when the place is full." Noticing our worried looks, Bee waves us off with a laugh. "It's just a family thing dears, don't worry. I'm not talkin' to no ghosts. Great-aunt Pixie liked to have all of us stay at her house all the time. She liked havin' someone sleepin' in every room, every night. Many of the neighborhood children would be invited to sleep-over and if she ever saw someone who looked put-out, she'd invite them in."

"So the place was destined to become a Bed & Breakfast?" I smooth the sheets by her side.

Bee has a far off look in her face. "I suppose. I try to keep the place filled. But with that new fancy Hilton that opened up last year and all the other hotels around the marina, it's hard to keep it up."

"But, Bee!" cries Margie, "They don't have your cooking skills. No one compares to your breakfast spread."

The compliment brings a big grin to her face; the wrinkles melt away when she smiles. "Well, you girls are goin' to have to fend for yerselves a few more days. They say I can go home tomorrow but I'm not supposed to be on my ankle for at least three weeks while the sprain heals, and then start the nonsense of rehab for the hip. They'll set me up with crutches, then."

"Bee, there are, like, a million steps in that house!" I rub my calves, "I should know, I've been climbing them all day."

"That's why I've never needed to go the gym." Bee winks at me.

"But you can't possibly do it on your own."

"I called my daughter. She doesn't like runnin' the place, but she's done it for me before when I've needed to take a break. Only problem is Cindy can't make it out for about a week." Bee slips into a frown again. "I should probably cancel the next wave of tenants. The place was booked solid for the entire month." Bee sighs and bites her lips, looking off towards the window of her room.

I can't believe what I'm about to suggest, but why not?

"No. You will not cancel your reservations. I will help you out."

"Melanie, that's so sweet of you." Exclaims Margie.

Bee studies my face. "You sure you can handle it, dear?"

"Oh, come on Bee. If you can do it, surely I can handle it. Besides, I don't have any set plans for my vacation. And I made it okay today. It can't be that hard to run the whole place." I just have to figure out how to grind coffee, cook bread, and you know, get over handling people's personal shit so I can clean their rooms. I must be insane.

Bee continues to study my face, hopefully she isn't seeing my internal debate.

"Come on, Bee. Say yes." Margie prompts. "You'll be home tomorrow and you can supervise her."

"I'll have to pay ya."

I shake my head. "No, no. You helped me out, I'll help you out."

"I loaned you earrings! This is not an equal trade."

I beam down at this woman who could so easily be my grandmother. "You did more than loan me earrings. I haven't cried in two days. Two whole days Bee. I need to stay busy. I…I need to do this."

She has a knowing look in her eyes. Biting her lip again she nods. "Okay, then. You can help me run the place till Cindy gets there." Wagging her finger at me she adds, "But when she arrives, you go back to your vacation you hear me?"

Margie stands up, "Great! All settled then." Turning to me she asks, "Ready to go?"

I shake my head. "No. You go. I'll get an Uber back. I have some questions to ask Bee so I can make a list to help out at Pixie's."

NINE

Oh. My. God. What am I doing?

Back at the B&B I look through the list again. She can't seriously do all of this in one day.

Make the beds.

Clean the bathrooms.

Vacuum all the rooms.

Sweep the steps.

Make bread.

Pick lemons and make lemonade.

Prepare the next day's breakfast.

Clean all the dishes.

Empty the trashes.

Water the plants.

Pick herbs from the garden.

Confirm the next wave of guests.

Restock anything that is used up. How am I supposed to know if it's been used up?

Well, I finished making the beds and already cleaned up the bathrooms. In the empty rooms, at least. I sprayed some water at the flower boxes in each window and dumped a cupful in the pots of the house plants. I looked at the garden, "Which are the weeds and which are the herbs?" But the songbird I asked didn't help.

The vacuum is some central line contraption. After a few trials to get the hose snapped into the port, it's pretty easy to get the vacuuming done. Starting at the third floor, I vacuum the empty rooms and sweep the stairs on my way down. But it takes me two hours to finish up. I still haven't touched the occupied rooms, although now I know where the spare keys are.

I made dinner plans with Karen for six and I still need to clean myself up. Since I can't cook anyway, I skip over all the preparation items. Bee told me where to find the coffee grinder and after a few trial runs, I've been able to set up the pot for tomorrow.

Bee gets up at 5am every day to get the coffee and breakfast made for Roger, the earlier riser. But that won't be happening. I slipped a note under his door that let him know I'd be up at six, and he could make coffee for himself before then. I even placed a full coffee serving set t on the kitchen counter by the pot, and another note with his name.

Charlie and I never played hosts. Growing up, we always went to other friend's places. We never lived anywhere large enough to have guests other than our closest friends. Those events usually consisted of a few extra blankets on the sofa and ordering a second pizza.

I have a sudden flash of Charlie's face, my mind filling in the expression he'd be wearing if he knew I was trying to run this place by myself.

I didn't even run my classroom by myself. I had an assistant to help deliver the lesson plans and mothers would volunteer to take turns coming in to teach special topics like knitting and painting.

But I know good service when I see it. And I want Charlie to be proud of me. I want Bee to be pleased with how I sub for her.

Time for a shower.

"Melanie?" Karen's voice is faint over the running water. "Mel?"

I yell out to her, "Karen! Hi, I'll just be a few more minutes!"

When I step into the room she is sitting on my bed, wearing a glittery black dress that is way too short.

"Where exactly are we going, again?" Pulling the brush through my hair, I eye her suspiciously. That's a lot of glitter.

"Just out to one of the bars that is debuting a local artist. I thought it would be nice for you to mingle with some of my friends. After all, you need to meet the rest of my bridal party."

I pull on some jeans and reach for my black tank top. At least I can blend into the background.

Karen pouts. "Really, Mel? Come on, you have to have brought something a little funkier with you?"

"Funky isn't exactly in my wardrobe these days, Kay."

"Well at least wear those lady bug earrings again." The jewelry is still sitting on my dresser. Sure, why not?

After a slight pause, I reach for the silk scarf and weave it through the belt loops of my jeans. Looking in the mirror, I'm pleased with my reflection. The scarf adds quite a bit of color to my ensemble. I sweep my wet hair up into a ponytail that shows off the ladybugs.

Slipping my sandals on, I turn to Karen and declare, "Ready."

Karen stands. Her dress is even shorter than I thought it would be. Her bright red hair is gelled into spikes that stick out in all different directions. Hanging from her ears, giant gold loops sway and hit her shoulders as she turns her head. Smears of yellow eye shadow enhance her eyes.

Standing next to her, I look dull. She's the flame. I'm the ashes left behind.

But dull works for me. I reach for my wedding band on the side table, having taken it off for the shower. Before sliding it into place, I have a different idea. I slip the chain off the butterfly charm and slide the ring on it instead, then clasp it around my neck.

Karen nods in silent approval, and I smile. We head down to her car.

Mike Tanner is standing on the porch talking on his phone. Sally is sitting in one of the rocking chairs, rubbing her belly as if it is already swollen and egg shaped instead of washboard flat.

Stopping over by Sally, I inquire about the interview.

"It went splendid! In fact, they want him to come in again tomorrow to meet with the boss higher up."

"That's fantastic, Sally. Congrats."

"The only problem is, we can't seem to find any other hotel to stay at. Everything is booked solid for the rest of the week."

"Why don't you just stay here like you had planned?" I gesture to the inn. "I'm helping Bee out while she recovers."

Mike points to the phone and gives a thumbs down sign.

"Looks like we don't have much choice really." Sally chews on her lip. "We do really like this place, but are you sure it won't be a burden...you're here as a guest, too."

"Not at all. It's just some coffee and some dusting. You might as well stay the night."

Mike has gotten off the phone now and puts his hand on Sally's shoulder. "Sorry honey, the Hilton is booked too."

"So, it's settled then. You guys will stay here. Bee will be delighted to know you aren't leaving."

"What was that all about?" Karen asks after we climb into her car.

"Oh nothing, just chatting with the other guests."

Karen's friends are insane. But what else would I have expected from her?

We've been snacking on bar food and sipping Cosmos all night. I've met the rest of the bridal party, all are artists and each seems to be in the punk scene along with Karen. I find the 'art show' on display hard to understand.

I take another sip of my Cosmo and study the white underwear attached to different briefcases. Someone tried to explain the concept to me as the underlying similarity between all of us; no matter what our profession, we all wear underwear. I totally don't get it.

I had hoped Eddie might be able to explain the art. I watched him chat up the artist for a little while before he came to check in with me. "Any clue where this concept came from?"

He ordered a club soda and then turned to me, "You'll have to wait to read my review." When I rolled my eyes, he simply responded with a wink. I tried to goad him to some sort of clue on what he really thought of the show, but he dodged each question masterfully. Before leaving, he informed me that Karen could stay at these things till the bar closes down which is why they always drove separately. "Did you want a ride home?"

It was tempting to say yes and slip out, but Karen was still floating around and I had nothing to do back at the B&B. After saying good night to Eddie I ordered another Cosmo and tried to just be in the space.

Everything in this bar is art. The bar top itself is a fish tank and you can watch them swim underneath your drink. Not a single chair or stool is in the same style. Even the Cosmos are made in various colors. I'm currently sipping a blue one that tastes like those raspberry slurries you can get at the movie theater.

I can feel myself fading. Between the lack of sleep last night and all the flights of stairs I climbed today, I'm beat. I've been sitting at the counter for the last thirty minutes or so, debating if I should call a car to head back to Pixie's. But Karen comes over and flops into a seat next to me.

"Great stuff, right?" She takes a swig of her yellow drink.

"Yeah. It's… different."

Karen laughs. "You don't have to like it, silly. Art isn't about making stuff that looks good anymore. All the best artists are making things people can't stand. Raw. Gritty. You know?"

I start to nod but then decide to shake my head instead. "No. I don't know. What's wrong with pretty?"

Karen throws her head back and laughs with glee. "Oh, I've missed you, Melanie. You should really come back home."

I put my drink on the counter. "Not you, too! Have you been talking to my parents?"

"Come on now, it wouldn't be the worst thing in the world. I'm sure you can get a teaching job here and we could find you a place to live not too far—"

"I don't want to teach."

Where did that come from?

"What?" Karen is staring at me the way I feel I should be staring at myself.

But that is how I feel. "I just...don't...I can't be a role model anymore. It's too hard, Kay. It's too much."

"Oh, Mel! Give it time. You'll see, some other guy will come along and you'll start over. You always wanted to have a lot of kids, you told me that was why you wanted to teach in the first place, to be around all those kids. It's all you ever wanted to do."

"Yeah well, now I want to do something different."

Drink in hand Karen peers at me. "Different huh?"

"I don't know what just yet. I haven't thought it all out." I swirl the blue liquid in my glass before downing it in one gulp.

"Melanie. There is one thing I know about you. You will come up with a plan. I'm sure of it. Just double check that you are making the right decisions, okay? Don't just react to Charlie's death by flipping your life upside down."

Karen really does have my best interest at heart. But what the fuck does she know? She's all giddy in love and planning her wedding. She hasn't lost anything the way I've lost my soul mate. My life is already flipped upside down. I'm trying to right it and bang out the dents. Salvage something.

"Mel...don't." She reaches out and strokes my hand, "don't cry, sweetie."

"Can we just go, please?"

"Sure, sure. I'll run you back to your place, just give me a second to say good-bye."

I blink back stinging tears. I've been *so* good the past few days, avoiding this depression zone. I don't want to lose it now.

Crap. Do I really want to stop teaching? I'm rolling this around in my head when I realize I'm being watched. In the mirror behind the bar, a man sitting a few seats down is staring at my reflection. He looks vaguely familiar, but the alcohol is pulsing through me and I can't be sure. I meet his eyes in the mirror, and he doesn't turn away. In fact, he cocks his head and smiles at me.

This is all I need right now. I do not want to flirt with some stranger. Not even one as handsome as this guy. I leave a tip on the bar where a goldfish under the glass immediately starts to check it out and I walk quickly towards the door.

I pass the chair where the guy is sitting, and he stands up.

"Hey, don't I know you?"

Without looking at him, I keep moving, but call over my shoulder, "Nope." And push my way outside.

TEN

I fight with the alarm. The alarm wins. *Crap!* Is it really 6:30 already?

I didn't end up getting to sleep until almost midnight after Karen drove me home. I scramble to change into clothes and get downstairs to put on the coffee.

Roger has scribbled a thank you onto the back of the note I left him. He placed it next to the dirty dishes he left behind.

With the coffee I ground yesterday, I get the pot going and the liquid it sputters out actually looks like coffee.

Now. Breakfast.

Bee strictly forbade me from buying anything else from Gus's. But I don't know what to make.

Oh, I remember. She said her plan for the last breakfast was to serve lemon toast with fried eggs. Well, surely I can fry an egg. And bacon. Larry will be happy if there is bacon.

I pull the ingredients out of the fridge and pour some oil into a frying pan that I pull from the pot rack. About two inches should do it, I think. Counting out two eggs for each of us, I set the bacon in another pan over low heat.

Okay. So far, so good. Now, onto the juice. Bee told me she juices her own oranges, which I find in a bin at the bottom of the pantry. The juicer is easy to locate in the cabinet of gadgets.

I cut a few oranges in half and turn the machine on. Seems easy enough. Just hold a half of an orange down over the twisting thing and…it's juicing!

Shit! The juice is coming out a little spout on the side and is spreading across the counter and dripping on the floor. I flip the machine off and throw some paper towels over the juice river.

Not to fret. All I need is a container to collect the juice. After opening a few cabinets, I find a large measuring cup. But it's too high for the location of the spout. I rotate the juicer so the spout faces the edge of the counter; I hold the cup up to it with my left hand and run the orange halves through with my right.

Ha! See, it's working now. I have about two cups of juice made when smoke catches my nose. The bacon!

Sloshing the cup of juice on the counter I grab a spatula and try to flip the bacon. But it's useless. The undersides are burnt to a crisp. I thought I had it on low but I must have mixed up the burners, my oil is still cold.

I rub my eyes in frustration. Immediately, my eyes start to burn. *What the hell?*

The juice. My fingers were covered in orange juice, and the acid is now in my eyes.

I dip my head under the sink and flush out my eyes, blinking them to clear away the tears.

Making breakfast should *not* be this hard. I just have to do what I've told my students a thousand times. That old cliché. If at first you don't succeed, try, try again.

I scrape blackened bacon into the trash and put a fresh batch on. This time, I double check my burners. The bacon is on low, and the oil on high.

I finish juicing the oranges and wash my hands. A quick sniff confirms I've rinsed all the juice away.

I flip the bacon. So far, it's not burnt. Now, for the eggs.

The oil looks nice and hot so I pick up an egg and crack it open into the pan.

Holy shit! Why is it sputtering like that!

I grab the handle to take the pan off the burner, but it scorches my skin. "Crap!" Using a dish towel from the sink, I get the pan off the flame, and the popping egg settles down. It looks horrendous. Bits of fried egg white float in the oil.

I've eaten fried eggs before. This does not look like a fried egg. This looks like white vomit.

I can hear some voices from the lounge and pop my head out the kitchen door.

"Oh, Melanie, good morning!" calls out Sally. "It smells wonderful, how's it coming in there?"

"Well, the coffee is made. I'll bring that right out." I smile at everyone and step back into the kitchen.

What am I serving for breakfast? So far I have coffee, orange juice, and bacon. Great.

In my class, one of the mothers comes in to show the kids different snacks. And I have an idea.

Fifteen minutes later and we have a home-made breakfast on the table for five. Coffee, juice, bacon, and apple wedges with peanut butter and raisins.

At first, everyone is a little baffled at the entrée. But after Margie reaches for a few pieces of apple, they all follow her example and load their plates, making do without comment.

"Is there more bacon?" Larry asks.

There would have been if I hadn't burnt the first batch to a crisp, but Margie responds first. "I have to get to the salon, and you do not need any more bacon." She shoos him out of the lounge.

I'm scrubbing up from breakfast when the phone rings.

"Hello....um, Pixie's," I amend.

"Yes, hi." Snaps back the caller. "Do you have any open rooms for this weekend?"

Oh shit. Now what? Bee said the place was booked but half the guests just left and I don't know what is going to be filled when. "Um, well for how many?"

"My husband and I, for Friday and Saturday."

I find a pen and a pad of paper by the phone and start jotting down notes.

"Right, two of you for two nights…okay, anything else?"

"So…you do have the room?"

"Maybe, I have to check."

"Okay." And then there is silence.

"Well, I can't check right this minute. Can I get your number and then I'll have the innkeeper call you back?"

"Oh. I see." The woman responds curtly. She gives me her number and I'm about to ring off when she asks me the price.

I didn't book this place myself and I have no idea how much Karen paid for it. "Sorry. You'll have to wait for Bee to ring you back."

"When can I expect to hear back from her?"

Geez. "Um, by this afternoon I'm sure. I'll make sure she gets the message. Have a good day now!" I hang up the phone before she can ask me anything else I don't know.

The hospice service arrives next door at 2 to set Bee up. By then I've taken five more requests for reservations, cleaned up the main rooms, and picked and juiced the lemons from the tree in the back yard.

I still have not been into the occupied rooms to clean them. I did clean my own room at least.

Bee is sitting in a wheelchair, arguing with the orderly when I arrive at the back door.

"No, no. Swing the bed into the doorway of the kitchen. Yes, the kitchen! I don't want to be in the den. The bathroom is right off the kitchen and I can use a walker to get there."

Trying to stay out of the way, I stand back and observe her in action. They get the bed set up and help her move from the wheelchair into it. Even in bed with her leg elevated on a square foam block, she is in total control of the situation.

She's been directing one of the guys to pull items off the top shelves of her cabinets. "No, no, not the green bowls, the blue ones, yes, those. And now in the cabinet to the right, let's see, I'll be needin' the gravy boat."

"Bee, I can get those things for you later when you actually need them."

"Melanie! I didn't see ya there. Come on in." Bee waves me over. When I get close enough, she leans in and whispers, "but that one there, he has such a tight backside, I can think of a few more things he can reach up and grab for me."

I pull back in shock. "Bee!"

"What? There is nothing wrong with my eyesight, young lady."

The man pulls down another bowl from the top shelf. He has to lift up onto his toes to reach, and the action stretches his white pants over his thighs. I have to admit, he does have a nice butt, which is clearly sans underwear.

When everything is as she wants it, Bee bids the gentleman farewell and I set about pouring her a glass of the lemonade I brought over.

She takes a deep gulp and then puckers her lips and gags on a cough. "What ratio of water and lemon did you mix into this?" she asks when she finally gets her throat settled.

Mix? "Um…"

"It tastes like straight lemon juice." Bee is eyeing the glass.

"Well, I made it just like I made the orange juice this morning."

Bee is looking at me incredulously. "You can drink straight orange, but you *cannot* drink straight lemon."

"Right. I know…I was just testing you. You know? Make sure all your senses are sharp." I try to kid with her. Bee's expression doesn't changed.

"Melanie. You just served me lemon juice. Please tell me ya didn't give this to anyone else?" I shake my head. "What did you serve this mornin'?"

"Well, I made some…stuff." I lift my chin in defense, and add,"Everyone ate it."

Bee regards me carefully. "You didn't buy anything from Gus?"

I shake my head.

"That's a start. Okay. What did you make?" Bee folds her arms across her chest, but then settles her hands in her lap while I dawdle.

I try to come up with a fancy name for the meal I served, I don't really want to admit that I served a children's snack as a main entrée to her paying guests.

"Manzana de…um…" What's the word for peanut butter? "Mani?"

"Nutty apples? Never heard of that dish, what's in it?" I should have guessed she knows Spanish.

"Apple wedges with peanut butter."

Bee gives me a stony stare.

"And raisins on top." I add with a bit of hesitation.

Her shoulders start to shake and I think she is going to cry. But her mouth splits into a smile and she laughs. I am laughing too and for a few moments the two of us are just caught up in giggles.

"Oh, that's rich." Wiping tears from the corner of her eyes, Bee lets the laughter peeter out. "I bet Larry was in heaven. He loves peanut butter."

"There was bacon, too. Plenty to feed everyone. But we're out of bacon now. You'll have to tell me where to buy more."

"You served bacon with the apples? Interestin' mix."

"Well, I was going to serve fried eggs. But I don't know what happened there. I thought I had the oil hot enough, but when I dropped the egg in, it didn't work."

"Which oil did you use?"

"The vegetable oil. I found it in the pantry." I start to twist my fingers as Bee stares at me.

"Hmm, maybe I won't ask for more details on that one." Bee screws her mouth up in thought, "Is the house cleaned up for the day?"

With my fingers crossed behind my back, "Yes."

"Okay, I have an idea. I'm stuck in the kitchen, right?" I nod, "And you need to learn how to cook some food, right?" I nod again. I think I know where she is going with this.

"So…you want to teach me?"

"Bingo! Pixie's B&B is best known for my cookin'. I can't have you marrin' my image with nutty raisin apples…no offense."

"None taken." But really, is it so bad to serve apple and peanut butter? It's healthy, cheap, quick. Maybe not fancy like a frittata or lime muffins, but it got the job done.

"What do ya know how to cook?" Damn it. If only I had used the cooking lessons Charlie had given me for my birthday.

"Ah, well. Toast. And umm…and bacon. I can make baked potatoes and popcorn. And today I made orange juice."

"And lemon juice. You still have to learn how to make lemonade." Bee smiles gently. "Is that it?"

I shrug. "Charlie always did the cooking. I made the salad. Or called for take-out."

"And what about before that? Didn't ya learn how to make anythin' at home? Some family recipes?"

I swallow. "Not really." Family recipes were Hamburger Helper and those instant rice packets that you add hot water to.

Pizza Fridays were my favorite. Each week we took turns selecting the toppings. Pineapple was my choice.

Letting out a big sigh, Bee scoots herself up in the bed. "Well then, I guess we have our work cut out for us. First things first, we need some ingredients from the pantry next door."

I go through half a dozen eggs before I am able to fry one successfully. It turns out you only need a little drizzle of oil in the pan! Of course, I figure this out *after* Bee yells at me for pouring two inches of it into the pot like I did earlier. They really shouldn't call it a fried egg if you ask me.

We've made lemonade that you can actually drink. Bee even had me pick some mint from the back garden and muddle it into the bottom of the pitcher and pour the lemonade on top to make it extra special. It is now safely tucked in the fridge next door for service when folks come back this afternoon. Muddling is fun, who knew?

Now she has me chopping up a papaya to make a fruit salsa to be served over the eggs. We've already diced up the onion and the pepper, and picked the herbs. This part is easy. No cooking involved, just chopping and stirring. But I had to run to the store for a few things, which gave Bee the opportunity to take a nap.

For one, we were out of bacon. And I needed to get a pomegranate to finish the salsa. Despite Bee's reassurance that baking fresh bread is really simple, I won the argument that we just don't have the time. She instructed me on which bakery to visit and buy a loaf to make toast for the morning meal.

I am feeling more confident about helping her out. I didn't really think it through when I made the offer, and after seeing the list of chores, well, it was more than I thought I could manage. But I have all day free. "One step at a time, Melanie"

Although it feels like she is still helping me out more then I'm helping her.

"Bee?" I call out softly when I enter her house in case she is still sleeping.

"Hmm?" She's sitting in her bed, flipping through some recipe books, dog-earring the pages she wants me to review for later this week.

Unpacking the bags from the store, I try to coolly ask, "Who's Harold?"

"Why do you ask?"

"You were saying his name yesterday when I first found you."

She puts aside the cookbook and folds her hands together. "Harold's my late husband."

"Oh." I start in on the pomegranate, although I have no idea how to work with it.

"He was a beautiful gent, that guy. Really nice backside." She sends me a wink. I smile back.

"How did he…" I wave the knife in the air. "You know?"

"Die?"

I nod.

"Cancer. It got him slowly. I took care of him right up till the end." Bee looks up and smiles.

I don't want to interrupt her memories so I keep chopping at the fruit on my cutting board.

"Melanie, tell me something?" I knew if I asked about her husband she was going to ask about mine, but curiosity got the best of me.

I prepare myself and look up at her with expectation.

"What did that pomegranate ever do to you?" It's not the question I expected.

Looking down, my hands and the board are stained red from the juices and little gelled seeds are splattered across the counter and, yup, even on the wall.

I shrug.

Bee clicks her tongue at me, "Oh dear. You really have a lot to learn, don't you?" She picks up the cookbook again, and starts reviewing more recipes.

ELEVEN

My fried eggs and salsa are a big hit the next morning. I served my very first one to Bee in her kitchen-bed, and when she gave me the thumbs up; I went back and made a bunch more for the other guests.

After I cleaned up the meal and prepared a new batch of lemonade, this one with muddled raspberries…seriously, muddling gets a lot of frustration out, good messy fun… I received two more cooking lessons from Bee. First, we got a quiche squared away in the oven, and then Bee insists I make bread.

"But the bread from the bakery is practically home-made." I protest. "I watched them making some when I was picking up yesterday's loaf."

"It's not the same. Buyin' bakery bread is only useful if ya need some stale loaves for pudding or stuffin', neither of which we need at the moment. And stop whinin'."

"I'm not whining!" I whine.

Bee regards me for a second from her bed. She's marked a few bread recipes in her cookbook and decides to stick with the simplest wheat bread she can find. She's determined we could make a flavored butter to go with it so it wouldn't be too plain.

The yeast is brewing away with honey and warm water in the bowl. I measure out five cups of bread flour to go in next.

When it's all combined with the yeast mixture, the whole thing starts to quiver.

"It reminds me of the school science fair." I remark. Last year, about half the students made the usual volcano pieces where you pour vinegar, dyed red, into a basin with baking soda to get an eruption.

"Yes, cooking is a science. Many things must combine in just the right way to produce the product you want. Mix it incorrectly, and you're going to have a mini explosion." I never did reveal to her what happened with the lemon bread dough she had left rising at Pixie's.

"Is it bubbling all over yet?" I bring the bowl over to her side so she can inspect it. "Yup, that'll do."

She turns the book to me and points to the next step. I read aloud. "Add some butter, more honey and salt. Then knead in the rest of the flour."

"Knead?" I mutter the question under my breath.

I'm staring blankly at the page. Bee gives me a look that says to get on with it.

I've melted the butter in the microwave—at least you can use the microwave for *some* of the bread making process—and I mix that in with the other ingredients.

But then I stop. I can figure this out. I watched the bakers a little bit yesterday while I waited my turn. Well, really, I was watching all the different cakes and tarts spin around in the showcase. They looked so delicious and I had to resist the temptation to buy one or two to try them out. But I do recall the bakers working in the background, and they were rolling the bread around on their boards.

The recipe says to flour a flat surface and I'm supposed to get another two to four cups into the dough. Why can't they make up their mind? Is it two or three or four? I decide to start with two cups and measure that out onto the counter. Then I dump the glob of dough on top of it.

I look up at Bee but she is just staring back at me with a blank expression. Okay. Nothing to do but knead it.

With both my hands I tackle the dough and try to roll it around, but my fingers immediately sink into the blob. When I pull them away, bits of dough is stuck all over. I try to rub it off but the goo is just sticking from one finger to the next.

Bee's expression is deadpanned. She shrugs and gestures for me to continue.

I pat my sticky hands into the flour on the counter and tackle the dough glob, again. This time my fingers don't sink in immediately. I try to push the mass around the way I saw the bakers doing it, but it rolls off my mound of flour and sticks to the counter.

Oh, this is not going well!

Bee is chuckling. In fact, she has a hand to her stomach as if she is trying to hold in the laughter. My cheeks are flaming. I can't possibly be this incompetent! Why am I trying to make bread? I should have just put my foot down and told her we would be buying bread while I was helping her out. I should not have to do things the exact way that she does it.

"Are you upset, dear?"

"No!" I snap, and stomp my foot. And immediately I regret it, I didn't mean to snap at her like that.

"You're getting' frustrated. Good." Bee replies simply. *Good?* "I know people have machines that do this now, but old-fashioned bread kneadin' is one of the best ways to get the tension out of your body. Of course, it shouldn't be the cause of the tension." Bee shrugs. "But ya have to start somewhere."

"I'm not tense." I say threw gritted teeth.

Bee nods. "Sure, sure. Your husband died when?"

She throws the question at me so bluntly, I'm caught off-guard. I pry the dough off the counter and spread out the flour so more of the counter is covered. "It will be six months soon." I answer softly.

"And how long were ya together?"

"Six years."

"Ah," is all she says.

I push the dough around some more so it's covered in the flour. This warm ball of dough in my hands is annoying me. It's just too perfectly round now. I thought Charlie was perfect; well-rounded.

Husband material.

But why did he do everything for me? Didn't he see I needed to learn some things? Like who I was supposed to call to turn off his cell phone service. Or which mechanic to take the car to. I don't even know which store he bought his favorite cheese from. Some special French cheese he always liked to have around, and they don't sell it at the normal grocery store.

Why did I even try to find the cheese? I don't eat it. And he isn't here to eat it. Stupid waste of my time to even try and look for it. But I did. I drove around to six different places looking for that one little triangular wedge of stinky cheese I didn't even plan on buying.

Stupid perfect ball of dough. I'm so annoyed I punch it.

"Bravo!" cries Bee.

I look up; I had completely forgotten she was there.

Looking back at my bread, my perfect ball now looks like a car ran over the middle. "I ruined it." I whisper.

"Course not! You can't be nice to the dough. You have to beat it up a bit, or it will never turn into perfect bread." Bee is trying to sit up taller, but she can't move much more. "Do that again."

"Punch it?" I give her a curious look.

"Turn it over on its side," she gestures with her hands and I follow with the bread, "like that. And push into it again."

I give it a gentler punch. But Bee shakes her head.

"Harder. Like you did the first time."

I punch into it harder and then roll it over and punch it again.

"That a girl. Keep goin'." Bee watches me punch it a few more times. "Now add more flour to your board. The dough is startin' to suck it up, see that?"

I keep going like this for several minutes. Rolling, punching. Adding more flour. The dough glob is getting denser. It takes more effort to punch it each time I do it. The shape is starting to bounce back at me after each punch.

"Melanie." I look up at her but I keep punching. "Did ya feel like cryin' earlier?"

I realize I did want to cry. I nod, and clarify, "But not now."

"When Harold died. I was devastated. It was a long time comin', but still. We were together for over thirty years. Raised our daughter, traveled to Europe, saw history happen. But right after he died, I moved in here with my mother. Took care of her till she died too. And then I was alone. For the first time in a long time, no one around me was dying and I had to start focusing on the livin'. It's not easy going out in the world alone. Not when you are so used to having someone else there to take care of ya all the time. But then I opened Pixie's, and anytime I felt sad or scared, or I was just upset at how unfair it was, I made bread. Kneadin' lets ya take all that negative energy and turn into somethin' wonderful."

I've stopped working the dough. It doesn't want to take any more flour and I know this because I can feel it. My upper arms ache and my face is sweating.

"Let it rest now. Cover it in a bowl so it can rise."

Following orders, I put the dough aside and wipe away the rest of the flour. "What now?"

"Now we wait for the yeast to do its thing."

"Well, for how long?"

Bee chuckles. "However long it takes. Ya can't put bread on a clock. It does its own thing in its own time. Each bread takes a different amount of time dependin' on the day and the weather and how much punchin' ya put into it."

"So…what do we do while we wait?"

"Well, I'm goin' to call back some of these people that want to stay here. You should go make up the rooms."

"Right." But all the empty rooms are still empty and I've cleaned those. Bee is already pulling out the new cordless phone I bought for her while I was out yesterday. "Bee?"

She looks up at me. "I…I don't…I'm not—"

"Spit it out, Melanie. You don't what?"

I have to admit that I haven't been following her daily checklist of chores. The three rooms with guests haven't been tended to since Saturday. But I won't tell her that. I offered to help her out and she is trusting me to do things to her standards.

"I don't know how often you change the sheets on the beds?"

"Oh. Every three days. And that means they are overdue if you haven't done it." She has a worried crease in her brow.

"Not to worry. I'll get on it."

"Good, good. By the time you get the rooms set up for the day, it will be time to work the bread again." She sighs out her last words and starts punching in a phone number.

I can do this.

I start with Roger's room. It's just him and he's never here. It can't be all that bad.

I open the door. It is a disaster His clothes are strewn all over the floor. There is a wetsuit draped over the shower bar. Shaving cream splatters the mirror and his toothbrush is sitting bristles-down in the sink.

I pinch his clothes between two fingers and move them one by one to a chair. With the floor cleared, I run the vacuum around and then strip the bed. But under the pillow is a writing pad with Roger's notes scribbled on it. I try not to look as I move it to the side table, but I can't help it.

Poetry. The beach bum can actually write sweet poetry. Of course, it's about crashing waves and sunsets over the ocean. But still, it's nice.

I toss the sheets down the steps and turn to the bathroom.

I never even liked touching Charlie's stuff. But I will myself to move Roger's toothbrush and clear everything off the sink and tub so I can wipe them down. Remembering Bee's arrangement in my own room, I line everything back up as neatly as I can.

But I have no clue what to do with the wetsuit. I'll just have to leave that where it is.

I survey the room. It's still pretty messy with all of his dirty clothes piled up on the chair. I start to fold them and arrange them on the bed until I pull out a pair of his underwear. Okay, I'm totally not doing this!

I get the other two rooms straightened up as best I can make myself do it. I doubt it's up to Bee's standards, but I've got the jitters now from trying to avoid everyone's things. At least all the sheets are going in the wash down in the basement.

I find Bee napping when I return to her kitchen, but the instructions for the bread are pretty simple. Punch it down and divide into three loaves. Then they have to rise again. The quiche has completely cooled and I carry that back over to Pixie's and leave it displayed on the central counter.

I made this! The crust looks so flaky that I want to cut a slice of it right now and give it a try. But I don't want to ruin the appearance. I have a plan to serve it whole tomorrow and let everyone cut their own slice. It even has a central design of basil leaves that Bee helped me arrange to look like a clover leaf.

No wonder I'm hungry! It's almost noon and I had promised my folks I would come by today for lunch. Working at this place has got my appetite back on track. I'm famished!.

I have to stop at the store to pick up more oranges for tomorrow, so I grab some pre-made sandwiches and head down to the marina. After getting buzzed into the gate I walk down the dock to my parent's boat.

Along the way, I bid good morning or wave to the other boaters who are lounging on their decks, early cocktails in hand. The boating world has its own unique set of characters. They all seem to have nowhere to go, and they never run out of alcohol.

When I turn the corner to the dock where the Sea Princess lives, I count three people on the deck. My father is laughing at whatever their guest is saying.

"Hi!" I call when I get close enough to the boat.

"Melon Ball! Just in time!" My father is not usually this animated nor has he used my childhood nickname since, well, I was a child. I'm on guard.

"Just in time for what?" I smile back at him. I turn to face their guest.

I've seen him before… where have I seen him? He's tall and broad, and deeply tanned, with intense grey eyes. His hair is shaved short but what is there shines golden brown in the sunshine. He's wearing fancy slacks and a crisp polo shirt.

"Melanie Murphy." He says as he comes to his feet. "It has been a long time." His eyes run down my body and back up.

I'm suddenly conscious of the fact that I'm still wearing the old jeans and t-shirt I had on while I cooked and cleaned today.

Why didn't I take the time to spruce up before I came out?

Why am I even *caring* how I look? Automatically I finger my wedding band on the chain around my neck. I kept removing it from my hand to work with the food, and it was just easier to leave it as a necklace. Bee already told me I could keep the chain after seeing the ring on it.

"Gibbs…its Melanie Gibbs now." I'm still trying to figure out where I know him. "You were at the bar the other night, right?" He nods.

"But you don't recognize me beyond that?" He turns around in a little dance and gives me a puzzled look.

"Sweetie," Mom exclaims, "its Ricky Carlson!"

"Ricardo now," he amends. "I stopped going by Ricky after high school."

Oh my god. Ricky Carlson is standing three feet in front of me. In high school, before we moved south, he was all I could think about. I longed to become high school sweethearts and doodled my name with his last on my notebooks. He had a smile that would stop your heart beating when he looked at you. Captain of the soccer team. Star in the school play. All the girls, and some of the boys too, wanted to be in his arms.

I was. Or I was supposed to be.

We saw each other on the track field when I was training. He raced me a few times, said it was a good work out to prep for his soccer matches. He was a senior and I was just a freshman. But one day after he beat me at a race yet again, he brought up homecoming and mentioned that I would look good as his date. I remember that all I could do was nod.

My friends were so envious. They kept wondering if he would kiss me at the dance, because then we were destined to be an item and not just racing buddies. I got all this advice about what flavor lip gloss to wear, and that I should eat a big lunch so that I wasn't hungry at the dance. Wouldn't want to get anything stuck in my teeth or sour my breath before the BIG kiss.

It was a magical night. The crisp October air, already chilly enough to need a shawl over my dress. I was the only one of my friends who had a date. And not only with a senior, but with the god of the school.

I don't know why he picked me. I was a nobody. Just Melanie Murphy.

He gave me my first real kiss. His hand on my back. The disco lights above us. Right at the end of a slow song that we had danced to. Before he dropped me off at my house he asked if I would like to go out to dinner with him.

Dinner with Ricky Carlson. Somewhere that we could be away from teachers and parents. Maybe he would hold my hand across the table and we would gaze into each other's eyes the way they do in all the movies.

It was pure ecstasy for all of 24 hours. I learned that weekend that we were selling the house and moving to Florida. I never had the time to actually go on that date with Ricky.

And now, he is standing on my parents' boat.

"What…what are you doing here?"

He reaches his hand out to me. I stare at it baffled for a minute. But I realize he is just offering me a hand while I step onto the boat. What a gentleman. But I'm newly independent and I ignore his hand and step onto the deck without the assist.

And promptly fall on my ass as a wake from a passing boat rolls the deck just enough that my foot misses the mark. Trying not to drop the bag with the sandwiches, I twist my body so they land in my lap.

"Mel! Are you okay? Are you hurt? Did you twist your ankle? Oh, dear! I hope you didn't twist your ankle." My mom is looking around helter-skelter. But she hasn't put down her soda. Priorities.

"I'm fine, Mom. Just bruised my dignity."

Ricardo reaches down and offers his hand. "Will you let me help you this time?"

After a pause, I take it and he pulls me to my feet. His hand is hard and rough. I didn't expect that after the way he is dressed. Working hands.

I get myself composed and reassure my mother two more times that I'm fine. She even makes me walk around in a circle so she can inspect me. I find a Diet Pepsi in my hand and mom is trying to top off Ricardo's.

"No no, Mrs. Murphy. You've been very generous, but I've taken up too much of your time already. I'll let you visit with your daughter."

"Are you sure, son? Why not join us for lunch?" *Son?* Did my dad just refer to him as family?

"Yes! Do stay for lunch!" Mom chimes in. *What is going on with them?*

"I only have three sandwiches." I look between my two parents as they both beam at Ricardo.

"See, it's not meant to be. I'll be heading out now." Ricardo stands up and shakes my dad's hand and then hugs my mom. When he turns to me, he isn't too sure what to do. After an awkward moment of offering and then dropping his hand, and stepping forward for a hug—to which I step back from— he waves. "Was good to see you, Mel. Maybe we can catch up before I head back to Jersey."

"Oh, you must!" Exclaims my mom.

"Mom!" I hiss at her.

"Your folks know where I'm staying. Just give me a ring and we'll set something up." With another wave, he heads off down the dock.

I watch him walk around the corner and turn to find my parents standing arm in arm, staring after him.

"What is with you two?" I shake my head and go into the cabin to set up the sandwiches.

Over salami and provolone on squaw, I learn the mystery reason that Ricardo was sitting on my parents' boat this morning. It's worse than I thought.

He wants to buy the family house.

Our *family* house!

I didn't even know my parents were considering selling the place. My dad grew up in it and his parents built it back when Long Beach Island was only accessible by boat. My grandfather lived in that house till the day he died. I have fond memories of spending my weekends there when my grandmother was alive; wearing pajamas all day, watching cartoons and eating snacks. Grandma would get down on the floor between us and watch the shows too. In the afternoons, we'd run to the beach that two blocks away from the house.

It is the last house on the north tip of the island overlooking the water where Barnegat Bay meets the Atlantic Ocean. Only an ice cream parlor and tackle shop sit between it and the water and you can see beyond them both from the second floor. The red and white lighthouse, Old Barney, can be admired from all the north-facing windows of the house.

Best of all, the house had a name. I don't know how long the sign has been there, painted by my grandmother and touched up over the years by various relatives. It is a white oval with a navy-blue outline of a young sea captain and the name 'Captain's Quarters.'

A nod to my grandfather who served in the Coast Guard for three decades.

The property even has a private garden in the back. A rarity on the island where everyone has such a small plot of land that they fill every legal inch with as much house as they can squeeze in.

I haven't been back there in years. Gramps would come to Florida for the winter and I would see him here over the holidays. Aunt Julia would join us in the South too, at least during the years when she wasn't vacationing in France.

Charlie visited the Jersey house with me once, when I wanted to give him a tour of the town I grew up in. We went in the winter though, and most of the island shuts down during those months when the ocean is angry and the beaches are too cold to walk along. Despite the temperature, we still got ice cream, and I showed him the Captain's Quarters.

All of those memories, and more, flood my brain as I listen to my parents explain why they want to sell the place.

My dad is saying, "With Gramps gone and everyone living in other states, what's the point?" Mom nods her head in agreement.

"We might want a place to stay when we vacation in Jersey," I try to argue.

"Oh, Melon, honey. None of us have vacationed in Jersey in at least five years. And if your mom and I want to go up there, we'd take the boat."

"You haven't even taken the boat around the horn of Florida yet, how likely are you to take it all the way up the coast?" I'm flummoxed. "But what does Ricardo want with it?"

I'm puzzled by his visit. Couldn't he just buy the place from Jersey? Why come all the way down here to see my dad in person?

"Well, Melon," Dad starts. "We haven't put the place on the market. Ricky had mentioned to my father that he wanted to buy it years ago. And after he passed, we got a few letters reminding us."

"So…" I still don't get it.

"Apparently, the property is an ideal location for a restaurant and Ricky wants to create a fancy bistro there."

"We've been given sample menus." My mom jumps in. "It looks positively scumpti-ly-li-umptious!"

"A restaurant? But it's set up all wrong for a restaurant. The kitchen is hardly big enough and everything is on the second floor. That can't possibly work."

"Sweetheart—"

"And what can you fit, maybe two tables in each room?"

"Melanie," Dad tries again to talk over me.

"And there is no parking. I mean there is space for what, four cars?" I continue.

"He wouldn't turn the house into a restaurant."

I look at one and then the other of my parents. I'm totally confused. They just said he wanted to put a restaurant there. "But then how—"

"He's going to tear down the house and build something new." He supplies.

"*What!*" I spring to my feet nearly spilling soda onto the deck.

"How...but...Dad! That's your *family* home!" How can he even *consider* selling it to someone who is going to tear the place down?

"Melon, we don't have any reason to keep it." Dad reminds me.

I try to find some reason, any reason to argue against selling. But I come up with nothing.

I guess he is right.

But it just isn't okay and I don't know why. Maybe I just need time to let it sink in.

It's not okay. It's just not!

It's been two days since I found out the plan to sell the Captain's Quarters, and I'm still boiling about it. Bee made use of my steam and we've knocked out three more bread recipes. I even attempted croissants. They came out all wonky and some of them unraveled in the oven. But they still tasted good. Once you cut off the burnt bits, anyway.

The Tanners checked out yesterday. Mike got the job and they headed back home to start packing for their move.

Another couple checked into the second-floor room, and Roger still leaves me his dirty plates every morning.

It's the Hellins' last night. I'm determined to serve them a proper breakfast, worthy of their anniversary in the morning before they depart. I'm going to attempt a cheese soufflé and the practice batch is in the oven under Bee's watchful eye.

She's already moving around much more than her doctor wants. I try to check in on her every two hours, see what it is she needs so she doesn't get up to get it herself. I even moved her computer from the upstairs den down to the kitchen allowing her to update her website and monitor the reservation requests coming in.

I'm in awe of her tenacity. Who would have expected Betsy-Lou Ringley to keep a blog? Apparently, a lot of her guests are loyal to Pixie's and they like to stay abreast of current events happening in Pelican Bay. With the news about her injury spread to hundreds of her former guests over the internet, get-well packages have been flooding in.

Many of the packages are fruit or cheese, jars of honey or jam. Some cooking gadgets and cookbooks, too. Bee particularly likes the cookbooks that are local to a certain town from where her guests live. These she reads cover to cover like a novel.

Every day at one o'clock the post arrives with get well cards by the dozen. She asked me to pick up some thank-you notes so she could write replies to everyone who sends something to her.

"You know, they don't expect you to write back." I told her.

"That's the point, Melanie. The unexpected little gestures are what gets ya into their memories and then they keep comin' back here to be my guests."

"Like the little pots of coffee outside the door in the morning?"

"Precisely." Hmm, I should probably try to start that routine again.

The little unexpected things. I found out she posts some of her recipes on her blog when her guests ask. She even sends out her jams and spreads for just the cost of shipping, which she asks for *after* they receive their goods.

When I asked if she was afraid of getting ripped off, she clucked her tongue at me. "People who stay here become like my own family." She informed me. "You trust your family, right?"

I wish I did. But I still feel like my parents have no right to sell my grandfather's house. They said Ricardo wanted to buy it years ago. Then why didn't he? If my grandfather had wanted to sell it, then he would have. Obviously, he didn't want to see it get torn down and turned into a bistro.

It gets easier to clean the rooms and move the other guests' stuff around each day I do it. No one stays at the B&B during the day. Everyone seems to have some busy life to run off to on their vacation. It's helped calm me down. The work is unrelenting, yet relaxing at the same time. I go about my routine now in fluid movements. Undisturbed by anyone, occasionally popping in on Bee, and by the early afternoon, I have everything squared away for all the guests to return.

I found extra rubber gloves in the basement which I wear to move their personal items. I just think it's more respectful that way if I'm not actually handling their things.

Okay. So maybe it just helps with my paranoia of touching their stuff.

Every time I find a discarded piece of underwear that I have to move, I keep flashing back to the art show Karen took me to at the bar. And when I think of that, I think of Ricardo sitting at the same bar. I catch myself wondering how different my life might have been if we had gone on that date. If I hadn't moved away and...

But then I feel guilty. I never would have met Charlie. He was my one true love and he can't be replaced. It's just, if we had never met, I wouldn't know what I'm missing. And I don't know which is worse.

Not that I can change the past anyway. Stupid to even dwell on it.

Margie must have bought some new lingerie. I move the slinky black thing off the bed and toss it on the chair with the rest of the clothes I picked up. Every morning the same thing. Their clothes from last night strewn about in their haste to get their hands on each other.

We were passionate, but not *this* passionate. Some of my co-workers talked about how their love lives had faded with each year they were married. I always stayed out of those conversations because mine was going just fine and I didn't want to brag.

But next to Larry and Margie's…well, really. Anyone's love life next to theirs would just be a sad, sad story.

When I finish wiping down their bathroom and lining up all their bottles, I catch my reflection in the mirror. It's a horrible sight. Skin is peeling off my nose from where it burned. My hair looks flat and frizzy at the same time. I've been pulling it back into a ponytail all week to keep it out of the way. I twist out the tie and try to fluff some volume into it and spread it over my shoulders.

Oh god, when was the last time I had it cut? The ends are brittle and split. What used to be bangs are long enough to tuck behind my ears. Peering at myself closer I realize I haven't tweezed my eyebrows in ages. I'm going to be celibate for the rest of my life!

As soon as I think that, my cheeks flush.

I can't even recall making love to another man. I absent-mindedly finger the ring around my neck. Thinking about Charlie, naked, handsome, moving over me.

I let the ring drop to dangle from its chain again. Well, enough of that for now. No point in getting worked up when I cannot do anything about it.

Heading back to Bee's I can smell the soufflé before I even walk into the kitchen. She's sitting in her bed diligently writing thank-you cards. But the dish is already cooling on a wire rack on the counter.

"Bee!" I remark. "You really need to stop moving around so much."

She just shrugs and keeps on writing, "It was done. Needed to come outta the oven."

"But how did you manage to pull it out and balance on one leg?"

"I used to be in the circus," she jests without stopping her card writing.

I dismiss her with a shake of my head and pull out a large spoon and scoop into the soufflé, serving out a large portion for each of us.

Licking the seal on the envelope, Bee puts aside the finished card and takes the plate from me. I pull up a chair and we both take a bite.

After chewing it with consideration she turns to me and asks, "It's missing something. What do you taste?"

I try another bite, chewing it slower, rolling it over my tongue. I shrug, it tastes fine to me.

"Salt. It needs more salt. Sprinkle some on and you'll see the difference."

I fetch the salt shaker and add a tap to each of our plates and try it again. Oh! She's right. That does make a difference.

"Otherwise, it's good, Melanie." We eat in silence for a moment before she continues. "You are doing splendidly, my dear. I've never seen someone take to cooking so quickly before. You're a natural."

"Huh!" I try to laugh. "You're just a good teacher Bee. I've tried to cook before, but I failed miserably every time. Charlie even got me cooking lessons...but I couldn't bring myself to go."

"Why not?"

I push some soufflé around the plate. "He grew up in a house where the family meal was a big event. He was always talking about the ham his mom served at Easter or the pies they had every weekend. He knew I couldn't cook when we met. I was really good at ordering out though, and it was safer that way. I didn't want to be compared to his mom. If I started to cook, how would I ever be able to live up to her recipes?"

Bee chuckles. "Every daughter-in-law feels that way, Melanie. I never wanted to cook for Harold's parents."

"But you're an amazing cook! I've seen all those requests from people asking about your recipes and ordering your jams."

"Yes, yes. That's true. Now." Bee holds out her empty plate and I get up to serve her seconds. "But back then, when we were first together, I could make sandwiches and that was about it. In the first year of our marriage, Harold's mother pulled me aside and accused me of trying to starve her boy." Bee is smiling with the memory, her eyes dance.

"So how did you learn how to make all this stuff?"

"I experimented. Harold was away a lot for work. So every time he left, I'd pick a recipe out of a cookbook and...just wing it. Sometimes I had to make it two or three times before it came out the way it was supposed to. But by the time Harold came home from whatever trip he was on, I'd be able to prepare a whole new dinner for him. Eventually I learned enough about the magic of makin' the ingredients work together that I was able to just experiment on my own. Makin' things up as I go." She forks in another mouthful of soufflé. "You'll get there too. You're not as incapable of this as you think you are."

"Can I tell you something, Bee?" I look down. "About Charlie?"

"Of course, dear."

"That night that he died. He was supposed to be coming straight from the office to our house. I had made dinner and was going to surprise him with it. But he wasn't coming from the office, the accident was north of our house and he works to the west." I grimace with the information that has haunted me since I found out what exactly had delayed Charlie that night. I hadn't told anyone about it yet. "He was coming from Mandy's."

Bee reaches out and grabs my hand in both of hers, "Oh! He was seeing another woman?"

I shake my head, "No. Mandy's is a local diner. Apparently, he went there to eat just about every night for an early dinner. It was so embarrassing!" I start to laugh.

After a moment, Bee starts to laugh with me, and it turns into a giggle fest.

Wiping tears from her eyes, Bee says, "He was cheatin' on ya with a diner."

I'm still laughing, "It's my cooking that killed him!" But my laughter starts to fall into crying and before I can stop myself, I'm sobbing.

Bee squeezes my hand again and tries to sooth me from her awkward position in the bed. "It's okay. There, there."

But it's not okay. "If I had just learned how to cook like this sooner. He wouldn't have been coming from that diner and he'd still be alive." I choke through sobs.

Bee moves a strand of hair off my face, "But if he hadn't died, you wouldn't have learned how to cook. No point in playin' that game. I did it myself long enough. If Harold had just taken a different job. If he hadn't been in at all those construction sites and breathin' in asbestos all the time. Maybe he wouldn't have gotten ill. Maybe he'd still be here now. But Melanie," she puts a gentle finger beneath my chin so I am looking into her eyes. Her sweet, knowing eyes, "you can't play the maybe game forever. At some point, ya just have to accept that he is gone and ya have to move on with things."

"But I don't know how." I whisper.

"Silly. You already are. Look at that." She points to the half-eaten soufflé on my plate, and then taps the ring hanging around my neck. "And this."

I snuffle and sit back in the chair. I brush the hair off my face and wipe my cheeks with the back of my hand.

Bee is looking me over thoughtfully. She reaches for the phone. As she punches in a number she tells me, "You need a new look. A fresh look for a fresh start." When the phone connects, she says, "Hello? Hi Eric, this is Bee. Oh, fine fine, yes, the ankle is healing just nicely. Look, I can't keep my standing appointment with you today of course, but can I send someone over to fill it? Sure? Great, she'll be there at two!" Bee beeps the phone off and looks back at me. "There, all set."

"What's at two?"

By 2:30 I am sitting under a blow-dryer dome at a hair salon with foils on my head and watching what used to be at least half my hair being swept off the floor by Eric, Bee's hairdresser.

I'm afraid to look at what is going on up there. The rest of the customer's all look like Bee. Grannies with short curly bobs. I never knew there were so many selections to dye your hair grey or white. Apparently even grey haired women get highlights and lowlights added in.

Eric seemed a little baffled at first when I walked in. As he tussled my hair around he mentioned something about how great it would be to work on young hair. I gulped down my fear of asking what he was planning on doing, and followed Bee's advice and told him to just 'make me new.'

So, now I'm on a timer, ten more minutes to process before we wash out whatever he put in. I hope it's not grey. He wouldn't do that to me. Would he?

All the magazines here are about golfing and retirement homes; I've been playing a game on my cell when a new text pops in. Probably just Karen bugging me about this weekend. She's been trying to get me to agree to drive over to St. Augustine's to visit the gravesite. But that will mean a full day to drive there and back, maybe even staying the night. And I can't leave Bee yet. Not until her daughter arrives, and Cindy still hasn't committed to an arrival date.

Plus, visiting my husband's grave isn't exactly something I'm eager to do.

But the text is not from Karen, it's an unknown ID.

> do you have plans tonight?

Must be a wrong number. The only people who would ask if I have plans are Karen and my folks. No one else would be asking me out.

I type back:

> Sorry, wrong #

The phone flashes a message symbol again.

> Melanie Murphy? its Ricardo, ur dad gave me the #

Oh, they did not, what were they thinking! Before I can respond, he sends another.

> how about dinner @ 6, we can catch up

I hit reply and type in a no thank you. But I pause before sending.

Bee has some friends coming over to play bridge tonight and I was on my own for dinner. My only plan was to sit around the B&B and read more cookbooks. She has me hooked on those.

I delete the negative message. In a daze I watch myself reply.

> Sure, why not

I don't realize I'm holding my breath till the phone beeps again.

> great! ill pick u up at 6, looking forward to it! :)

I'm rereading the message for the umpteenth time when Eric comes over and switches off the dryer.

"Okay my lady! It's to the sink with you now!" Eric leads me over to the washing station and tilts me back in the chair.

While he scrubs the chemicals off my scalp, I can't help but feel giddy. *I'm finally going on a date with Ricky Carlson!*

I have a date. Oh, my god! I have a *date*.

Is this a date? No. Two old friends catching up over a meal. It's just a dinner…date.

I can't date.

This is all wrong. Suddenly my hands are sweaty and I try to sit up.

"Ah-aa." Scolds the hairdresser. "We aren't done yet, honey."

I focus on taking deep breaths to steady myself. It will be okay. I'll just cancel. Just one quick little text and this will all be resolved. I hold my phone up over my face and try to punch the buttons but Eric is scrubbing my scalp so hard my head is bobbing and I can't focus on the little screen.

I can wait. I can cancel it in a second. No big deal.

"There we go." Eric sits me up and holds my hair in a towel. "Back over to the other chair."

I bring the phone up again but as soon as we sit down he brushes hair across my eyes.

"Bangs, right?" And he starts to clip at my hair.

With the bangs cut I get a glimpse of my new do while he sets up to blow dry it.

"I'm a red-head!" I exclaim. Not red like Karen's hair. Natural, subtle. Still more brown than red, but definitely a glow of red.

"Auburn, brings out the Irish in you." Eric says and he flips on the dryer. I can't stop watching myself as he dries the hair around a large brush to pull it straight. The color gets even more intense as it dries, revealing the gentle streaks of red spread throughout. He's cut my bangs thick and blunt, the way I wore them in high school.

We both admire it as I swivel my head around. My hair is blown completely straight and it just hits my shoulders now. "I love it. I absolutely love it!"

Even my eyebrows look good again; Eric waxed them right after he put in my color. I still have skin peeling off my nose, but you can't fix everything at the salon.

I've pay, adding on a generous tip, and walk out of the salon. Flipping my hair in front of every mirror that I pass, I remember I never sent that text to Ricardo.

I pull out my phone while I'm waiting for the Uber.

Crap! My low battery alert is on the screen and the car is still three minutes out. I don't want to risk being stranded again and if my phone dies the car might not find me.

I'll just have to call him from the inn when I get back.

But I can't call him when I get back. The phone died on the way here and my phone charger is not to be found. And without being able to get the phone on, I don't know his number.

I tried calling my parents from the inn's phone but no one answered. It's already half past four, they are probably at the stupid early-bird dinner at the marina. Why on earth do they eat so damn early!

I'm at a total loss as to what to do. I have to cancel. This is all wrong.

I pop into Bee's for advice but her friends were already setting up for bridge. They all remark at my new hair color and Bee just looked too happy for me to burden her with more of my troubles.

I grip the kitchen counter and bang my head lightly on the surface.

"That's an interesting way of getting the kitchen prepped. But hey, whatever works for you!" Roger has snuck in behind me and is peeling a banana he snagged from the fruit bowl.

I peer up at him from my bent over position on the counter.

"You're a guy, right?" I blow a wisp of my hair that falls over my eyes. For maybe the first time in my life, it actually blows back in place.

Roger stops the banana in mid-air. "Last time I checked, yes. I could check again if you need me to." He makes a mocking gesture of undoing his trousers.

"If you ran into an old friend of yours, a female friend, and you invited her out to dinner to catch-up," I make air quotes to emphasis the last two words, "would you consider that a date?"

Around a mouthful of banana, he asks, "Is that what the new look is about? You have a date?"

"Ohhh." I groan and put my head back down on the counter.

I spend the next hour grating cheese for the soufflés tomorrow. I've grated all the cheese I had in the fridge, which is about three times as much as I needed to prepare, but the clock is ticking so damn slowly!

I've thought of all the possible ways I can convince myself that this is not a date. He's married. He's gay. He wants to talk about the house so it's a business dinner. But it's no use. Whatever reason I come up with, it still feels...well, wrong.

The last date I went on was with Charlie. Six years ago. I mean, we had 'date nights,' but its different when you know the person you are with. You end up going to the same restaurants and you can practically order for them without looking at the menu. You know exactly who is going to sit in the booth and who will take the chair. Whether or not they want ice in their water. What type of service will earn the waitress a good tip.

By 5:45 I've changed my clothes three times. At first I put on the yellow dress I wore to Karen's. Nope. Too flirty. Then I put on the oldest clothes I have with me, the ones I've been cleaning in. No way. Too depressing. I finally settle on a brown summer dress. Figure flattering to show I'm in shape, but not overt enough to draw attention. Perfect for a business meeting, because I've decided that is what this is.

I put on make-up and then scrub it all off. Except I put the concealer back on to cover up the sunburn across my nose. And I dab some on my shoulders too. Stupid Irish skin. Where are the freckles that my brother has?

Looking myself over one last time I finger the ring around my neck.

After a few seconds, I unclasp the chain and slip the ring off and slide it back onto my left hand. It feels cold against my skin and it's tighter than it usually is. I spin it a few times and think about Charlie.

See. It's not a date. It's just dinner. My heart belongs to Charlie. It will always belong to Charlie. No matter what.

Ricky Carlson is sitting across from me. *The* Ricky Carlson. He is just as dreamy as ever I imaged he would be. A little older, more filled out than he was in high school. But...dreamy.

He picked me up in a Mercedes and we are now sipping white wine on the terrace of a French restaurant. It's similar to the one he wants to build, and he's been going on and on about the menu and the décor and everything he and his partner plan on doing with their new place.

This is obviously a business meeting. Not a date.

I looked carefully at his left hand, no ring. But also, no tan line from a missing ring. And the way he keeps talking about this other guy, Jeff, combined with the fancy attire and the overtly macho car...he must be gay. He even has a gold chain around his neck. Bill wears one like that, if I remember correctly, so that confirms it. Which I know, makes me racist or sexist, or some such category like that.

I breathe a sigh of relief when I come to this conclusion, and I'm much more relaxed now then I've been all afternoon. I'm even enjoying the wine and the view.

There is soft violin music playing in the background and the ocean is glistening from the sun sitting low in the sky. There is still plenty of daylight out, but the candles on the tables are already lit.

"So, what do you think?" Ricardo asks after the waiter serves us the salad.

"This dressing is pretty great." I actually cannot stand blue cheese, but the crumbles are big enough I can push them to the side.

"Not the salad, my restaurant proposal." Ricardo locks his smoky grey eyes on me as he lifts the wine glass to his lips.

"Oh, that." I push a few more chunks to the side and stab some lettuce onto my fork. "It sounds great, just great. But can't you find a different location for it?"

"Your grandfather's house is the perfect spot, Melanie. I've done all the research. The view of the lighthouse, the way the sun sets off the west side, the proximity to the beach and the fishing pier. It has all the right ambiance."

"Sure, sure. But it also has a lot of meaning to me and my family. You can't just tear the place down like it never existed." I have a lot of memories in that home, the thought of it simply not existing any longer is horrifying.

"Oh, I wouldn't say it never existed. There would be pictures of the place in the lobby of the bistro and little plaques with the history of your family." Ricardo's voice is sugary sweet, he's probably used to getting what he wants and this conversation with me isn't unsettling him at all.

"But you'd still tear the place down." I point my fork at him before popping a pecan into my mouth.

"Well, yes. It's not exactly built to hold a restaurant at the moment." He gives a slight shrug.

"My point exactly!" I sit up and square off with him, a challenge to make eye contact but he declines.

Ricardo keeps eating his salad and I pull a roll out of the basket and start tearing off little chunks of it.

He eyes me before asking, "Are you going to eat that or just turn it into bread crumbs?"

"We're supposed to be catching up." I remind him. "Tell me, what have you been up to since high school? College?"

Ricardo shakes his head. "No. No college for me." Really? I thought he would graduate valedictorian or at least close to it. College bound all the way.

He takes my expression in stride and goes on. "I know, everyone makes that face at first. But I needed some time off from school so I joined the Coast Guard, like my father and his father and so on. Then one year turned into two years….and well, it just kept going."

That explains the tan. And the rough hands. If he's out on a boat all day long, he's certainly not going to have baby smooth gentleman's hands.

"A water cop."

Ricardo chuckles and sits back in his chair. "Yes ma'am, at your service."

"Speeding boats and reckless jet skis."

"Most of the time." He pours us more wine, and swirls his glass before taking a long drink.

"I always wondered, does the Coast Guard set up speed traps like the cops do? Hide out under a bridge or behind a big rock just waiting for someone to swim by you." I swirl my wine too, but some of mine sloshes out of the glass.

"Oh, trade secrets." He runs his fingers over his lips and twists, zipping them closed.

I can picture him, Ricky Carlson, shirtless, driving around in one of those long red boats with the siren blaring. Lifting a megaphone to his perfect lips and calling out orders to the renegade boat he is chasing.

Okay, so he wouldn't be shirtless. But just maybe he was in the middle of changing into a swimsuit. Could happen.

A flush is rising to my face. I put the wine down; it has to be the wine.

"So, have you saved a lot of people?"

Ricardo picks up a roll and starts pulling it apart, too.

He nods. "Tourists usually. Most people should never be allowed to get on those watercrafts. Then you have the fishermen who start drinking beer the moment they bait their hooks in the morning, and don't wrap up till they've drunk a whole case. Those bastards are always falling off the pier and getting beat up by the waves."

The waiter clears our salad plates and tops off our water glasses. After he leaves, Ricardo continues.

"But it's not the saves that count. We do that all day, every day. It's the losses. The ones you don't get to in time." He picks up his wine glass and takes a big gulp.

"Is that why you want to get out?"

"Get out?"

"You know, to open the restaurant."

"Oh, no. I'm not going to be leaving the Guard. Jeff is going to run the place. He's going to be the manager and the executive chef. I'm just backing it."

Our entrées arrive and I squeeze the lemon over my fish before cutting into it. "You guys must really have a great partnership to decide to go into business together."

"Sure. Jeff is a great guy. I wouldn't trust anyone else with this venture." Ricardo pops a shrimp into his mouth and snaps off the tail.

I don't need to ask where the money is coming from. Ricardo is a Carlson. The Carlson family practically own the island. Being an only child, he'll undoubtedly inherit all the businesses his family owns.

"So, where do you and Jeff live?" I'm imaging they have an ocean front house, one of those ridiculous modern ones with all the weird angles and colors. They probably have a mailbox in the shape of a manatee. Or a flamingo.

"I live by the Coast Guard station. I have an apartment across the street. Jeff doesn't live on the island. He runs a restaurant over on the main land, near the high school actually. But he'll probably move close to the restaurant once we get it going."

"Oh, sorry. I shouldn't have assumed you two lived together." This fish is really good. I find myself considering ways I can turn this into a breakfast dish…but halibut in the morning doesn't sound too good.

Ricardo is giving me an odd look as he pops another shrimp in his mouth. "So, what about you? Your mom filled me in a little. A teacher, huh?"

"Well, for now." I don't comment further, I haven't *actually* decided to change careers. Yet.

Ricardo nods, "Right, you're moving back here."

"What? No!" I practically yell the words and I know my eyes popped at that one. Geez, why would he think I'd be moving back to Florida?

"Okay." He puts his hands up in defense. "I guess I misheard them. I thought for sure your mom mentioned you would be moving here."

I can't believe her! *Arghhh*. I could just scream!

"And she told me about your…" He trails off and is looking at my left hand. I slip it under the table. Ricardo clears his throat. "Right. Do you want to try a shrimp?"

THIRTEEN

My cheese soufflé is a hit! I had so much cheese grated, I put a second one in the oven as soon as the first was out and thank goodness, because the guests finished them both off.

There are now eight people staying at Pixie's, although the Hellins leave today, but Bee informed me the place would be filled by the end of the weekend. Plus, Cindy finally confirmed she was coming on Monday. Bee insists that I can still get cooking lessons from her…if I want to waste some time with a little old lady.

Larry is wetting his finger and pressing it around the edge of his plate to pick up the crumbs. I swear that man would prefer to eat alone so he could just lick it clean. The Hellins seem to be having a pretty rough morning. Margie isn't even sitting at the table. She made herself a Bloody Mary and is sipping it on the couch by herself. Well, sipping might be the wrong word. Is that her third?

Everyone else has already left for the day, and while I'm clearing away the dishes I keep glancing between the two of them. Margie is just staring at the photos under the coffee table' glass and Larry has found every possible crumb, but still sits with his fork in hand. Bee would butt in. I wouldn't. Bee would though, and I'm filling in for her, so…

"What is with you two, today?" I ask hesitantly.

Neither of them respond. In fact, have they said anything all morning? I stack the last of the plates and carry them into the kitchen. No. I'm pretty sure everyone else did the talking and they didn't chat at all. That's the norm for Larry. But Margie is usually a chatter box regardless if anyone is engaged in conversation with her.

I walk back into the lounge and put my hands on my hips. "Okay you guys. I feel like we've become friends over this week. Margie, you helped me out with Bee, thank you. And Larry, you let me borrow your car to run some errands, thank you."

Still nothing.

I pull a chair out and sit next to Larry. "I see you guys every night, completely in love with each other. And every morning you are so cold. Forty-two years right? Come on, whatever you are fighting about you can get past."

Larry slowly looks up at me with sad puppy dog eyes. But still, a vacant stare.

"Margie?" I call to her. "Margie!" That at least gets her to turn her head to me. I'm good at resolving small fights at school. You just need to get both kids to sit next to each other. They never want to look at the other, their eyes always downcast. But you get one to tell you the story first and then the other, and they get to hear each other mumble what the fight was about. Then you tell them to both apologize and hug. They usually run off holding hands. All better.

But they were seven-year-olds. Their fights are about who was playing with the dump truck first.

"Come on guys." I feel like whining, but I keep my voice steady. "I don't want you to leave Pixie's like this. I know we can resolve whatever it is. Just tell me what started it and we'll go from there."

I look at Larry but he's turned his face away from me. Margie however is still staring at me. In fact, she looks like she's angry at me. Me?

In a slightly less convincing voice I repeat, "Just tell me what started—"

"You!" Margie finally speaks, "You are the cause of this …spat!" She tilts the glass up to her lips and gulps down the last of her Bloody Mary.

"Um…me?" I mumble, my hand pointing to my chest as if I'm not sure she actually meant *me*.

"Yes, you! I trusted you with my secret and then you went and exposed me. And now Larry hates me. *Hates* me!"

Okay, I'm totally lost. I certainly did not pull Larry aside and reveal any dirty little secrets.

"Margie. Don't blame her," he stabs a fat finger in my direction, "when it's you who can't be trusted!" Larry's voice booms across the room. But he still hasn't turned to look at his wife.

"I did what I had to do, Lawrence! If you only understood—"

Larry pushes off from the table and stands up to face Margie. He is practically quivering.

"Oh, I understand. I understand plenty! You think I don't find you attractive. You think you are old and fat! Well look at me honey!" Larry puts his hands in the air and twirls around. "I'm older and fatter."

"You didn't want me anymore." Margie shrieks. "You went for months without touching me. What was I supposed to think?"

"What are you supposed to think?" Larry turns his head to the ceiling, "Margie, we've been married for four fucking decades. Is it so wrong to be content just being with you?"

"But you used to have such a healthy appetite and then it just went away." Margie pouts. I look at Larry. Really? He still looks like he has a healthy appetite to me. "I thought you must be seeing someone else. Someone younger, and thinner. Sexier." With this last word, Margie bites on the celery stick. Tears are threatening to spill from her eyes.

I feel like I should point out they are at it like rabbits every night…but I don't really want them to realize how much I've heard.

Larry walks over to the couch. "Did you really think you needed to slip me Viagra?"

Oh, crap! He found out.

Oh, double crap! I knock myself on the forehead. I remember now. When I was cleaning their room yesterday and lining all their toiletries up, the pill bottle was amongst them.

Margie looks up at her husband and nods her head. He sits down onto the couch and slips an arm around her.

"Honey. I've never been with another woman and I never will be. You," he taps her chest, "are all the woman that I need."

Margie sobs, "We weren't making love."

"Maybe we weren't having the buck wild sex we've been having the past few years, but we were always making love." Larry leans in to nibble on her ear.

Ooooookay. I should probably retreat from this conversation. I start to walk backwards out of the room.

"Let me show you how I make love to my wife without those pills." Larry is stroking Margie's collarbone and sliding his hand down her shirt. I'm trying to tiptoe back into the kitchen around the table just a little bit faster

Margie wipes at her nose and giggles.

Larry leans into nibble her neck. "Oh, Larry!" And more giggling.

Okay, screw the tiptoeing. I turn tail and get back into the kitchen, turning the sink on full blast and making as much noise as possible getting the dishes ready to wash.

That was not like solving a fight between seven-year-olds. *Not at all!*

"Melanie?"

Margie's ash tinged voice startles me and I drop the plate I was scrubbing back into the sink, splashing water onto the counter.

"Sorry, dear. Just wanted to ask if we could check out a little later? We um…still want to use the room." Margie nods her head in the direction of the room.

"Right, right, sure! You go ahead!" I can imagine the ridiculous smile I've plastered on my face. My cheeks feel inflamed.

She winks at me and slips back out of the kitchen.

The dishes can wait. I pull the rubber gloves off and make a mad dash to Bee's house.

I replay the Hellin's fight to Bee while we put pumpkin muffins in the oven. I had her laughing to tears when I tried to imitate Margie's voice.

Wiping the corners of her eyes, Bee tells me, "Do you know how many years I wanted to expose that woman's secret? I was always tempted to line that pill bottle up with the rest of the stuff."

I've been rearranging the newest batches of get-well jars while the muffins bake. We agreed to arrange the jams alphabetically and I've just reshuffled the entire shelf to squeeze in a huckleberry jar between the grape and jalapeño varieties. I didn't know huckleberries were real fruits.

Reaching for the next batch, my attention is caught by the gift tag.

"Bee?" I inquire. "Did you see this basket from Gus?"

"Humph. Of course, I saw it. It's nothin' special, just put it with the rest of the stuff."

She's being indifferent. Too indifferent. With each new package, she *oohs* and *ahhs* over the contents, spontaneously thinking of ways to use the items and jotting notes to herself for future recipes. Surely, she looked at this box, too. The centerpiece of the arrangement is a small jar of saffron jelly.

I've been doing my homework at night, reading Bee's cookbooks, and I know that saffron is one of her coveted spices. The most expensive spice there is. And here is a whole jar of it, albeit a small one.

"Bee. You saw this, right?" I hold it up so she can see.

But she only looks at it from the corner of her eye. "Yup, another jelly. Just put it in order with the rest of them."

I shrug at her lack of enthusiasm for it and about to put it on the shelf when I realize the label is handmade.

I roll it over to where the ingredients would normally be listed and read aloud, "*Ingredients: Saffron, sugar, water, two glasses of champagne, dinner, and a movie.* Bee," I look up at her, "I think he's asking you on a date."

"Don't be ridiculous. Hand me the thank-you cards, I have some writin' to do." She snaps her fingers at me with her outstretched hand, still refusing to look up.

I pick up the cards and walk over to her, but when she reaches for them, I pull them away. "Spill it."

"Spill what? Give me those." She reaches for the cards again and I pull them further away.

"I've met Gus, remember? He seems nice and he sent those roses to the hospital for you. Now this saffron jelly with a personal note on it. Come on, he's *into* you."

I bring the cards around and she snatches them from me. "Oh, what would you know? He just wants to sell me his pastries. He's always sending stuff over here for me to sample and trying to swindle me into usin' his store more. That's all it is." She begins in earnest to write out the next thank you note.

"I don't know—"

"Trust me. He ain't got no interest in me. Just my business." I want to keep on her, but I can tell she has a wall of defiance up, no point in pestering her further. I turn back to arranging the jellies and silently, we waited for the muffins to finish cooking.

As I'm popping the muffins out of their tins there is a knock on the door. It opens to reveal Margie and Larry, holding hands.

"Bee, Melanie." Larry turns to both of us respectively. "We just wanted to thank you for another lovely week."

"Yes, the food was just perfect, Melanie." Margie adds. "You have a good helper there, Bee."

"Yes-sir-ee. I heard she fixed you two up just right. I expect you'll be back next year then?" Bee asks.

They both nod. With a wave, they retreat, pulling the door shut. "Drive safe!" I call after them.

"Hope they have enough energy after their mornin' exercises." Bee deadpans.

"Bee!" I toss a dish towel at her. We both grin.

"We should all be so lucky to have a love like theirs." Bee adds wistfully.

"We did, Bee. We both had that." I finger the ring, secured back on the chain around my neck.

"Yes, we did."

FOURTEEN

I agreed to play a round of golf with my parents this weekend, but I had to convince them to take a later tee time than they normally prefer so I could get breakfast set up at Pixie's beforehand. Today's fare is an array of yogurts, granola, and fruits that I sliced up last night. Bee and I selected some of her jams that didn't fit in the cabinet and I placed those out next to an assortment of muffins and biscuits we've been baking all week. I was quite proud of my buffet set-up, and even hand-wrote little tags for each item and a big sign that invited everyone to help themselves.

Now it's 8am and I have four hours before I need to be back at the inn to greet the new guests arriving today.

My parents could be twins, the way they are dressed. Identical white shorts, yellow plaid shirts and socks halfway up their calves. The only difference is their heads; mom is wearing a ridiculous straw hat with a red bow, and dad has a Dolphins baseball cap.

I feel out of place. For one thing, no one else is wearing jeans. I looked. Not in the lobby, not in the rental shop where I checked out clubs, not even the gardener we passed when we first got the cart. Between the floppy hat Bee lent me, and the white splash of thick sun block across my nose, I should at least be able to keep the sun away. My mom tried to rub it in when she first saw me, but then realized I had done that on purpose.

With my phone finally working again, since I bought a new charger, I pleaded with Karen this morning to come up with some emergency that could get me out of this activity. She apologized, saying that she was at a crucial place in a sculpture and hadn't slept in two days trying to get it done.

So, golfing it is.

I hate golfing. Mainly because I suck at it. I enjoy mini golf; the kind with the windmills and little labyrinths you putt the ball through. But I'm always way over par on every hole. Charlie used to keep score and would usually just give me par anyway. Not that it mattered; he always won even with the skewed counting system.

"Okay, who should go first?" Dad asks after we are all standing around the first tee. We look at each other and shrug.

"Oh, I know!" Exclaims mom, "Just like in the old days, remember Melon? When we were trying to decide if you or Todd would be sitting up front in the car when we went out. Remember what we did?"

I have to think about that, "Rock, paper, scissors?" I guess.

Dad shrugs, "Okay then, count of three. One, two, thr—"

"Wait, wait Richard dear. Are we throwing on three or after three?"

"On three. Ready? One, two, three."

We all throw a paper and I quickly ball up my fist. "Oh, looks like I'm out. You two now."

They throw again and Mom gets Dad with rock over scissors.

"There you go Gloria, all yours." With a mock bow to the tee, Dad stands back and we watch as my mom places her purple golf ball in place. She takes a practice swing and then hits her ball with a loud *whomp*.

"Excellent, dear!" Dad cheers when the ball lands…well, somewhere out there.

Dad follows with a similar show and tells me his ball is just shy of where Mom's fell. Maybe I need to see the eye doctor when I get home; I didn't track either of the balls.

"Okie dokey, Melanie, your turn!" Mom seems positively excited that I'm playing with them. She's been calling me every night with a countdown reminder of when we were going to golf. Why can't their hobbies consist of going to the movies or walking at the park?

I pull a club from the bag and set my ball up.

"Um, Mel…you sure you want to use that club?"

I look down at what I'm holding, it looks fine to me.

Turning back to my dad I shrug. "Why not?"

"Well, you should really use a driver and that's an iron."

I walk back to the cart and slide the iron into the bag and grab another one. Pulling it out just a few inches I see my dad shaking his head. I touch a different one and he nods.

Back at my ball, I take a practice swing like they did. But I bump the ball off the tee and it rolls a few feet away.

"Oops!" I giggle and set it up again.

I square myself up to the ball, get my club centered, look up, look down. And swing!

Man, I really do need glasses. Where did it go? I'm searching the horizon to see if I can watch it fall when Dad clears his throat.

"Melon…"

I look back at him and he is pointing to my feet. Where the ball is still safely nestled on the tee.

"Oh." Seriously, hiking on the beach would be a nice hobby. They should try it some time.

"Perhaps you should hit it from the woman's tee? I'm so used to your mother giving me a run for my money back here I didn't even think of adjusting our normal game for you." Dad is pointing to another tee spot a few yards ahead of us, but I just want to get this over with.

"No, I'll just try that again!"

This time I do hit the ball, I actually hear it, and it lands about half as far as my parents' balls.

"Atta girl! You're a natural!" Mom cheers. She's even doing a little jig. I have to smile in spite of myself.

By the third hole it's apparent that I am *not* a natural. I'm fifteen over par and we agree that I'll just putt the ball once we get to the greens while they play the entire course.

From the safety of the cart, I watch them tee off at the seventeenth hole. The two of them share lively banter the entire time. In fact, they've had something to say to each other the entire day. How is that possible? They are retied and live on a boat. They are around each other all day, every day, yet they never run out of things to talk about.

I didn't have that with Charlie. We were...quieter. We'd chat over dinner about each other's day, sure. But then we would retreat into separate quarters of the apartment and work on our own stuff. Half the nights we went to bed at different times, so there wasn't even conversation as we drifted off to sleep.

It's been nice at Pixie's. Every evening when people come back in for the night, someone is inevitably in the mood to chat. Either sitting out on the front porch drinking lemonade or in the lounge over a game of cards. There is always someone to talk with, and the conversation almost never stops until everyone has retreated into their rooms.

I didn't realize how much I needed that type of connection before.

"Onward, ho!" Mom climbs back into the cart and Dad secures their bags on the back.

"Gloria, you are now..." Dad is calculating their scores, "three...wait, no, four strokes ahead of me. You're having a great game, love. Looks like you'll be winning this one." In the mirror, I watch him lean forward and kiss her on the cheek.

"Oh, you still have a chance to overtake me, Richard. Remember the game we played with the McCreadies?" Mom claps her hands together with the memory.

"That was just pure luck." Dad nods.

"Still, it could happen again!"

"What happened?" I ask from the front seat.

"Well, we were out with the McCreadies playing golf." Mom leans over the seat before going on.

"Yup, I got that part."

"Right, so Polly was ahead at first...you remember Polly don't you, dear?"

"Umm..." I shake my head.

"Polly and Frank McCreadie? I swear I introduced you to them the last time you came around. They have a boat that is docked just one pier over from ours."

"Two piers." Dad corrects.

"Two? I'm pretty sure it's only one, Richard. The Parkers are two over and the McCreadies aren't docked on the same pier."

"No Gloria, David Scott is one pier over. The Parkers are three over, and that makes the McCreadies two over."

"David Scott? I thought it was Scott David. Why must people have first names as last names, it's just so confusing."

I can practically feel Dad rolling his eyes.

I pull up to the balls and turn around in the seat to look at them. Mom is looking up to the sky and diagramming out the piers in the air with her fingers. After a second she nods her head in agreement. "Oh, you're correct. The McCreadies are two over."

They both climb out and select clubs. Okay, so maybe they talk all the time, but they don't seem to be in a hurry to get anywhere with what they have to say.

"Anyway..." I try to lead in.

Dad is practicing a swing but opts for a different club before approaching his ball.

"Anyway what, Sweetie?"

"The story? You were playing golf and got lucky?"

"Oh, oh." He says and takes another swing with the new club. "I got a hole in one." And with that he walks over to his ball and successfully hits it onto the green.

By the time I get my ball in the eighteenth hole, my score is almost an even match for theirs. I'm actually proud of myself! So what, they played the entire course and I just did the greens. On paper, no one would know that.

We're dropping the cart back off at the lodge when mom cries out, "Ricky! What are you doing here?"

I look up in time to see Ricardo break away from the two guys he was standing with to come and hug my mom. Great.

"Mrs. Murphy. Mr. Murphy." He takes my dad's hand. "I met up with some acquaintances for a round of golf. If I'd known you were coming, we could have played teams." He nods in my direction.

Oh, thank god he didn't show up earlier! That would have been positively humiliating.

"Melanie, how are you doing today?"

"Fine, just fine." Why do I feel flustered around him?

"I really enjoyed our dinner the other night. We should try to get together again before you head out."

I nod and busy myself getting the clubs off the cart. I can feel mom eyeing me. She asked if I had met up with him, and I avoided the question. I mean, it's not like it's *wrong* to have gone to dinner with him. It was just two people catching up on each other's lives. Besides, he has a partner. So, no big deal. Right?

Ricardo has turned back to my dad. "Mr. Murphy, I talked to the bank and confirmed we are all set to go. I just need a fax number and I can have my lawyer send you all the paperwork to look over. You of course can consult your own attorney, but I can assure you everything is in place."

"I've known your dad my whole life, Ricky." Dad claps him on the back. "I wouldn't doubt a Carlson for a second!"

Ricardo smiles. "Well, good then. I've lined up an inspector to look over the property tomorrow and then we can get everything signed and sealed by next week."

"Sounds great!" Mom adds.

"And of course, I'll bring over a check for the twenty percent down we agreed to, just as soon as you give me the thumbs up when you get that contract to review."

Dad writes down the fax number for the marina and they bid Ricardo good-bye.

"Mel, I'll be seeing you." He waves and climbs into the waiting cart with his friends.

As they drive away I turn on my parents. "Really? Do you really have to sell Gramp's place?"

"Sweetie—" Dad tries.

"No! You can't do it. He's going to tear the place down, the whole entire house! And then he's going to serve what? Escargot and brie pie in the same spot that we used to dip Oreo cookies in milk. And there will be stupid French drapes in the windows where we used to play Eye-Spy at the passing ships."

"Melon—" Dad holds his hands up and tries to shush me. I know I'm making a scene. But I can't help it.

"Why can't we keep it? Rent it out or something, just the way it is." I look between the two of them, but they both have their pity eyes turned on. I hate pity eyes.

"Melanie. Please just listen. It would need to be renovated if we rented it out." He shrugs, "it's just easier to sell it."

"Can't it just sit empty then? How much can you even be getting for it? Aren't the memories worth it?"

Mom mumbles something under her breath that I don't quite catch.

"Two what? Two hundred thousand? Our family history has to be worth more than that. You don't even the need the money, do you? Do you?" I'm panting with the effort of not yelling. Although I am in fact, yelling.

But they are both shaking their heads. Mom leans in and whispers louder this time, "Two million." She looks around nervously to see if anyone has overheard her.

"Two point three." Dad corrects and holds up three fingers but quickly puts them down

I'm speechless. Two…million dollars. True, they really don't need much money since downsizing to the boat and budgeting for the fixed income of their retirements. But I can instantly get that they aren't taking a crap deal, that M-word has a lot of power in it. I'm not going to win. I don't even know what I want to win.

I veer off to the ladies' room to try and get myself together.

Gripping the sink with both hands, I take deep calming breaths. It will be okay. I have the memories. The house can go. They are right after all, we aren't using it. That much money could go a long way with our family. I'm sure they will do good things with it; my parents are pretty frugal to begin with. Hell, that's why they live on a boat instead of in a house with a boat as a toy like sane people.

Okay. I'm good. This will be fine.

I look up into the mirror.

Crap! Batting at my nose with both hands I quickly rub the sun block off.

FIFTEEN

Cindy is not at all what I expected. With Bee's friendly take on everything and her welcoming smile, I just assumed her daughter would be the same way. Or at least close. Yet she's the polar opposite. Cindy is some high-up executive at an energy company and the moment I meet her, I can't imagine her ever running Pixie's.

I had stepped outside the moment I saw the sedan pull up. But now I've been standing here for an awkward five minutes and I feel stuck. I can't very well go back inside now, that would be rude. When she finally emerges from the back seat, I smile and wave, reminding me how I first met Bee when I arrived in similar fashion.

As Cindy approaches, I stick out my hand, "Hi, I'm Mel—"

My introduction is cut short by a dinging and Cindy raises her cell to her ear, flicking her eyes at me as she steps inside the inn.

Her jet-black hair is pulled back in a tight bun and she is dressed head to toe in a black suit. The driver of the sedan has unloaded a single piece of luggage from the trunk and deposits it at my feet before taking off.

"Right." I click my teeth, trying to decide if I should leave the bag or bring it in. Sighing, I pick it up and walk inside where Cindy continues to make sharp comments into her phone. She follows me up the stairs.

I have set her up in the Nutmeg Room, and had written out the schedule of who was staying where, and when the guests would be checking in and out. I had planned to go over it with her, maybe chit chat a bit about some of the inventory in the kitchen and supply closet so she had a heads up on what was getting low. Now, I have the sense it would be a waste of breath.

I've been waiting patiently at the door for her to put the phone down. But she's just busily going about unpacking and talking to her office. I'm not even sure she knows I'm still standing here. Finally, she tells the person on the phone to hold on. She covers the mouthpiece and looks at me with a question on her face but, doesn't say anything. I guess her talking is reserved for phone calls only.

"I thought perhaps we could look things over together so you know where I've left everything?" Her eyes are beady. No make-up and no jewelry. If it weren't for the skirt, I'm not sure I'd be able to determine she was a girl.

"No need for that. Just…you know…enjoy yourself." Turning her back on me, she resumes her call.

With that curt dismissal, I retreat to the kitchen. I've already cleaned up from the waffle breakfast I put out this morning to rave reviews. Bee's idea of mixing honey into the batter was brilliant.

About now is when I would start working on the rooms. The sheets are due for a change over in some of them and the Morrisons checked out this morning, their entire room needs to be reset…but I wrote all this down for Cindy. I'm sure she'll have it all under control.

Back up in my room I look over the books I've brought up from the Rosemary Lounge, but I've read them all. I suppose I could go to the beach. Or maybe walk around some of the knick-knack shops. I should really pick up a gift for Freddie to thank him for taking care of Buca.

But my eyes keep coming back to the stack of magazines Karen left me to look through. As the maid of honor in her wedding, she wants me to pick out the bridesmaid dresses. She's marked the pages that have looks she likes and will fit her wedding theme.

Which is of course, fairies.

"Wings and all!" She'd said. One of her friends from the gallery she shows her stuff in is helping with the décor. They have this whole grand scheme for turning a banquet hall into an enchanted garden. I heard something about lots of twinkling lights and even live butterflies being released when they say their vows.

She gave me these magazines over a week ago, when I was at her place for dinner. But I haven't wanted to look through bridal books. Just the thought of it made me nauseous.

Pulling open the desk drawer I look down at the photograph of Pixie and her groom that I stashed there when I first arrived. I've found all her photos now, a portrait in every room. Bee was correct; she was married four times from what I can tell. In this one she looks younger than all the rest.

They look so...okay, they still look like zombies...but I can imagine they were in love with each other despite the style of the actual photograph. Pixie is wearing her hair piled on top of her head, seated with her lace gown spilling all around her feet. Her husband's hand is on her shoulder and the other on the hilt of the sword he wears on his hip.

Did he die in war? Or perhaps he ran off. Maybe she left him. Something happened to make her available to marry again. And then again and again.

Hanging the picture back on its hook, and grabbing the stack of magazines, I head out of the room.

Cindy's door is open when I walk by. She is sitting on the bed typing into her iPhone and doesn't even glance up as I head down the stairs.

At Bee's I'm greeted with a big smile and I just can't imagine these two women being related. Granted, they do have the same nose. And maybe the same chin.

"Good mornin'! Did Cindy get in?" Bee is sitting on the floor with her elevated leg sitting out to the side with cards strewn all around her.

"Yeah, she's…unpacking. What on earth are you doing, Bee?" She's using the kitchen shears to cut out a little mouse from the front of one of her get-well cards.

"What does it look like? Arts and crafts!" She gestures to the cast the doctor added to her ankle when he realized she wasn't abiding his orders to stay off it. Already glued onto her boot are bouquets of flowers, rainbows, Snoopy, and other characters from the cards she's been receiving. With the mouse cut out, she reaches for the glue bottle and dabs a little to the back.

"Now, where should this little guy go?" Rolling her leg to the left and right she spots a place she likes and presses him down.

"Why are cutting up all your cards?"

"I've read them all and thanked everyone, what else is there to do with them?" She shrugs as she picks up another stack of cards and selects one with roses to start cutting.

"Don't you want to keep them…and I don't know, read them again later?"

"Melanie. If I kept all the cards everyone had ever sent me, I'd fill a whole room with them. Besides, the moment is over, gone. No need to read them again. This way, I get to look at all their lovely images all day long." She glues the rose in place and picks up the scissors again.

I've kept every card I'd ever been given. Filed by sender and then chronologically. Once I thought they should be chronological and then by sender and I reorganized the whole batch, but I ended up not liking that system and sorted them all back. It's the only collection I have that is organized at all, and not dumped in a pile.

But I never do read them a second time.

"What do you think of my daughter?"

I put the magazines down on her bed and join her on the floor.

"She seems nice." Taking the pile she hasn't cut up yet, I start sorting them by type of image.

"Right. Nice. Has she put her phone down yet?"

"Nope." Guess it's the norm then.

Bee sighs. "One day she'll slow down and actually enjoy life. Cindy is just so…eager to be on top."

"There is nothing wrong with being on top." I shrug. I hold up a card with a picture of wine glasses, that should go into the food category.

"Ha! There is when you have no interest in the rest of life. I swear I'm destined to never have any grandkids. I don't even know the last time she had a date." Bee sounds sad. The only other time I've seen her like this is when she was in the hospital and thought everyone might check out of Pixie's.

I sort a few more cards into piles. Who knew rabbits were so popular for sympathy cards? I received a lot of cards like this after Charlie passed. But I couldn't tell you what was on them. Or in them for that matter. I read a few, but they all basically said the same thing.

And now they are safely filed with the rest of the cards. Right next to the holiday greetings and birthday wishes. That's why I like the system of filing by sender, you get to mix up all the good ones with the sad ones and they get lost in the shuffle.

"Is it really all that bad to focus on work? It's safer I think. If you work non-stop, you don't have any room left over to fall in love. And if you don't fall *in* love, you can't be hurt. If you work all the time, you don't even think about all that." Flippantly I add, "I know I haven't."

Okay. I have. I still think about it a lot. But I don't have time to be sad. There are beds to make and dishes to wash, people to muddle lemonade for.

"I haven't cried in days, Bee. *Days*." She looks up at me from cutting out a daisy.

"Well, that is a good thing, dear. Very good. But you're not *just* workin' now are ya? You are connecting with other people. Relaxing over there in the lounge or on the porch in the evenin's, right? Ya even went on that date the other night with that cute fella."

Why is everyone obsessed with Ricky?

"It wasn't a date. It was just dinner. Besides, he has a *partner*." I emphasis the last word with a flip of my hand, "if you get my drift."

"Still. Ya went out and had fun." Bee looks at the wall as if she can see through it and into Pixie's. "Cindy doesn't know how to do that. She'll do the bare minimum that needs to be done here and she'll spend the rest of her time glued to her reports or that minicomputer she talks on. Then she'll complain about how she's missin' some important meetin' or grumble about how much time it takes my machine to wash all the sheets and how I should really get an industrial size one so I can do more in each load."

"Why did you ask her to come, then?"

With a shrug, Bee sighs, "She's my only daughter. I like spendin' time with her near-by, even if we don't actually spend time *together*."

We sit on the floor, sorting through the cards and cutting out images for over an hour. I make us some tea and we share a leftover pumpkin muffin. I never would have thought to make pumpkin-anything during the month of March, but Bee pointed out that it's just a flavor and like all other flavors, it should be enjoyed year-round. Of course, before I met Bee, I wouldn't have known *how* to make anything with pumpkin, period.

Cindy popped over to say hi to her mom. But she still had the phone in her hand and had barely set foot in the door when it rang. She mumbled an apology while backing out the door.

With the last of the cards cut up, Bee admires her adorned leg.

"Well?" She asks me while twisting and tilting the cast to show off the wrap.

"Um….it kind of looks like a garden party that is being invaded by rabbits who are going to get drunk on wine."

We both laugh as I help her get back to her feet.

"Oh!" Bee grips the kitchen counter and squeezes her eyes shut.

"What? What is it? Did you tweak your leg? Is something hurting?" I look her over in panic.

"No, no. Just a head rush. Will you help me back in the bed?" I support her elbow and she hops over to the hospital bed. When she gets a solid grip on the bed rail I let her go so I can move the magazines out of the way.

Bee gets herself propped back up onto the mattress. "God, I can't wait till I can get back into my own bed. This is an awful contraption."

"It's only been a week Bee; you have to be more patient."

"Bah!" She moves a pillow under her cast and picks up her teacup. "What do doctors know anyway? I've been climbing four flights of stairs to take care of Pixie's every day for over a decade. They think I'm some old ninny, but I'll heal faster than they think."

I have no doubt she will. In just this past week I've noticed a change in my own muscle tone. I can make it all the way up to Roger's room and back down with the bundle of sheets in my arms, and not be out of breath by the time I get down to the basement.

I pull one of the wooden kitchen chairs around and pick up the stack of magazines again.

"What are those, dear?" Bee puts her tea to the side and nibbles on the shortbread cookies I put out for us to share.

I hold one up, *Best Brides*. "My friend wants me to pick out my own dress for her wedding. Thought you could help me out."

She wiggles her fingers at me and I pass her half the stack. Bridal books weigh a ton. Each page is a full color ad for rings, cakes, favors, invitations. You name it; there are probably twenty retailers for every possible component of a wedding competing for your attention in these things.

Bee flips open to the first tabbed photo and makes a face.

I watch with mild humor as she opens to the next two tabs and her face gets even more skewed.

"Not liking anything yet?" I try to keep the laughter from my voice.

Flipping to the next marker she turns the book around for me to see, "What on earth is your friend tryin' to do to ya?"

The post-it has an arrow drawn on it pointing to a girl wearing a dress with little silk flowers stuck all over the bust and drapes of flowing pink and red chiffon. More flowers are spilling down from the waistline all the way to the floor.

I flip open one of the magazines in my lap and turn to the first note and hold it up for Bee to see. A gothic black velvet dress with gold ribbons laced across the front and long v-shaped sleeves that drop down from the elbows to touch the floor.

"Now, just image this dress with wings on the back for added flare." I put my arms up in mock wing form.

"That dress has enough *flare*." Bee makes air quotes on the last word. "What on earth does it need wings for?"

I nod and shrug at the same time. "Karen wants to be a fairy princess, and we are all supposed to wear wings that some art friend of hers will be constructing to match the dresses."

Bee widens her eyes and nods while pressing her lips together. "Ya know, in my day, we just wore a white dress and that was that. All these theme weddings everyone is havin' these days is somethin' else." With a sigh, she flips through to more of the marked pages.

I flip through all of the post-it notes in the first book and drop it loudly on the floor. Picking up the second I turn it to a purple garment that is more shoelace then dress with all the crisscrossed tied-knots snaking over the model that is positively hideous. I love Karen, but no way am I wearing that! Shaking my head, I'm about to turn to the next post-it when my breath catches in my throat.

On the opposite page is an ad for engagement rings and there is a photograph of a couple, the man on bended knee and the woman standing with an astonished face as he holds the ring out to her with all the hope in the world.

The man looks exactly like Charlie. I trace the line of his chin and hold it up closer to my face. No, not so much like him, slightly different features.

"See somethin' ya like?" Bee asks.

I smile and turn the page around to her. Tapping the man, "He looks like my Charlie."

Bee reaches for the magazine and I pass it to her. "Cutie pie."

I stroke the ring on my neck and close my eyes, bringing up his face in my mind. I can think about him now, like this, without breaking down into tears.

I shocked myself the first time I did this a few days ago. A scene of Charlie and I canoeing together had played through my mind. Charlie kept threatening to flip the canoe over. We splashed cold water on each other with the paddles, screaming as it hit us and we tried to dodge. Our roughhousing caused the boat to flip anyway. Dragging the canoe to the river's edge and flipping it upside down, Charlie pulled me underneath it, and we stripped out of our wet clothes.

We were both shivering hard from the cold water, but he started to kiss me. First my lips and then my ear, down my neck. I can remember arching into him and feeling the passion as clearly as I remember the way the stones felt under my back. We made love under the canoe and promptly got each other warmed up. We lay there for at least an hour hoping our clothes would dry in the sun across the top of the canoe, but they were still damp when we finally pulled them back on.

I can remember times like that and it only hurts a little now.

"Bee…" I start, but trail off.

She hands me back the magazine and I stare down at the Charlie look-a-like. Tracing his face one more time, I flip the page to the next gown choice.

"You were going to ask me something, dear?" Bee volunteers.

"Have you…did you…" How do I put this? "After Harold passed…do you ever think about getting married again?"

"I am married, to Pixie's."

"That's not what I meant to ask, really. I mean, did you ever date anyone? Don't you have…you know…urges?"

"You mean like Margie Hellin?" Bee smirks at me. The image of Larry and Margie going at it slips into my mind and I shudder.

"She *really* loves him, doesn't she?"

"Most definitely. And to the other question of yours, yes." I watch her flip through a few of the flower ads before she continues. "But you get to my age and they are easier to ignore."

"Did you ever think about trying again? You know, going out there and meeting someone new?"

She shakes her head. "Oh no. Not me. I'm not a young attractive girl like you, Melanie. No one would want to date this old body."

"Gus does." I prompt. I have to admit, I like watching her face flush pink when I mention his name.

"I already explained what Gus wants. But are we really talkin' about me, or are we talkin' about you?"

Fidgeting with a page, I mull that over. "I didn't think I would want to, you know? The whole idea of falling in love again is...scary. Even dating seems like it would take so much effort. But I've been looking at those photos of your great-aunt and she seems happy in all of them. Four husbands?"

Bee nods. "Four." And holds up four fingers to emphasis the fact.

"So, maybe it wouldn't be so bad to go through it again."

"No, I should think not."

"Maybe you are more like your daughter then you realize." I suggest, slightly changing the topic

"Now how is that?" Bee crosses her arms and narrows her eyes at me.

"You just said you were married to Pixie's. No time to date. Sounds just like what you said about Cindy." I point out the window where Cindy has been pacing back and forth, still on her phone. We can only hear the ebb and flow of her voice, but it's been nonstop since she took the call.

Bee frowns while she stares at her daughter's shadow passing by the window yet again.

"And you also just said you were more spry then the doctors give you credit for, so surely you could still act on those...um...urges if you met the right person." This is an awkward conversation, even after becoming such close friends with the little old lady sitting next to me. Strange to think, I haven't really made any girlfriends in all the time I've lived in

San Diego. Not the kind I'd be talking to about relationships and sex, and Bee isn't the kind of person I would have pegged for becoming my confidante, either. Funny how life brings you the people you need right when you don't even realize you needed anyone at all.

"I suppose ya have a point." She finally concedes.

I turn to the last marked page, and after a second turn the magazine around to her. It's a simple dress, a cream-colored top with wide shoulder straps. The cream fades into an autumn orange on the knee-length skirt. The model has gold rope wrapped around her waist, and ivy woven through her braided hair. "This one."

Clasping her hands in thought, Bee taps her lips while looking over the page. "I agree."

SIXTEEN

The next couple days pass without much ado. Cindy somehow gets the rooms cleaned up with the phone attached to her ear the entire time. She doesn't do things the way Bee would do them, and I have to stop myself from following her around and turning the bottle labels to face front or fluffing up the pillows on the couch.

She doesn't cook breakfast either. She bought a Keurig and supplied an assortment of K-cups for the coffee option. There has been fresh fruit available every morning and Cindy left out a box of Pop-tarts with the toaster on Tuesday, and this morning she had set out little boxes of cereal with milk. Looking in the fridge I found store-bought orange juice. I thought Bee would be livid, but she just shrugged when I told her about it and said, "That's my Cindy."

I wanted to ask her why I was forbidden from serving store bought goods, but her daughter could. I refrained. Where would I be now if I hadn't been forced to fry an egg?

Since Cindy took over the breakfast preparations, if you could call it that, Bee decided I should learn how to cook a few dinner items. Tonight, we made a basic tomato sauce and ate it with pasta and fresh meatballs. After I bagged up the leftover meatballs and placed them in her freezer, I headed back over to Pixie's for the night.

I've gotten used to company. Sitting on the rocking chairs in the setting sun, sipping the lemonade, which I still make from scratch, I mingle with the other guests. Everyone shares their story. And I encourage with questions of where they came from, what brought them to Pelican Bay and what they did for the day. With all the different travelers, you never hear the same story twice.

It's not like my students who tell the same story over and over, and every time you must nod and comment on it as if it's the first time you heard it. And the knock knock jokes, the endless parade of jokes, always the same punch line.

Only a few more days before I'm back in school and telling them to be quiet, settle down. Back to teaching them about the big wide world from the confines of a little square room. The closer it gets to going back, the less I want to return.

Maybe my mom is right. And Karen.

Maybe I should just move back to Florida this summer. I can't possibly stay on that boat with my folks. But perhaps I could stay at Karen's place till I get one of my own. Until I can figure out what to do next.

I've been back to the beach, this time properly coated in sun block. I searched the shoreline, but failed to find a matching shell for my collection. Sitting under the shade of a palm tree I watched the other people on the beach.

I particularly looked at the guys to see if I could imagine falling in love with any of them. There were tall guys, short guys. Some were gleaming with a tan, and some of them desperately needed a tan. I watched couples walking the beach hand in hand, and others romping in the waves. I looked at the families chasing their kids around.

Not one person stirred something inside of me. But nothing made me upset either, not even the couple that were making out as if there was no tomorrow, and for that, I was grateful.

I keep thinking about Pixie and the fact that she found love so many times. How did she do it? There weren't any singles clubs or online dating sites back then. The Merry Widow blog site where widows and widowers can meet. Yes. I checked it out.

I'm not ready to date, but I want to know that I will be. Bee might find it okay to be single for the rest of her life, but let's face it, she's a lot older than me and she was married for over thirty years. That is a long time to be with one person. I can understand her hesitation with not wanting to date again.

I'm not even thirty yet. I can't be defined as a widow and stay that way forever. I want to come home to a husband. Maybe have kids someday. Move on.

When I get to that part - the moving on part - I retreat.

It's one thing to look at other people and consider what type of boyfriend they might be, to think of the flowers they might bring home. But when I think about a wedding, about a child. I can't help but think, it would have been better with Charlie. Or, nothing will compare to how Charlie did it. Or that time he...

That wouldn't be fair to who ever the next guy is. To always be compared to my husband. My late husband. Why do they refer to it that way? Late. What could he possibly be late for now? He's just gone. 'Former husband' is not any better because he is still my husband, even if he isn't here anymore.

It's times like these that I slip the ring back onto my finger. But mostly, I continue to wear it around my neck.

Cindy noticed the ladybug earrings in my room and commented that they looked just like something her mom would wear. I keep forgetting to take them back over to Bee's house. Maybe tomorrow.

No, not tomorrow. She has to go to the doctor's and convinced Cindy to take her grocery shopping and run some other errands. A sly way to force her daughter to spend time with her.

Although I imagine Cindy will be on her phone the entire time.

I pick up my own phone and shoot a message to Karen asking if she wants to get lunch tomorrow.

The phone beeps with a reply while I'm brushing my teeth.

> I never thought ud ask! Y dont u come to my hotel n we'll leave from here

Hotel? Confused I look back at my sent folder. Oh, I didn't! I sent the message to Ricardo instead of Karen!

I'm typing in an explanation of my mix-up when he shoots another note over.

> im @ the Bayfront. lets meet @ noon. cant wait to c u again!

Arggh!!

> No, sorry, wrong number.

Holding down the backspace, I delete that. That's just dumb.

> Noon? No, I can't do noon. Never. Let's do never.

Jokes won't help. I delete again and roll my eyes at myself.

It's like a practice date. The man is gorgeous and he's totally not available, so it would be safe to experiment a little and see how I handle this. I mean, it's just lunch. Totally benign.

> Sounds great!

Ricardo is waiting for me out front. I look him over from head to toe as I get out of the car. Even though he is fully clothed, you can see the power of his muscles underneath. All those guys I saw on the beach yesterday hold nothing to Ricky Carlson.

He has on a pair of high quality sunglasses and I see my reflection as clear as a mirror when I approach him.

Putting away his phone, he steps forward to hug me, but pauses to see if I back away again. I don't.

"Melanie! I was so happy to get your text yesterday."

"Sure. You know, I was just bored anyway, nothing to do all day. Figured why not. Just lunch, right?"

I'm a blabbering idiot.

"Do you like Mexican? Just up the beach they are set up for spring break and serving lunch out in the sand. Margaritas, yeah?"

When I nod, he extends his elbow and I take it. So far, so good.

"So, I hear you've been volunteering with the elderly?" He asks as we walk away from the hotel.

Confused, I mutter an "Um...?"

"Your mom told me you were helping out with some old lady that broke her arm. Cooking and stuff?"

Mom! Can't leave my personal life alone and then doesn't get the details right.

"A friend of mine sprained her ankle and I'm helping her out is all. No big deal." Or just the best thing that has happened to me in the past six months.

"Well, I tried some of that lemon bread you made and it was quite good. I even told Jeff about it, he'd love to get the recipe." I had left some baked treats with my parents after our golf outing. Ricardo must have been over to see them since then. Just how much time was he spending with my folks?

"Sure. Oh!" I turn to him, "Jeff doesn't mind that we're having lunch together, right?"

Ricardo laughs. "No. Why would Jeff care who I have lunch with? You think he's afraid I'm going to replace him with someone who bakes bread? He's the best chef I know. You'll see. When we get the bistro open, you'll have to come try his food."

I pat his arm. "Of course, of course. I just wanted to make sure." That damn bistro or restaurant or whatever abomination they want to replace Gramp's house with. I'm determined *not* to discuss it today.

As we get closer to the restaurant I can see what he means about them being set up for spring break. A whole section of the beach is roped off with umbrellas and picnic benches. Tan college students are everywhere, drinking green margaritas and shaking to the music. A live band is playing a fun mariachi beat, and people are dancing in the sand in front of the players.

"What do you think? If it's too loud, we can go somewhere else."

"No, this is perfect!" I raise my voice over the music. It's a little loud, but that means there will be very little talking. Which makes it ideal.

While we wait for a table Ricardo tells me about his golf game. "I got a birdie on the ninth hole."

I gasp. "You killed a bird?"

"You have no idea how to play golf, do you?"

"I was pretty much just driving the cart that day." He stops talking golf. We just stand there looking around not talking till we are seated. After our margaritas and a plate of nachos arrive, he starts up the conversation again.

"So, we never fully discussed what is going on in your life, Mel. When I knew you before, I never saw you as the teacher type." He lifts a mountain of nacho toppings into his perfect lips. He carefully licks a drizzle of cheese off his finger. Why is that sexy?

"We don't really *know* each other Ricardo. How could you possibly know what type I am? Or was?" What is a teacher type, exactly?

"I remember this one time after we raced. While catching our breath you looked up at the scoreboard at the time and totally went berserk. Not about your run, but about the actual time. You ran off before I could tell you they hadn't reset the clock for daylight savings." Ricardo laughs.

"I don't remember that."

"And you never volunteered to be the facilitator in any of the team practices. Don't you kind of have to, you know, be in charge to be a teacher?"

"How do you remember so much about me?" I don't remember these things.

"I liked you, Mel. I'd been trying to get up the nerve to ask you out for months. Come on, why do you think I asked you to the dance?"

I shrug and put a nacho in my mouth so I don't have to answer. Ricky Carlson was nervous about asking *me* out?

"Anyway. I always thought you'd be a painter. Or maybe a writer or something. Something where you didn't have to worry about clocks or giving orders." He grins at me.

"I'm not that good with art, crafts are more my style. Things with glue and yarn." I said , still trying to catch up with his story details while wrestling with the memories they are bringing up.

"Well something more...quiet. But kids? I don't know, I just can't imagine you as a teacher. What drew you to it?"

I don't really know anymore. I just ended up there. I had taken a bunch of random courses and in my third year of college my advisor suggested I focus on Early Childhood Development since I had already taken a lot of classes that counted towards that degree. And I always wanted to be a mom, so it made sense. I did my internship during senior year and they hired me as a substitute. Then I met Charlie and just kept going in that direction.

Why did I never realize this before? I've been working as a teacher for six years and I never really selected that path. I just kept going forward and no one stopped me.

"Kids." I say at last. "I wanted to have kids, so it was like a quick fix you know? Being around other people's kids. But I don't think I want to do that anymore."

Ricardo waits me out while we both crunch on the nachos. But I stay silent. until he prompts, "What do you want to do then?"

"I haven't figured that out yet." Our tacos arrive, and I add a spoonful of guacamole before diving in. Ricardo follows suite and we are silent again for a few minutes enjoying the food.

"Do you still want to have kids?"

Do I? "I haven't figured that out either."

"Well, I do. I'm getting old!" Ricardo clicks his tongue. "As they say, the clock is ticking!"

He was only three years ahead of me in school, can't be older then 30, 31 maybe? "Do you plan on adopting or using a surrogate?"

He raises an eyebrow and tries to respond around a mouthful of tacos, but starts to cough. "Sorry! None of my business. What else has been going on? Tell me about, I don't know, something with your work?"

While we finish our meal, he tells me about one of the rescues he did which involved a twelve-year-old-boy, a collapsed sailboat, and a dog. He got both the dog and the boy but the way Ricardo retold the story, I found myself wondering if they were both going to make it.

"The kid is screaming at me and hitting my shoulders as I'm getting him into the life jacket, 'You have to save Bandit, save Bandit!', and I'm doing all I can to not just drop him and go get the dog first so he'll be a more cooperative victim."

I was hanging on his every word. I could just picture him on his boat with the American flag and the guard insignia rippling in the wind. The thrashing seas with the boy and his dog, both outfitted in a bright orange life jacket, calling for help. The boy with his arm looped through a buoy and another around the dog. Refusing to get into the coast guard boat until the Labrador was safely loaded.

And Ricardo, again shirtless in my mind. Why was I obsessed with this man's chest?

"I am stuffed!" I exclaim and put the last of my taco down.

Ricardo downs the last of his margarita and stands. Pulling me to my feet he says, "Come on, we can dance some of it off."

"But I don't know how to dance to this!" I try to protest. The band has switched to another style of Latin music that I don't recognize. Something with a fast tempo.

"Just look around. No one knows how to dance to this." Ricardo is bouncing his shoulders at me and snapping his fingers. He looks utterly ridiculous.

I glance around and realize he's right; no one is dancing the same way. Most are vaguely on beat. Arms are flying all over the place, hips are shaking and smiles are plastered on all the faces I see.

I tilt my head back and laugh. If it weren't for the margarita, I'm not sure I would be doing this. But I try to match Ricardo's movements and then I let my arms go up over my head and shake them out. Oh, this is liberating, it's so free!

"There you go!" Ricardo yells to me over the music. "Try this!"

He squats down and pops up on one leg, then bounces down and pops up on the other. "Isn't that Russian?" I ask with a wide grin.

"Who cares, just dance! I love it when you smile."

"What?" I lean towards him and ask. Over here the music is too loud for normal conversation.

Ricardo leans in and says. "You look great!"

I smile back at him. This is going so much better than I thought it would. I am totally ready to date. Lunch, dancing, light conversation. I can do this. For once I'm grateful Ricky Carlson showed up here, so I could practice my new social status.

We dance to three songs in a row and we're both sweaty. Even though the dance area is under a tent, it's still the Florida beach, and the air is humid. I'm about to suggest we sit down when the band changes to a slow song.

Ricardo doesn't hesitate to pull me into his embrace, his hands firmly on my waist. He's already swaying and I have to put my hands on his shoulders just to keep from tripping.

This close to him, all I can do is breath in his aroma. The heady scent of a man. It's been so long since I've touched a man like this, been in someone's embrace.

"Just like the last time we danced together." Ricardo says in my ear. "I'm afraid I'm not any better now than I was then."

But I have my eyes closed and a smile on my face. I can remember dancing like this with Charlie at our wedding. All of our family standing in a circle around us. Looking up into the eyes of my beloved. We were on top of the world. The day had been so very long and exhausting. I remember I could feel the fatigue setting in by then. But we still had to dance and cut the cake and socialize more before we could escape into each other's arms. Alone.

Charlie hadn't wanted to take dance lessons. We rocked slowly to the song, *Come Away With Me*, and I forgot all my worries about us not putting on a good show. I forgot how tired I was. I forgot that my feet were throbbing from the stupid shoes that were pinching my toes. I forgot about Aunt Julia who was passed out drunk at her table.

In that moment, I forgot everything but what I had ahead of me. A future for Charlie and I as husband and wife. The way he was gazing into my eyes, watching him mouth the words to the song as if he was saying them to me from his heart. And when the song came to an end, he brought me into a passionate kiss with everyone applauding and cheering for us.

Oh my god! I'm kissing Ricardo.

I open my eyes and push away from him.

"What—" He starts.

I clasp my hand over my mouth and stare at him.

"But you're gay." I say, and at the same time he says, "Is it too soon?"

"I thought you were Charlie." I cover my face with my hands, "I mean, I was thinking about Charlie."

"I'm not gay." Ricardo is looking perplexed.

"But you said Jeff was your partner. And…oh god." I cringe. *Holy crap.* I'm wrong, but I didn't want to be wrong. I wanted him to be a practice for dating, later dating, with other people.

"Jeff is my *business* partner. Nothing more than that." Ricky's face is contorted with confusion and hurt.

Then this was a real date. And he thought I had asked him out.

My pulse is racing and my cheeks are hot. I have to get out of here.

"Melanie." He comes after me as I rush back to our table to get my purse.

"Here. We'll go dutch, okay?" I grab a twenty out of my wallet and put it on the table.

"Melanie!" Ricardo calls after me. I look back as he's trying to find the waiter to get the bill. The tears have started to run down my cheeks and I run across the sand to a bench.

I am so embarrassed.

My insides are twisting and I squeeze my eyes shut and try to breathe through it. I'm still racked with sobs when I hear Ricardo approach. He stands there, somewhere behind me while I get myself together. When I'm certain the tears are over, I blink open my eyes and turn towards him.

"Sorry." I mumble.

He sits beside me and reaches to put his hand on my shoulder but he sees me flinch away and lets it drop.

"I guess you're not ready for any of that yet."

I shake my head. "No. I thought it would just be good practice." It sounds like a silly idea now. Practice.

Ricardo sighs. "I've never lost anyone like you have, Mel. So, I won't pretend to know what you are going through. But I did have a pretty bad break-up."

I risk a glance up and he continues. "Susan. We were living together and I was away for a training mission. Out of state, no communication for a couple weeks. The details don't matter. Anyway, I came home and she was gone. Not just her, but all her stuff, a bunch of my things too. She didn't even leave me a note." Ricardo picks up a shell and flings it as far as he can but it falls short of the water. "I spent months trying to figure out what happened, where she went." He continues. "But I never found her. Took me almost a year to start dating again. Another year after that to start trusting anyone."

The breeze catches my hair and whips it across my face. I turn my head into the wind and it throws my hair back. The smell of the sea comforts me, I take a deep breath and feel myself relaxing again.

"You really are a beautiful girl, Mel. Maybe one day, when more time has passed, we can go on a real date?"

Looking back at him, my hair whips across my face again. He reaches up and tucks a strand behind my ear, and this time I don't pull back.

I nod. "Yeah, maybe someday."

We sit there in the wind and watch the waves crash on the beach in silence.

"Could you do me one small favor?" I request.

"What's that?"

"Don't buy my grandfather's house. Not just yet."

Ricardo picks up another shell and tosses it again. This time he hits the water with a little splash. "What is with you and that place?"

I dig my foot into the sand and decide to tell him the full story.

"I took Charlie there once. I was showing him around where I grew up. The school, the race track, and the park I always went to with my brother when we were little. You know the one on Concord?"

Ricardo nods.

"And of course, my grandfather's house. Even though it was cold out, we got ice cream from next door and we were sitting in the side garden. Gramps was down here for the winter and we didn't have a key. So, we were just sitting outside, freezing and eating ice cream and I'm telling him about all the things we did at that house when I was growing up."

I look over at Ricardo, he's still gazing out at the ocean, but I know he is listening so I go on. "And my ice cream fell on the ground. So, Charlie gets down on the ground to pick it up and we realize he's on bended knee, and looking up at me and I can see the light bulb go on, you know? So, he gets into this theatrical mode and says a few bravado lines, tosses his own ice cream over his shoulder and takes both my hands in his. And he says 'Melanie Murphy, I love you more than life itself and mark my words, one day I will marry you!' We both laughed and I pulled him back up off the ground."

"Sounds like a romantic guy." Riccardo shuffles his feet in the sand and folds his hands together.

"It was the first time he ever told me he loved me. There in my grandfather's garden. And I just can't let that go." I fling some of the sand with my foot. "Not yet."

Ricardo sighs. "Your dad already signed the papers, Mel. All I have to do is give him a check and file with the realtor back home."

"Oh," is all I can manage.

We both continue to stare out at the ocean. But how much longer can I really hold on to things like *that* and not keep having meltdowns like *this*?

SEVENTEEN

I can't get the Captain's Quarters out of my mind; it's all I can think about.

Okay, that may not be entirely true. I also woke myself up dreaming about Ricardo. One of *those* types of dreams.

Over my coffee this morning I was picturing him running across the sand in nothing but shorts with one of those life preservers strapped across his chest. Slow motion, with the sand flying up from his feet and hair bouncing softly around his face. Then I realized it was the opening sequence to every episode of *Baywatch*. And he's not a lifeguard. And his hair is practically shaved bald.

But in between the sultry images of Ricardo running through my head, I can't figure out what to do about Gramp's house. I know he wouldn't want it torn down. He built it with his own two hands and he lived there his entire life. My dad and Aunt Julia were born there. Literally.

The bridge connecting the mainland to the island was done by then, but the nearest hospital didn't have a birthing center. Gramps liked to tell us he tried to convince my Grandma to get in their boat and they would get to one of the docks on the mainland and have an ambulance pick them up from there. But January in the Barnegat Bay is not only freezing but also hazardous.

A few of Gramp's old Coast Guard buddies argued over who was the one to deliver the babies. Aunt Julia is technically ten minutes older than my father, but when they finally did get to the hospital, they processed my father's birth certificate first. It's a bone of contention between them even after all these years.

I just can't wrap my head around it. The families that have lived on that island are like legends, going back for generations. When the parents go, the children move in. The family always stays.

The Murphys shouldn't be leaving either.

I Uber over to the marina and find my dad down in the battery well changing the filters. I help myself to a Diet Pepsi while he's washing his hands.

"Your mother is at a Mahjong match today. She's in the quarter-finals you know."

"They have tournaments for that?" I shake my head, at least my parents stay active.

"Oh yes. Your mother just loves that game. She'll be sorry to have missed you."

"I really came to talk to you today, Dad." My father is tall and lean, suntanned skin contrasting with sun-bleached hair that is stark white. Still a looker after all these years.

"I need to test out the new filters, if you don't mind taking a quick trip around the harbor?"

"I'd love to!" I appraise him as he settles into the driver seat and turns the motor over. He worked as a professional fisherman for years, and his body still looks like it could pull a hundred-pound tuna over the side rail. If it hadn't been for that stroke, he'd probably still be out doing it. But the doctor told him he had to retire after that; if he had another one while he was out on the ocean, he might not make it back.

It's one of the reasons they never take the boat away from the marina for more than a quick afternoon trip.

I jump out and untie the ropes that anchor the boat to the dock. Bringing in the bumpers I give him a salute and he eases us forward. It takes almost fifteen minutes to crawl out of the marina and into the open harbor where he tests the engines with a few quick surges before driving us out of the main path and cutting the engine.

I haven't floated on the water like this in years. The gentle rocking is soothing.

"Tell me the story of how you met mom." Dad smirks and pops open his soda. After a long drink, he looks out over the water.

"You know that story well enough to tell it yourself."

"Okay. You were seventeen, still in high school."

"The same school you went to, Melon." He says with pride.

"The school I started in," I remind him. "And it was summer break. Back then you worked at a bait shop because you were too young to work the boats themselves. Every morning you got up before the crack of dawn and went down to the bay line and unloaded your traps. If you had time, you dug for clams with your toes."

"I can still do that you know! But there are no clams down here, the water is too warm." He frowns a little. That man loves his fresh clams. In New Jersey, he'd stand waist high in the water next to our boat, bringing up one clam at a time with his feet. Shuck them where he stood and slurp them back raw, then toss the shell over his shoulder while he continued to knead his toes searching for the next one.

"And one morning you were out doing this, digging for clams and the sun was just rising over the water and you saw a mermaid."

"Your mother." He toasts the air with his soda can.

"But you didn't know who she was and she didn't see you there as she swam in the shallow water. But your bait selling job ended at 10am every day, and most of the fishermen were already out on the water by then. So, you would help Grandma out in her store."

"And there she was. My Gloria." He takes over the story, just like I knew he would. "She was applying for a summer job to work there and I knew Mother didn't like to hire teenagers. She always thought they were more likely to steal things. I had to beg her to hire Gloria. I still don't know why she listened to me, but she did."

"Then you started to work more in the shop, right?"

He nods and continues. "Yup, I found all sorts of excuses to be there. Before I knew it I was running the place because Mother hardly needed to be there with both Gloria and me taking care of everything."

"But she wasn't there for very long was she?"

"No, she was just a summer tourist. I didn't know if I'd ever see her again." He sits quietly for a minute. "And then the next summer, I kept looking for her. My mermaid. By the end of June, I thought she wasn't going to be back that year."

"And then Grandma needed a light bulb changed."

"Yup, Mother needed a light bulb changed. I got out the ladder and I was in the middle of the store changing the light bulb. When I was done, I went to step down but I couldn't move my foot. It just wouldn't move. And I looked down to see what was wrong."

"And you saw mom." I add.

Dad smiles big now, "I saw my mermaid. She had tied my shoe laces to the ladder rung and I had to slip my shoe off to get down."

"And you were never apart after that."

"And we were never apart after that." He echoes.

In silence, we sip our sodas. I let the story sink in before I ask my next question.

"Why would you ever sell the Captain's Quarters when it holds memories like that?"

"Oh, Melon." Dad stands up and faces the bow. "How many times must we discuss this?"

"As many times as it takes for me to understand, Dad." I stand next to him and look out over the water. A pelican is resting on a channel marker that protrudes from the water. His throat long and full of fish.

"What is there to understand? It's empty, we don't need it, someone wants it. It's simple."

"No. I don't believe you." The pelican flies off and I walk to the other side of the boat to watch as it disappears in the sky. "I've been thinking about it all week. We all have memories there, and it's the last connection the Murphy family has to the island. If you sell it, that's it. You've cut our ties. And if there is one thing I learned from you, Dad, it's to never cut your ties."

The Irish blood runs firmly in him. He's mellowed out since the stroke, but he used to have so much pride in his heritage that it flowed out of him to anyone who would listen. Traditions were hard for him to break.

"Two million dollars is a very generous offer from Mr. Carlson." He's being formal now? *Mr.* Carlson?

"You know your grandfather only paid seventy-five dollars for that property when he bought it. Before the bridge of course, when everyone thought the island was useless as anything but a local fishing spot. Two million dollars." He repeats wistfully.

"Two point three." I remind him, and he nods. "But what for? You don't have any expenses. You sold the house, you live on this boat. Todd and I are both grown up and on our own." I have to steady myself after I say this. I am on my own.

"Ah, Melon. Your mother is going to give me a talking to after this." He turns the motor on and adjusts our position. The pelican flies off at the sound of the engine and I watch as he soars out of sight.

When the boat is a in a good spot again, Dad cuts the engine and sits down facing me where I lean back against the railing.

"You know how your Aunt Julia is in France right now?" I nod. "Well, the thing is. She isn't really in France."

I wait while he shuffles his feet. I don't usually see my father nervous.

"We just say she's in France because we don't want everyone to know she's in rehab." Dad turns to me and takes my hands as he says this, his face somber and his eyes sad.

"But…" this is confusing, "she goes to France every year."

Dad nods.

"Oh." I take a seat next to him, bringing my hand to my face. "Oh!"

"Yeah. My sister can never quite give up the drink." Dad has been sober now for over twenty years. He proudly wears his AA pins on his ball cap.

"I didn't know she was trying to." All my memories of Aunt Julia involve her passing out somewhere. But we never really spent any time with her outside of big family gatherings, and the alcohol is always flowing at those events, right next to the copious supply of Diet Pepsi for my parents. I always drank more than usual at those gatherings, too.

"You don't know how much debt she has racked up over the years. These…trips she takes, they cost a lot. And she really needs to go someplace better. But the better places cost a lot more, Mel. Your mom and I, we've been looking into them and we really want to help her out. Get her set up someplace with a lot of support and get her well."

"That's great, Dad. I'm sure Aunt Julia will really appreciate that. But it can't possibly cost two million dollars to get her set up can it?"

An unhappy laugh escapes his lips, "You'd be surprised, Melon. She's remortgaged her house twice and maxed out all her credit cards. To clear her debt and get her set up, it will take over nine hundred thousand dollars. We can't sell just half the house, now can we?"

"No. I suppose not."

"So, now you know. Don't tell your mother I told you." He holds out his hand, he wants to shake on it.

I reach over and take his hand, "I'm sorry, Dad. I just thought…I don't know what I thought. I just can't believe we have to sell the Captain's Quarters." I feel hollow inside, selfish for fighting the sale in the first place.

He squeezes my hand and taps it on his leg. "I know sweetie. Trust me, we've thought of every possible solution. But family first, memories second. We have to take care of Julia now that Gramps is gone."

I want to feel sorry for my aunt, but I really feel sorry for Dad. All these years, I had no idea that his sister needed so much help. We never really talk about Aunt Julia and she's always been away in France. I do remember asking her to teach me French once…now I know why she said she couldn't.

"So, have you given any more thought to our suggestion for your next step? Will you be moving back to Florida?" I get it, he wants to change the subject.

"Dad, I just don't think that is going to work for me. Besides, it sounds like Aunt Julia needs you right now. I'm a lot more independent than you think." I really am starting to think I can be on my own and be okay, now. Although, it would be nice to be around family.

"I know that, sweetheart, but you know you can always come home." He gives my hand another squeeze and steps back up to the wheel. "Will you be staying for dinner? Your mother should be done with her tournament soon."

"Sorry, I have something planned for tonight." I wink at him as he gets the engine going and we head back through the harbor.

Cindy is sitting in the lounge when I get back to Pixie's. Her laptop is open, and binders of paperwork are strewn across the table. It reminds me of how Charlie would set up his work at our house. Her phone is sitting on the table, silent, and she is sketching out a chart.

"Cindy, did you get my note earlier?"

She holds up a finger at me and taps the Bluetooth in her ear. Of course, why would she actually be *off* the phone?

I disregard her and carry my bags into the kitchen. Unpacking I lay out all the ingredients I bought. Apples, yams, green beans, mustard, garlic and pork chops. I open up the cookbook to the applesauce recipe.

So simple. Why did I never learn how to make this when Charlie was still around? I peel the apples and get all three pounds of them sliced up and into a pot with water and start cooking them down.

I reread the pork chop recipe three times and decide to make one of them now as a test for later. Getting the juicer out, I make a fresh batch of orange juice. I add in some mustard and garlic, a few sprigs of basil I clipped from the garden, and salt and pepper.

"There!" I swirl the mixture with my finger and give it a taste. Not bad.

I set a skillet on medium heat and add a little butter. To think, two weeks ago, I was torn between Taco Bell and KFC. Now, I'm trying my hand at pork chops. *Oh*, it's still slimy raw meat. Yuck. I use the tongs to pick up a chop from the paper packaging and place it down into the butter. Recipe says to brown it on both sides and then pour in the orange sauce.

I have to flip the chop over about six times before I consider it browned. I make a mental note about that for later. When the liquid hits the pan, everything immediately begins to sizzle and it only takes seconds to come up to a boil.

I'm placing the lid on the skillet when Roger walks in theatrically smelling the air.

"Mmmmm, what is that?"

He tries to peer in the skillet but the lid is already fogged over from the steam.

"Pork chops with an orange glaze."

"Please tell me you are serving that for breakfast tomorrow." He begs. "If I get served one more pop tart!" He shakes his fist in the direction of the lounge.

"Well, if you stick around, this is my test batch; I could use a taste tester."

"You'll hear no complaints from me." Roger pulls out a glass and fills it up with the remaining orange juice. Digging a fork out of the drawer he holds it up and says, "Ready!"

I have to laugh. "Well, *it's* not. I need…" I check my timer, "three more minutes. And then I need to make the glaze."

"Well, what do you have in that pot?" He reaches in with his fork and spears an apple slice.

"Wait! That's going to be hot!" I cry out as he pops it in his mouth.

Holding his mouth in an "o", Roger sucks in some air to try and cool his throat down. Taking a swig of the orange juice he swallows and shakes his head. "Yowzer!"

"I tried to warn you." I shrug.

"Hat is weally haught." He's sticking his tongue out to try and see if it's burnt. I try not to laugh, but it's hard.

"Do you spend every day at the beach?" I push the meat around in the skillet and put the top back on.

Roger refills his glass with ice water and chugs it down. "I try to."

"Why?"

"Why not?" He shrugs. Man of few words.

I pull the chop out and put it on a plate with a piece of aluminum over the top to keep it warm. I measure out the cornstarch and add it to the liquid in the skillet. Looking back at the recipe to double check the amount of water…oh crud, I was supposed to mix the cornstarch with water before I put it in the skillet.

I add the water anyway and stir. But the starch has already clotted into little lumps and the liquid is not getting any thicker.

"Well, you're going to have to judge me on taste alone, afraid this isn't going to look quite right." I spoon some of the liquid over the chop, trying to avoid the clumps, and hand it to Roger.

He starts blowing on it to cool it down. I smile and turn back to the apples. They look pretty cooked down to me. I add the sugar and give it a toss and turn off the stove. Those can sit till later, when they cool I'll mash them.

I watch Roger slice off a piece of the chop with a knife. He looks it over, twirls it in the orange glaze and pops it in his mouth. He chews comically, moving the meat from one side of his mouth to the other and chewing in fast little chomps. After making a dramatic swallow he taps his chin with the bottom of the fork while looking at me.

He raises a finger and opens his mouth as if about to speak but then pops another piece in and starts the routine over again.

I am laughing out loud now. "Roger!" I make a motion to knock him in the head and he ducks his blond curls out of the way. "How is it?"

Still not responding, he puts the plate on the counter, carefully lays the fork and knife across the top and smooths down his t-shirt. Taking a deep breath he says in a booming theater voice,

"There was a lady of Pelican Bay,
Who made a fine pork chop, I say.
It tasted so good, It gave me some wood.
Now I shall go jump in the bay!"

And while I'm still laughing he makes a royal bow and heads out the door. I really cannot make that man out.

I cut off a small piece of the pork chop and taste it myself. Oh, it's perfect. Now I just have to get the yams peeled and snap the beans, and I'll be all set for later.

Bee is propped up in her bed when I enter her kitchen with a tray of cheese and crackers. I breathe a sigh of relief when I see that Cindy did get my message. Bee is wearing the blue shirt that brings out her eyes and she has on her bumblebee earrings.

I set the tray down on the kitchen island and pull out two place settings. Folding the cloth napkins down the center, I lay out the fork and knife.

"Melanie, what on earth are ya doin'?" She asks when I pull a candle out of the drawer, light it and place it in the center of the island.

"I told you, I want tonight to be special! My way of thanking you for all that you've done for me."

It takes some effort but I get the wheels unlocked on the bed and push it next to the island. Everything is within reach from her bedside. When Bee is munching on a cracker with Brie, I start to walk out the back door.

"I thought I'd get a start on everything over at Pixie's and just finish it up here."

Bee laughs, "Well, that's sweet, but also ridiculous. Why don't you just bring everythin' over here and finish cookin'."

"Nope, it's a surprise. I'll be back in a second."

I jog back over to Pixie's and shoot off the text I drafted earlier. When the reply comes back, I pocket my phone and fix up the salad plates. I used store bought dressing but everything else about this meal is homemade.

I stand outside between the two buildings holding the salads while I wait. The sun has already set and I can hear the chatter coming around the corner from the front porch where some of the guests are sitting.

I hear the car before I see it. The headlights swing towards me and I take a deep breath. I hope this goes well!

Walking back into Bee's I place the salads down.

"Just a salad, Melanie? That's what ya couldn't fix over here." Bee raises a skeptical eyebrow at me.

"First course. How is the cheese?" I'm just spreading the Brie on a cracker when the doorbell rings. "Now, who could that be?"

"Could be FedEx, they haven't stopped by today with anythin'." Bee calls after me as I head to the front of her house.

When I come back to the kitchen I see Bee is prepping a few of the crackers with the cheese and arranging them around the tray.

Glancing up at my empty hands she says, "No package?"

"Hello, Betsy-Lou." Says the man who followed me into the kitchen.

Bee freezes. "Gus?"

"I brought some champagne. And I have flutes too, I didn't know if you had any here." Gus holds up the two plastic glasses he's referring to.

"Here, let me take that for you." I get the champagne open while Gus takes off his hat and pulls up a stool to the island in front of the second plate.

"Wha—" Bee is looking between the two of us, still too stunned to say anything.

"You look stunning, Betsy-Lou." Gus prompts.

"It's Bee, you…you…ah!" Bee puts a cracker in her mouth before crossing her arms and turns away from him. I stifle a giggle.

"Now come on, Bee. Play nice." I hand Gus a glass of champagne, but Bee refuses to take hers so I leave it next to her plate.

"I can't believe you're doin' this to me, Melanie." She says in a huff.

"Doing what?" I say innocently.

"If I wasn't stuck in this damn cast I would storm outta here right now."

I lean in closer to her and lower my voice. "Now, give him a chance. He isn't after your business and he really does like you. I chatted with him the other day and he told me he's been courting you for almost five years. The least you can do is have a meal with the man."

I pull away and announce that dinner will be ready in fifteen minutes and head back over to Pixie's.

The yams are already cooking and I turn the green beans on to steam. The pork chops brown up and this time I only flip them four times. While the orange mixture is simmering over the chops I whisk the cornstarch in with the cold water. Lumpy glaze avoided!

Cindy steps into the kitchen and surveys my progress. "You know, I just want to say thank you for setting Mom up on this date and for taking care of all this." She gestures to the stove.

I smile back at her, "There will be—"

The phone rings from the other room and Cindy holds up her finger and runs out with the door swinging behind her.

"—extra if you are hungry." I finish. Oh well, it was worth a try.

With the pork glazed I plate a meal for two. Chops with homemade applesauce, yams, and a side of green beans. Charlie's favorite meal.

When I get over to Bee's kitchen I can hear her laughing. I knock on the door with my elbow and Gus opens it for me.

"*That* looks good." He compliments as I walk past him.

"Oh, Melanie! This is wonderful." Bee exclaims when I put the plate down in front of her.

"Everything going okay?" I hesitate to ask as I top off their champagne glasses.

Bee looks me in the eye, "I'm still not happy with ya at the moment for settin' this up, but," she glances over at Gus and leans towards me and whispers, "he's not half bad."

"Half bad? Old woman, you're only half bad yourself. If we cut out the rotten bits we make one pretty good apple."

They both laugh.

"Well then, I'll just leave you to it." I look between them one last time. Bee is shooting Gus a sidelong glance and a subtle smile.

"Go on, shoo." Bee says to me when I stand there for too long.

"Okay, okay. Good night!" I call out to them as I close the door behind me. I hum to myself as I walk back to Pixie's, fully satisfied with my execution of this surprise for my mentor and friend.

EIGHTEEN

I promised Karen I would spend Saturday with her. Eddie is out of town looking at a very old painting they found in a church basement somewhere in Mexico that might be a missing masterpiece.

But really, did our day *have* to start this early? Five a.m. and I'm knocking on her door while draining the last dregs of my first cup of coffee I brought with me from Pixie's. Karen opens the door wearing what I can only describe as repugnant.

"Are you trying out for an 80's fitness video revival?" I mock.

"I'll have you know, everyone in my yoga club is wearing this. It's the latest trend!" Karen steps back so I can enter her apartment. The gum tree has a lot more color on it; she must be chewing pieces nonstop.

"If you expect me to wear that, I'll leave right now." Karen has her hair pushed back by a purple headband. The navy leotard is bisected by a rainbow striped elastic belt. There is a bright pink shrug tied just under her breasts and on her calves are two different leg warmers, yellow over orange.

Karen laughs and takes my mug to fill with fresh coffee from her kitchen.

I didn't bring any workout clothes; it's not exactly my *thing*. Karen really wanted me to go to this yoga class with her and convinced me I could fit into her clothes even though I am at least two sizes bigger than her.

"Your clothes are in my bathroom, go get changed, we have to be there soon." I take my coffee back from her and head to the room she points to. I pat Daisy, the Maltese, on the head as I walk by, but she barely opens her eyes at me. Why does *she* get to sleep?

Karen's bathroom is the opposite of the rest of the house. Where everything else is white, punched with color, the tile in here is a glossy black. The sink and toilet are a matching red. The mirror above the sink is a mosaic of broken shards of glass and I have to duck down an inch to find a piece big enough to actually see my reflection while I pull my hair up into a ponytail.

The clothes hanging on the back of the door are at least normal enough for me to wear. Grey yoga pants and a plain black top. I slip them on and rejoin Karen in the living room where she is just pulling a piece of blue gum from her mouth.

"I will be soooo happy when this tree is done. My jaw is really getting a workout from this piece." Karen turns to me and gives me a once over. "Comfy, right?" I nod. They fit quite nicely.

"Great! Let's go." She picks up a bag and slings it over her shoulder.

"What is all that for?" I thought yoga just required a few mats and getting your body all contorted into odd shapes.

"Just a few things. Here, grab the water bottles." She points to the two liter bottles on the counter.

I give her a look.

"You can never have enough water with you." She explained.

Okay... "When did you become such a fitness buff, Kay?" I don't recall her ever talking about going to yoga before now. When I knew her in college, well, she was the definition of lazy when it came to physical workouts. She might get on a treadmill with a book and walk while she read.

With a shrug, "It comes and goes. And we need to go."

She gives Daisy a kiss, to which the dog replies by rolling over for a belly rub. Then we head out to her car and she tosses the bag into the back seat.

Punching a button on her stereo, the car is filled with a punk rock song. I turn the volume dial down to more reasonable decimal.

"Sorry!" Karen ejects the disc and swaps it for another from the holder strapped to her sun visor. With the new one in, the soft sounds of Enya start up. "There we go. Much more relaxing, right?"

I sip my coffee and close my eyes as she backs out of the driveway. Despite the caffeine, I could really fall asleep right now. Since Cindy arrived, I've been staying up later to chat with the guests, then sleeping till seven. Last night, I kept waiting to see when Gus would leave but at 11pm, I gave up and went to sleep. Getting up at 4:30 this morning was beyond painful. I try to stifle a yawn but I can feel myself drifting off.

A little nap on the ride there won't hurt.

Blinking my eyes open, I stretch my arms out in front of me. I feel really well rested for taking a nap in a car. The car is still moving, but we must be close by now. Karen is humming along with a Mark Anthony ballad, I could have sworn she put in an Enya album, but maybe it was a mixed set. Retrieving the coffee cup from the holder, I bring it up to my lips but it's cold.

"Karen…how long was I asleep?" The clock above the stereo says it's after seven, but that can't be right.

"About two hours." She says this without taking her eyes off the road.

"Oh, my god, I slept all the way through your yoga class, I'm so sorry! I must have been really tired." I look out the window at the sign for the road we are turning onto, I-4 East to Orlando. I sit up straighter but the sign has already gone by.

"Karen…"

"We aren't going to yoga. Don't worry, you didn't miss anything."

"Karen." I say more sternly.

She turns to me with a perfectly innocent expression on her face. "I packed some snacks and a lunch in the back. If you get hungry just help yourself. We still have another three hours to go.

"Karen!" I'm not angry, not really. But I am yelling.

"What! You weren't going to agree to go so I had to trick you. I had to, Mel. Don't be mad. Please?" She pleads. "You know you need to do this and I've been trying to get you to agree to go all week, and you just kept coming up with excuses. I understood when you were helping Mrs. Ringley out, but you told me her daughter is there now. You can't hide from this forever. We'll be quick, just go there, visit, and then leave. I know you think this isn't important, but it is. It totally is."

"I had things to do today, Karen. You…you've kidnapped me!" I fold my arms across my chest and slide down in the seat to pout. I guess I'm not making coconut muffins with Bee today. And I really want to find out how her date with Gus went last night. They were certainly hitting it off when I left.

"It was just a stroke of luck that you fell asleep. I thought I was going to have to pretend to get lost on my way to the yoga club so I could get onto the interstate without you figuring out I was lying. I hate lying to you, Mel." Karen frowns and I can see the fight leave her.

All I can do is shake my head and stare out the window.

"Mel?"

I refuse to look at her.

We spend the next three hours not speaking. Or rather, Karen tries, but I don't respond. When she asked for pretzels, I got them from the back seat and opened the bag for her. She wanted the map, so I opened it, but I only pointed to the road she was asking about. I needed a restroom, but thankfully she did too so I didn't have to ask her to stop. I'm starting to feel guilty, but my stubbornness keeps me from saying anything.

By 10am I spot the first sign that says St. Augustine and I start to get nervous. I snag some pretzels from the open bag wedged between our seats.

"Karen?" I whisper. After all these hours of silence, I'm afraid to speak.

"It will be okay, Mel." She replies softly.

"What do I say?"

She keeps looking forward, but shrugs. "Just tell him what you've been up to."

What I've been up to.

"Will you go with me?"

At that, she turns to me and smiles, "I am already with you, Melanie."

We pass a few more ramps before she turns off from Dixie Highway and onto the small streets of St. Augustine. I haven't been here in years; Charlie's parents travel a lot, so they usually came to see us. There is a new shopping complex that has sprung up, and more palm trees than I remember.

Charlie's parent's house is just off this street, and as we sit at the stoplight, I stare down the road to see if I can find the front porch. We had our wedding here, the limo was parked on the front yard and our guests' cars filled this entire block. But you can't see it from the intersection, and when the light flips to green, Karen turns in the opposite direction.

"Karen?"

"Yeah?"

"If we weren't ever going to yoga, what is with that outfit?"

Karen looks down at herself as if she can't image what I'm talking about. "What's wrong with a little color?"

"A little? Karen, you look like Rainbow Brite." I laugh.

"You don't like it." She deadpans, trying to make a sad face at me.

"Oh sure, sure. If you were trying to date Richard Simmons it would be perfect."

Karen's face cracks into a laugh, "I saw this at the thrift store by my house and couldn't resist. I have a change of clothes in the back. You're wearing my real yoga clothes. And I actually do attend."

I'm chuckling when I realize she is slowing down. The ivy covered stone wall that lines the Evergreen Cemetery is running along the side of our car. I can see the rows of headstones on the other side. Todd and I used to play this traveling game when we were kids; we had to hold our breath whenever we drove past a cemetery. I never thought about how you would do that if you actually *went* to a cemetery.

"Oh, I didn't realize it was this close to their house." My stomach is twisting, but pretzels are not going to help this time.

"Do you know where he's…you know?" Karen pulls the car into the entrance and stops. This place is massive. After driving through the roads lined with stores and houses it is odd to see open, rolling hills.

I don't make a habit of visiting graveyards. In college, I used one as a location for a photoshoot to complete an assignment in my Intro to Black and White course. Karen was dressed in a white nightgown and I had her sit on top of some large grave while I took pictures, trying to make it look like she was a ghost resting on her own stone.

She had long blond hair then, and makeup that made her look extra pale. We also tried some shots where she ran and jumped in the air to make it appear that she was floating. I thought they came out okay. But I only got a C on the assignment. We had both forgotten she was wearing sneakers and that ruined the effect.

Karen winds the car slowly along the path towards the little office. There are rows of graves on the left and an open field to the right. I catch myself thinking that there is still plenty of room for new arrivals. Everyone checks in and no one checks out. Always surrounded by people and no one to talk to. Who decides they want to run a graveyard? People who don't like to talk much, I suppose.

I stay in the car while Karen goes into the office to inquire about Charlie's location. She looks completely preposterous wearing the leotard and leggings entering the office of a cemetery. She comes back out with a map that someone has highlighted with a path that leads us to a little "x". Like a pirate map, find the gold where "X" marks the spot. I want to find that humorous; Charlie is indeed a treasure buried here, but I cannot muster the energy to smile.

Following the map, Karen winds around to a newer section of the cemetery; all the stones here are polished and reflect the sun that is high in the sky, now. Flowers are placed in front of many of the plots; a few tiny American flags are sitting idle with no wind to make them flutter. Just ahead, a man is erecting a white canopy over a pile of dirt. Another man is setting up chairs nearby.

We park on the side of the road and get out. I close my eyes, breathing in the scent of fresh cut grass. I suppose someone is out cutting grass all day, every day here.

Karen comes around to my side of the car and we both lean against its side, surveying the row of headstones in front of us.

"Are you ready?"

I shake my head and look at her, "I don't think I can do this."

She pushes off from the car and offers me her hand, "Come on." Wiggling her fingers at me she repeats with more force, "Come on, Melanie."

I let her pull me forward. We have to walk halfway down the row to get to his spot. I scan the names of his neighbors, the new people he hangs out with these days. We pass by a grave with the name Brandon Gibbs, Charlie's brother.

When we stop walking I turn to face the stone and slowly raise my eyes up to read "Beloved son and husband" written just above his name. My jaw starts to quiver but I hold the tears in. I don't want him to see me crying. I've been doing so good with that, the not crying over every little thing.

"I didn't know his middle name was Theodore. Like one of the Chipmunks." Karen breaks the silence.

"Charles Theodore Gibbs. Always in our thoughts," I read.

Karen envelopes me in a hug and gives my cheek a kiss. She holds me tight in her arms till I get steady. When I nod my head, she lets me go.

"I'm going to walk around for a bit, give you some privacy." Rubbing my arm she steps away, "Just talk to him, Mel."

I watch as she heads back down the row before turning back to the cold gravestone. Sinking to my knees I reach out and trace the engraved letters that make up Charlie's name.

Suddenly I realize I must be sitting on top of his head, and I quickly shuffle to the side. This is silly, he can't see me cry and he doesn't know I'm sitting here, and he can't hear me if I say anything. I look around for Karen, but she isn't in sight.

Damn her.

I lean against the side of the stone and tuck my knees up to my chest. Slipping my sandals off, I play with the blades of grass that peak up between my toes. A breeze comes through and I watch as the little flag in front of the stone across from me lifts a bit in the wind. Two birds chase each other through the air, one chittering at the other as they fly into a tree.

"I made pork chops last night. They came out real good. You would have liked them." I tap my fingers on my knees. What is the point of this? Rubbing my calves, I feel how defined they've become, and I laugh a little.

"And I've been climbing stairs. Every day. Loads of them. You would have liked this place; good food and exercise all rolled into one. I know how to make bread now. Did you ever hear of strawberry bread? It makes pretty good French toast."

The breeze stops and the flag falls limp. I lean my head back and close my eyes to the sun. I wonder again how Bee's date with Gus went. Will she be mad at me for tricking her like that? She can't be, it was for her own good.

Oh.

Just like Karen did for me.

I start telling Charlie about Karen's gum tree. And about Eddie. I tell him about Pixie's and about how I've been learning to cook from Bee. I even tell him about my mix-up with Ricardo.

"I hope that's okay, that I kissed him? I was thinking about you at the time, but it was nice, you know? To be in someone's arms and to have their affection. Even just for a second. But that's all it was, just a fleeting moment." The two birds have come out of the tree and are hopping through the grass. Occasionally one picks up a blade of dry grass and it flies back to the tree. Making a nest, I assume. Starting a family.

"Ricardo is buying Gramp's house. Do you remember that place? It's the first place you told me you loved me. God, I miss the way you would say those words. I should have said it back to you right there, but you took me by surprise. I thought you might be joking, but you weren't, were you? I don't know why, but I feel like letting them give that house up is just...wrong. I know they have to sell, Dad explained it. By the way, Aunt Julia has never been to France. Can you believe that? Decades of lies about that. I just…I don't know. If you were here, I'd ask you what I should do." I twirl the grass with my finger, "What can we do to save the house?"

A cough comes from behind me and I turn to see Karen standing there, changed into jeans and a t-shirt. "Sorry to interrupt, I thought you might be hungry." She hands me the sandwich she brought with her and one of the water bottles, and then walks away.

"No, stay," I call to her.

Karen backtracks and sits on the ground across from me, leaning next to the headstone with the flag. "Hello Mr. Timothy Winterbottom. Hope you don't mind me joining you for lunch." She says to the stone.

We sit in silence while we eat. People have started to gather by the chairs, and I watch a hearse come up the road towards the canopied area.

"Are you still mad at me?" She questions.

I shake my head and pass her the water. "You always butt in when I need you to, even if I don't want you to."

"That's what best friends are for."

I raise my sandwich in a toast to her and take another bite. We watch the coffin get unloaded from the back of the car and when it's set in place, one of the mourners drapes a rose blanket over the top.

"I should have thought to pick up flowers, too. Sorry about that." Wadding up the plastic our sandwiches were wrapped in, Karen stands. "I can go find some if you want more time."

"No, I've said everything I can think of."

I turn onto my knees and push off the headstone to sit up. The ring drops out from under my shirt and swings forward on its chain to clink on the stone. Standing up I run it through my fingers.

Karen watches me as I reach back to unclasp the chain and slide the ring off. I catch her eye and I know she can tell what I'm thinking.

"Are you sure?"

I chew on my lip and think about it again. I nod. "Yeah, it belongs here. I need a new start, Karen."

"If his head is just by the stone, then his heart would be about...here."

I kneel down again and try to dig through the ground. The grass has grown tightly over the area and I rip at the blades till I get a small bald spot. The dirt is pushing into my nails as I dig a little hole. A harpist has started playing a hymn at the burial and it seems fitting for what I'm doing. When I get the hole about three inches deep, I kiss my wedding band and place it into the soil. With one last look, I push the dirt back over it and pat it all down.

Standing up I brush my hands together and look down at the headstone.

"Okay, let's go home. Good-bye, Charlie. I love you."

Okay, so that was a stupid idea. On the ride home I'm using a tissue to try and get all the soil off my ring. As soon as we pulled out of the cemetery I made Karen turn around and dug it back up.

What could he possibly do with it anyway?

I do feel lighter though. Even with the ring safely back on the chain and under my shirt, I feel...freer. Like I got to say my piece.

"Oh." I sigh.

Karen glances at me and then back at the road as she gets back on the highway. "You okay?"

"Yeah, just thinking about all the work I still have to do when I get home. I need to take all his clothes to the thrift store, sort through the boxes they brought over from his office, figure out how to turn his cell phone off."

"You still have his phone?"

I nod. "It's on auto billing to one of his accounts and I have to cancel all the auto bills before I can close the account. That would mean calling everyone and explaining that he's dead and doesn't need their services anymore." I chew on my lip. "I tried to cancel one of his magazine subscriptions."

"Yeah," Karen encourages me on.

"And it was the hardest thing, you know? I talked to one operator and they said I had prepaid for the whole year and I couldn't get a refund but maybe I could get the magazines to stop coming. She sent me to this other person who said I couldn't discontinue receiving them, and then they sent me to yet another person and they said if I wrote a letter to their headquarters explaining the situation, they might be able to stop the magazines. And every time I got connected to a new person, I had to repeat that my husband was dead. Dead. Dead. Dead. I got off that call and cried my eyes out. And I'm still getting that damn magazine."

"You just made it through a whole visit with his gravestone and you didn't cry."

"I started to." I point out.

"But you didn't." She points back.

I pull some pretzels out and crunch on them. I didn't cry. I feel good about that.

"So...I didn't mean to eavesdrop, but who is this Ricardo person you kissed."

I can feel the heat rush to my cheeks and I fill my mouth with more pretzels.

"Oh come on, Mel! Spill it!"

"He's just this guy." I say it nonchalantly, as if it's no big deal.

"Yeah, where'd you meet him? Is he staying at the B&B?" It's fun to hear her animated and wanting to chit chat about boys, like we used to.

"No, he's someone I knew in high school, back in Jersey."

"Well, that's a coincidence."

"He's just visiting." I twist off the top to the water and take a few gulps. I pass the bottle to Karen, she drinks some too. God, I miss hanging out with her like this. Where we share everything, do all sorts of activities together, and never have to ask each other what we need. When I'm hungry, she's brought me a sandwich, when she's thirsty I offer her a drink. We're in sync with each other.

Maybe it wouldn't be so bad to move back to Florida. I could be near Karen, help her chew gum for her tree. Maybe get a job at an art gallery and sell her art, be around adults all the time.

Although, her friends are a little bit too wild for my taste. I don't think I could handle going to all those late-night events, drinking fluorescent cocktails all the time.

"He was here to visit you?" When I shake my head, she adds, "Who then?"

"My parents. He's stealing my family heritage."

"Drama Queen! You mean the house you were talking about?"

"It's not just any house, Kay, it's the Captain's Quarters."

"I don't get it." She shakes her head and looks at me for an explanation. I spend the next two hours telling her about the place. How my grandfather built it, the marathons, all our family memories, and conclude with the ice cream story. Maybe it's just transference, but I almost feel more upset about losing the house then I do about Charlie.

"Okay, so why don't you just buy it?"

"Ha! Karen, I don't have that kind of money. Two point three *million* dollars. Million!" Was she not paying attention?

"That's what he is offering them, but you said your Dad needs less than one million to take care of your Aunt, right?"

"Yeah, but—"

"And your Dad doesn't actually *want* to sell the house. So, you just need to be able to buy it for the amount he needs."

"But—"

"So, what's the big deal, buy it."

I hold my hands up in protest. "Wait. Even if I could afford it, what would I do with it?"

Karen lets go of the wheel and tosses her hands in the air. "Move there, live in it. I don't know, rebuild the knick-knack shop your grandmother had there when it was first built." She pulls over and stops the car so she can look at me. "And what do you mean you can't afford it?"

"Nine hundred thousand dollars, Karen. What do you mean, 'what do I mean'?"

"Well…what did you do with the insurance money?"

"What insurance money?" I am so lost, what on Earth is she talking about?

"When I was out in Cali with you, I talked to Charlie's boss, and he said Charlie had upgraded his life insurance policy from the usual one they give their employees, to the premium package. Something about how he wanted to be able to tell his clients what he had purchased so they felt confident in him to buy the same kind."

That does sound like Charlie. He was only just getting into the sales game, but he did like to make his clients feel like he was their equal. Hence all the expensive suits and the Italian shoes he spent a bundle on.

"So?"

"So…didn't you get it?"

"Get what?"

"Oh gosh, Melanie! You really didn't handle any of the paperwork I left for you?" I shake my head. I know she got a lot of things in order for me when she was there, but it's just one more pile of papers I kept meaning to get to.

"All you had to do was give them a copy of the death certificate and they would cash out his policy to you. I even made copies for you and addressed the envelope. Didn't anyone talk to you about it when you cleaned out his office?" She's looking at me anxiously, not exactly scolding me, but she kind of wants to scold me.

I didn't clean out his office. His co-worker brought everything to my place and Freddie accepted the boxes for me. His boss called a few times and left me messages about closing some accounts. But I just thought he'd do it eventually on his own.

"Mel. Didn't you and Charlie ever talk about this? What would happen if one of you died." I shake my head numbly.

"I don't even know if he wanted to be buried."

"Well, I guess he doesn't have a choice on that one now." Karen smirks. "Mel, Charlie left things in order for you. All you have to do is sign, and return the papers they need when you get back. You could have done it months ago."

"So, how much am I getting?"

Karen shrugs. "I don't know, but that guy I spoke with made me think it was pretty high."

My mind is swirling as Karen turns onto 95 South, towards Miami. How could Charlie have never discussed this with me? Did he try, and I just didn't hear him? I tried to care about his work, I really did. But why wouldn't he have sat me down and made a point of this?

I get my phone out and place a call, "Freddie? It's Mel. Good, good, I'm glad Buca is keeping you company. Listen, I need you to do me a favor."

NINETEEN

By Sunday morning I am all packed. My flight isn't for several hours but I move my suitcase down to the lounge so Cindy can get a head start on fixing up the room for the next guest. She tries to get everything done first thing in the morning so she can concentrate on her "real" job for the rest of the day.

Freddie was able to locate the documents, and I got in touch with Charlie's old boss while Karen drove to Pixie's, and he and I finally had that chat about closing accounts. At first I was floored when I found out how much he had left for me. But after we hung up and I found my voice again, Karen talked me through my plan. When I get back to San Diego, all I need do is bring them the death certificate and it would all be taken care of for me.

If only I had found the courage to work on all that paperwork sooner.

My parents were expecting me for an early lunch. I called them last night and asked if Ricardo had brought them the check yet. I was in luck; he wasn't coming by until this afternoon. For whatever reason, he must have listened to me when I asked him to stall. Now, I almost feel bad for him. Almost.

I use Pixie's kitchen one last time, making up a plate of apple wedges with peanut butter and raisins, and then walk over to Bee's. Knocking on the door as I walk in, I see she is on the phone. I make us tea while she finishes her conversation.

"Sounds good. Yes. Correct. Okay then, I'll see ya at four on Monday. Bye-bye." She merrily signs off and folds her hands in her lap.

"I thought the place was already booked, did you have a cancellation?" I hand her the tea.

"That wasn't a guest, dear." She blows on her cup and flicks her eyes up at me. "It was Gus. He's comin' over for dinner."

"Oh!"

Wagging her finger at me, she says, "He insisted on makin' me dinner from his store. I still think he's just tryin' to get me to be a customer."

"Ah huh." I nod.

"Now, don't you be smug about it."

"I'm not smug about anything," I say smugly.

"Well," she falters, "he was good company. And while I'm stuck with this stupid cast, I might as well make a few new friends."

"Does he have a nice backside?" I duck out of the way when she tries to swat me.

Bee wipes her eyes when she is done laughing. "Now, what did ya make for breakfast today?"

I show her the plate of apples and she starts to laugh. "Of course! Your debut meal here at Pixie's! How wonderful." She picks up a wedge and we both crunch away on our apples.

"Will you be okay?" I ask, when we've finished our meal.

"Will *I* be okay? Cindy is here and she may not express it very well, but she's gonna take care of everythin' and I'll be up and runnin' again in no time." Bee reaches out a hand to my shoulder, "Melanie, it's you I'm worried about. Did you figure out where your happiness is?"

I nod contently. "I think so. It's going to take a lot of work, but I think I know where I'm headed now. I wouldn't have gotten there if it weren't for you, Bee."

"Oh, ya would have found your way eventually. I might have just given ya a kick in the ass. Now, give an old woman a hug and get yourself outta here. Go have fun." She reaches over to the table and hands me a book. "And here, I want ya to take this one with you."

"Oh, Bee!" I take the cookbook from her hands and give her a hug. I scan a few pages. In the side margins are Bee's notes about the different recipes that she's tried. Additives, suggestions, smiley faces next to the ones that came out well, stars next to the ones she really liked. "This is just perfect!"

I decide to take my paperwork down to the beach to prepare for my meeting with my parents. It feels odd to think of this as a meeting, but I need to make sure that they know I can do this. On my own. I would lay out my full plan, the timeline, to-do list, all the people I would need to contact. But first things first, I have to make sure Ricardo doesn't get the Captain's Quarters.

It's confusing stuff. I had to convince my Mom to fax Ricardo's contract to me at Pixie's. She couldn't understand why I wanted to review it, but I eventually got her to send it over. All thirty-three pages of it, including a sample menu for the bistro.

I've made it through the first five pages when I take a break and move closer to the water. Sitting on the sand with my feet out in front of me, the waves just barely make it to my toes after crashing onto the shoreline and running up the beach. There are so many numbers, and the inspection report, the legal terms. My head hurts just thinking about it all.

With my eyes closed, I listen to the sounds around me. The kids playing further down the beach, the seagull flying above. I should really go to the ocean more often. I keep forgetting how calming it is. I can do this. Melanie Gibbs can figure out how to proceed, one carefully placed step at a time.

I can feel the instant lack of warmth when a shadow blocks the sun from my face. Squinting my eyes open, I find Roger standing over me. He's holding a surfboard and is dripping wet.

"Hi, Mel!" He sticks the board in the sand and plops down next to me. With one hand, he slicks his hair back, spraying salt water on my face and onto the papers.

"Hey!" I squeal.

"Oops." He says, as I shake the paperwork and switch it to my other hand, away from his dripping body.

"Ugh, it will be okay. I needed a break anyway. How is the surf?"

"Oh, I wasn't surfing." Okay, so why the board? But he doesn't explain it, he gestures to the papers instead. "What are you doing with those?"

"Um, just trying to understand them."

"You buying a house?" How'd he know that?

As if reading my mind, he adds, "It says 'Home Purchase Agreement' on the top." Oh.

"Trying to stop someone else from buying a house." I purse my lips.

"Can I see?" Why not, I can't make sense of it. Roger takes the papers and holds them to the side so he doesn't get them any wetter. After flipping through a few pages, he looks up at me and whistles. "Wow, expensive place you're after. Did money already change hands?"

I shake my head.

"And the seller," He points to my Dad's signature, "does he want to back out of this contract."

"My parents are supposed to hand over the contract later today."

"Ah, you're trying to stop your parents." He nods as if he understands.

"Well, they don't really need to sell the house; they just think they have to. But I don't believe they need to anymore. It's a long story." I don't really want to explain it again, not to Roger.

"So, the buyer hasn't gotten any of this yet?"

I shake my head again.

"Then it's simple. Just convince the seller, your Dad, to rip up the contract. If they don't sign it and they don't accept money, then there is no sale."

"Really? That's it?" It can't possibly be *that* simple. Could it?

Roger stands and yanks the surfboard out of the sand. "You want to go for a swim? The water is perfect this morning."

"No thanks."

"Suit yourself, adios!" Roger turns on his heel and splashes out into the waves.

I still don't understand this guy.

I stand and brush sand off, and bend over to get the papers. Underneath them I spy a shell, buried in the sand. I dig it out and hold it up. Perfect white shell with a bright purple inside, no chips and no cracks.

"I was looking for you." Pocketing the shell, I trudge up the beach and back to the road.

By the time Ricardo arrives at my parent's boat, I really do feel bad for him. My parents and I have already worked it out. It didn't take as much effort as I thought to convince them not sell the Captain's Quarters. In fact, once they got over the shock of learning how much I was getting from Charlie's life insurance, they were relieved they didn't have to sell the house after all.

I'm going to set up a trust for Aunt Julia's "trips to France," get all her debts paid off, and in return, my dad is going to turn the deed to the house over to me. That leaves me enough of Charlie's funds to remodel the house and get my new life started.

Ricardo is carrying a bottle of champagne and has a big smile on his face. I hate knowing that I'm going to squash his dream.

But I'm putting my own dream first. I'm not just going to do what everyone expects me to do anymore.

"Mr. Gibbs!" He calls out when he gets to the boat deck. "Oh, Melanie, hi." His smile gets even bigger when he sees me.

I give him a feeble wave.

"I wasn't expecting you to be here. I thought you would already be on a plane by now."

"Soon. I have to be at the airport in an hour."

"Ricky, so nice to see you again!" My mom comes out from the cabin and gives him a hug. Leave it to Mom to not realize she shouldn't be so peppy right now.

"I brought some champagne...and of course a check!" He hands the bottle to my mom and reaches into his breast pocket to pull out the check. "Two hundred and fifty thousand dollars."

With a beaming smile, he holds it out for my dad. Dad shuffles his feet and shoves his hands into his pocket.

"Ricky, I'm sorry, but we've decided not to sell the house after all."

Ricardo just stares at my dad and shakes the check at him. "Sorry, what?"

"I'm sorry, son. We just can't do it." Dad drops his gaze to the floor of the boat.

Laughing, "I don't understand, you said you needed the money to take care of some family issues. Did they just go away overnight?" He snaps his fingers and looks between my dad and mom.

Mom purses her lips into a frown and shrugs. "Kind of."

"Okay, okay. I get it." Ricardo folds the check. Reaching around to his back pocket he pulls out a checkbook. "How about two point five million? I can write a new deposit check now and we can open that champagne."

Dad shakes his head. "Look, son—"

"Two million seven hundred thousand! Three hundred thousand down, right now." Ricardo clicks a pen and is prepared to write out the check. "And I'll name a dish after you." He looks at my mom when he says this.

"That's awfully generous of you Ricky, but no-can-do." Mom says while rocking on her heels and playing with the tab on her soda can.

Ricardo has his tongue pressed to his top teeth. He looks between my parents and then puts his checkbook away. Turning to me he says, "You did this?"

Meeting his eyes, I nod. "I'm buying it."

He takes a step towards me and scoffs. "Melanie, what are you going to do with it?"

"I'm going to live there, Ricardo. I'm going to move back home."

"Ah Mel, I'm offering almost three million dollars to your family. You're going to get in the way of that for what…memories? You're going to grow herbs in that dinky little garden? I know that house means a lot to you, sugar, but think about what you're doing."

"She's going to open an inn!" Mom chimes in.

"An inn? Really? Oh, that's precious." He chortles. "Do you know how much needs to be renovated on that place to make it useable? It's going to take a lot of work and a lot of money. Money my family has and which you do not. And what do you even know about running a business? This is the dumbest thing I've heard all week, Melanie."

"I knew you'd be upset, Ricardo, but I didn't think you'd be cruel. I know that bistro meant a lot to you, but it's just a business. This is a family matter." I hold my chin up to him defiantly and look him squarely in the eye. "The Captain's Quarters will become a great Bed & Breakfast, and I hope you'll be there to show your support for my grand opening."

He scratches his head and then picks up his champagne. "Okay. Sure. Open an inn. And when you go bankrupt in a year, I'll make the offer again. But don't expect me to be as generous, next time. You'll be begging me to buy the place off of you. Begging. I can wait." He shrugs and steps off the boat.

"Poppycock. My little Melon Ball is going to be a big success." Mom to the rescue, yay.

"Such a shame, Melanie. I thought you and I had a spark the other night. Thought we could build something from that." Turning towards my parents he nods. "Mr. Gibbs, Mrs. Gibbs."

"I'm sorry, Ricky." Dad replies.

"It's Ricardo. Stop calling me Ricky." And with that, he strides away from us. His beautiful butt marching angrily down the pier till we can't see him anymore.

My parents hold each other's hands and when I turn to them they embrace me in a hug. It's a family thing. They are going to support me in my new adventure and I'm going to support them in getting Aunt Julia help.

And the Captain's Quarters is going to be great, just great.

There is nostalgia here. The furniture, old. The window trims, old. The wall sconces, old. The carpet…okay, forget nostalgia. Everything in this house is just old. Including the smell. I can't quite describe it. Mildew combined with old coffee grounds and a touch of Bengay perhaps? The place has been boarded up tight for over a year.

"Okay Buca, first order of business is to air this place out." The cat springs from the carrier where he's been cooped up for the last several hours on the drive here. His orange tail wraps around my calf as he weaves between my legs, and the stare he gives me says I had better set up the litter box before I open the windows.

I chuckle, "Okay, you first, then the windows." A quick scratch on the head to reassure him I'm coming back, and I go down the steps for the cat supplies in the car.

In the foyer are three doors, one with a stained glass door that leads to the office, one that enters the retail space currently being rented as an art studio, and one that goes outside to the parking lot. The office door is open and the pile of boxes the moving company delivered before I got here are spilling into foyer, calling to me. But so is the cat who has followed me down and is sitting on the steps eye level with me.

"Right, I know." Back upstairs with the supplies and Buca happily chowing down on a can of tuna flavored mush, I go 'round the room opening windows. The bay side opens easily enough, being the newest in the house. The bedrooms are more difficult, and I fail to pry anything open in the master bedroom.

But there are two entrances to this room and with both doors open, it should get enough of a breeze.

Better start a repair list, these things all have to function before I have any guests.

In the drawing room, I pause to take in the view. This is the last house on the island. Just beyond the ice cream parlor and the tackle shop there is a perfect view of Old Barney. The white and red lighthouse was refinished sometime after I moved away, and they say the light shines again, every night, guiding the boats back in through the narrow, rocky entrance where the ocean meets the bay.

You can't see the ocean from the house, just the bay before it disappears behind the trees that surround the park where the lighthouse sits. If you listen closely, you can hear the ocean waves crashing onto the beach that is just two blocks up the road. But it's this view, from right here, that will make the Captain's Quarters a sought-after retreat.

Well, the view and hopefully my cooking. I've been practicing ever since I got back to San Diego. As a thank-you to Freddie, I insisted on making a big Saturday breakfast for him every week, right up until we moved. I also made muffins and bread to take into the teacher's lounge at work.

I even gave Principal Jackson a basket of assorted cookies when I handed in my resignation. He wasn't shocked in the slightest that I was leaving the school. He told me he could tell teaching was not my passion.

The last day of school, I brought in cupcakes with pink frosting for all my students. I didn't tell them it was to make up for their missed Valentine's Day party.

The Captain's Quarters have been left untouched since Gramps passed. My dad and Aunt Julia removed his personal effects and some keepsakes they both wanted, but it was boarded up with all the furniture, the art, even the water glasses still in place. A thick layer of dust coats everything in the kitchen cabinets.

Aunt Julia is now in one of the best substance rehabilitation centers in the area, a six-month program. Before she checked in, she made a few requests when she learned what I was going to be doing with the place. The dining room set had to stay exactly as it had always been, so did the parlor. But I could upgrade the bathrooms and the kitchen as long as the style was kept in line with the rest of the house. I was going to convert the downstairs office to my own room; there was a half bath, but it needed a shower added.

For now, the people running the art studio will finish out their lease, but I am hoping to convert that into an additional three bedrooms. That would let me sleep twelve guests, plus me of course.

With the rest of the car unloaded, I poke around the rest of the house. Buca is curled up on the sofa, peering at me from slit eyes, pretending to be asleep.

Ding, ding, ding, dong.

Who on earth is ringing my doorbell already?

Getting back down to the foyer I open the door to find a Postman standing on the doormat and looking at a note in his hand.

"Are you…Melanie Gibbs?" He looks up at me.

"Yes."

"I'm Scott, you'll see me on this route most of the days." He offers me his hand, which I shake. "I didn't know anyone had moved back into this place. You just buy it?"

"It was my grandfather's house, just got here today, actually."

"Well, we've been collecting some mail for you, it was on hold till tomorrow but I saw the car out front so I thought I would try you." He reaches into his bag and pulls up a rubber banded stack of envelopes and hands them to me. "One second, I've got a few parcels in the car."

I snap off the band and sort through the cards. Most of them are addressed to the Captain's Quarters, and I don't recognize any of the sender's names. I rip one open and pull out a card with an image of a mailbox on it. Inside the handwritten note says: *We'd love to be put on your mailing list!*

What? I open another card and it has a similar message, but Scott is back at the door before I can get to any more. In his hands are two boxes which he carries into the foyer and puts on the table.

"There you are! Do you have any outgoing mail?"

I shake my head, "No. Are these," I hold up the envelopes, "for me? Are you sure they aren't for the tenants in the shop."

"I'm sure. Their address is on Fourth Street and yours is Broadway. Besides, these are addressed to the Captain's Quarters, they don't use that name."

"No, I guess they wouldn't."

"Well, you have a good day!" Scott steps out and leaves me to ponder the cards.

I look at the largest box and see it's from Karen. Smiling, I open it up to a box full of Styrofoam nuts. A few bounce onto the floor as I dig out the bubble wrapped contents. The cat decides they make a perfect toy and starts to bat them around.

"Buca, don't make a mess!" I laugh.

Pulling the plastic off, I find in my hands a three-foot high sculpture of a mermaid. It's made up of thin strips of metal twisted around to form the figure. She's raised up on her tail with one hand up to her face, and the other down by her hip...or fin, or whatever you would call that. I find the note inside with Karen's handwriting.

Happy Birthday, Mel! This is from my Leftovers collection; it's made entirely of the handles from Chinese take-out boxes. Love- Karen

My birthday was last week but I was so close to moving, I told everyone not to bother sending me any gifts. There is a save-the-date card in the box, too. The wedding is planned for this fall; they had to push it back so her friend could finish making all the fairy wings.

Turning to the other box, I see it's from Bee. She and I have been talking almost every week. When she found out I was going to open my own Bed & Breakfast, she couldn't wait to start telling me all of her trials and errors with getting Pixie's up and running.

She helped me figure out what insurance I needed and how to register as an inn. Without her guidance, I wouldn't even know where to start. Ricardo would have been right, if I had been on my own, I would probably fail. But I'm not on my own. And my personal mentor is going to help me with every step.

In the box is a set of muffin tins and a jar of saffron jelly. I laugh when I pull the card from the enclosed envelope. It's a collage of the images she must have peeled off from her cast after they took it off her leg. She did prove the doctors wrong, and was using crutches just one week after I left, had the cast off after just a month and had sent Cindy back home a mere eight weeks after her fall.

I can only hope to be as strong as Bee when I get to her age.

Dearest Melanie,

I wish you the best with your new start! I know you will be a success.

Warmest regards,

Bee & Gus

PS I wrote to all of my guests about the Captain's Quarters in case they were looking for a place to stay further north than Pixie's.

Oh. That explains the rest of the cards.

Gus has stuck around and Bee seems to be bursting with joy about it. Almost every time I call her at night, I hear him in the background saying hi to me. It's cute.

I sigh and run a hand through my hair. I haven't heard from Ricardo, but I didn't expect to, yet. I tried to talk to him last month, when I confirmed the date for my arrival here. But I only got his answering machine. With the Carlsons owning the tackle shop next door, and just about every third store in the area, I'm going to have to mend that bridge eventually. Maybe I'll make some muffins this weekend and take them down to the Coast Guard office.

Well, if I can get the kitchen in working order.

I clear the boxes off the table and pick up the Styrofoam nuts since Buca has gotten bored with them. I place the mermaid statue in the center of the table and stand back. Pulling the necklace out from under my shirt, I spin the ring through my fingers.

"What do you think, Charlie? Will this work?" In peaceful silence, I let a smile come to my lips. I am truly happy, now. I've found my purpose, my passion, a new project that I can really dig my soul into.

"I know what this needs." Buca follows me upstairs while I rummage through my luggage till I find the bag I'm looking for.

Back downstairs, I lay out all ten shells around the base of the mermaid. Perfect. This will be the centerpiece my guests see when they first check-in to the Captain's Quarters B&B.

"Alright. Let's see if that stove is working!" I scratch Buca's head and we go up the stairs to get started.

ACKNOWLEDGMENTS

I originally wrote this book eight years ago while I was taking a break between jobs and traveling the world. I had no intention of it sitting unfished for such a long time, but alas, life had other plans. Of particular thanks is my very first reader who read each and every chapter the same day I emailed them to her and who diligently wrote back with comments immediately. Jessamyn, I may have never finished the first draft without you.

When the first manuscript was "done", I emailed it off to three more readers while I went into cyberspace oblivion and emerged a few weeks later to find insight and comments from all three. John, Sabra, and Beth, thank you for supporting me in those early days.

Returning to the States and starting a new job caused me to put the book on pause. Where it stayed for much too long. I could not believe how much had changed in the world in just the few years since I had written the first version of the story and I had to update the technology and the cultural aspects of Melanie's life. In the revised version, I have to thank Derek for catching the details that were still not up to snuff.

From there, I joined a Meetup group for writers and I have a dozen people to thank for encouraging me to expand my craft and who introduced me to my editor, Kate. Sitting in an Ikea showroom, making use of one of their staged offices, I learned more about copy editing in thirty short minutes than I had learned in years of reading books and advice columns. After she had edited the full manuscript and we had sent it off to the beta-readers, she helped me brainstorm the future of Melanie's life that will hopefully turn into the second and third book in the series. And which I promise will not take eight more years to produce.

I owe special thanks to Matt, who volunteered as a beta-reader specifically to stretch his own craft as he is not the intended audience for this story nor is it written in a genre he would not normally read. He read it twice. And provided the most valuable insight to the minor storyline details that needed to be tweaked just a little more before the final version could be declared complete.

And there would be no book at all without my family who unknowingly have supplied various character traits to this story. While no one character is based on any single person in my reality, they have quirks that stem from somewhere. Most of all, there needs to be credit given to Seaman's Landing, the real live house that my real live grandfather owned on Barnegat Light that I really did daydream about turning into a bed and breakfast. It has been sold and is on its own journey in a different direction now, but in my heart and in my head, it will become the Captain's Quarters, a thriving operation that Melanie Gibbs will renovate and open for business in her next chapter.

Anna grew up in New Jersey and lived in San Diego for over a decade before relocating to Georgia. She daydreams about opening her own bed and breakfast someday. As a rescue mom to many animals, she did indeed have a cat nicknamed Buca.

www.ingramcontent.com/pod-product-compliance
Lightning Source LLC
Chambersburg PA
CBHW031308280626
47169CB00017B/866